AF420867

The Empathy Circuit

The Empathy Circuit

James W. Salkeld

Copyright © 2026 James W. Salkeld
All rights reserved.

ISBN: 979-8-9894163-5-6

QSynQ Publishing
QSynQ.pub

This novel is entirely a work of fiction. The names, characters and incidents portrayed in it are the work of the authors' imaginations. Any resemblance to actual persons, living or dead, events or localities is entirely coincidental.

DEDICATION

To my wife, Ellen, for many reads, rereads, and helpful comments.

ACKNOWLEDGMENTS

The author thanks Vicky Annette Larkin for her thorough reading and many valuable comments and insights and the Trilogy Lake Norman Adventures In Writing group for helpful critiques.

I have been studying how I may compare
This prison where I live unto the world;
And, for because the world is populous
And here is not a creature but myself,
I cannot do it. Yet I'll hammer't out.
My brain I'll prove the female to my soul,
My soul the father, and these two beget
A generation of still-breeding thoughts;
And these same thoughts people this little world,
In humours like the people of this world,
For no thought is contented.

Richard II Act 5, Scene 5
William Shakespeare

Contents

Of Mice and Moloi
May 2078

Nomusa Moloi woke to the sounds of grinding and digging. The mice were restless. She threw the blanket off and pushed herself up onto her elbows. "Hush, little ones," she said, addressing the caged mice. "I will check on you soon." She stood up from the couch and walked over to a small basin in the corner to wash her face and brush her teeth.

Nomie, as her friends called her, contemplated the mice and her future. Not that there was much to contemplate. The journey from her village in Botswana had been an exciting and eventful one. A scholarship to Oxford led to a doctorate at Harvard and, finally, this research fellowship from the Phillips Foundation.

Her chosen field was highly competitive. She was a newcomer to the study of cognitive enhancement and had to feed on leftovers. The small grant she won paid for the mice, a basic cloud server, and Tim's salary. Fortunately, the Phillips Foundation wanted mouse trials for their drugs, which were targeted at combating cognitive degeneration. The foundation needed to measure the efficacy of the drugs. Nomie's nanobot brain implant design would do that. The Foundation agreed to produce the implants based on Nomie's design. A win—mostly for the foundation.

The University allocated her the small windowless lab she was in now. She suspected it had once been a storage room. Still, it was big enough. Nomie needed little for herself. There was sufficient room for a couch, a table and a kitchenette. Cages of mice took up one wall, twenty-four in all. There was a mouse maze near the other wall. She frequently slept on the couch, monitoring the mice while Tim went home to get some sleep.

After checking on the mice, she sought coffee grounds for the machine. It was a fruitless search. Maybe Tim will remember to bring coffee this time. He should arrive soon, probably bringing in breakfast for her. Tim was a nice boy and a talented nanobot programmer. She sighed. At least when this project finishes, he should be able to get a better position.

Nomie's grant was based on what seemed like a simple idea: try out several cognitive-enhancing drugs and use nanobots to record the effect, if any. It had worked for Algernon, remembering the short story she had read as a child. And it *should* work. Nomie and Tim had injected the mice with nanobots yesterday. Testing this morning confirmed that the nanobots had taken hold. They had connected to various sensory parts of the brain, allowing Nomie to record to the cloud server everything the mice perceived.

She heard the door to the lab open, and turned to see Tim coming in, bearing a package, hopefully sustenance. "Good morning!" said Tim. The skinny youth was chipper as ever, grinning as he put bags on the small table they used for lunch. He was dressed in his usual jeans, t-shirt, and sneakers. His long hair was still damp, likely from a recent shower. "I brought your favorite food! Bagels! Still warm with *lots* of cream cheese."

"Thanks, Tim. Right now, everything is my favorite food." She grabbed a bagel and spread the cream cheese on it, her stomach reminding her she had skipped dinner again. She raised an eyebrow. "Just how much am I paying you? You are always bringing me food."

"A pittance. Luckily for us, Jared has a proper job. You can thank him for the food drops."

"I will," replied Nomie. "How is he doing, by the way?"

"Jared? He's fine, always fine. He wants to know when you'll finally come over for dinner. You have a standing invitation."

"Soon. Once we get some data, I'll have some time."

"Sure. And then you'll say you need to analyze the data. And so on." Tim shrugged and took a bite of his bagel. He looked over at the cages. "So, did everyone sleep well? No issues with the implant injections? They all look bright-eyed and bushy-tailed! Remind me, which one is Algernon? I'll bring some flowers for him next time."

"Stop it, Tim! Just because you don't read the classics is no reason to make fun. I have named none of them, of course. It is best not to get too attached. You know that— the nanobot batch serials associated with Greek letters identify them."

"Yes, I know. It just seems sad. They work so hard, and they have no names, really. No identity."

"Of course, they do! If one of these drugs works, then they will tell us. Or at least, the server logs will. By the way, did you recalibrate the communication protocols from the nanobots to the server? I want to be sure they are correct before we start. Oh, where is the coffee? All these bagels and no coffee!"

"Sorry, Jared won't let me drink it anymore. Makes me jumpy. Yes, the protocols are correct. I ran a feedback diagnostic last night just to be sure."

"OK, finish your breakfast. We have work to do!"

"Yes, boss." He tossed the food container into the composting bin and went to the locked drug cabinet. "Which drug should we start with?"

"None. We need a baseline, remember? I appreciate your programming skills, Tim, but you are a terrible scientist; we'll make one out of you yet. Take Alpha to the maze and get him ready."

"Right." Tim took the mouse to the maze across the room. "Let me get the protocol connection set up." He went over to the server console. After a few clicks, he announced, "Ready."

Nomie had walked over to the maze. "OK, here goes." She released the mouse into the maze. Alpha hesitated briefly, then began navigating it. After retracing its route after a few dead ends, it came out the other end and got its cheesy reward.

"Alpha took three minutes to complete the maze. Nanobot perception data has been logged to the server," reported Tim.

"That was an about-average time," confirmed Nomie. "I'll get Beta." She returned Alpha to its cage and retrieved Beta. She set it in the maze. "Ready, Tim?"

"Switching the protocol to Beta and recording

perception data. Anytime."

Nomie released Beta. It didn't hesitate; it started the maze immediately and took fewer dead ends on the way to its prize.

"Two minutes and logged to the server," reported Tim.

Nomie frowned. "Odd, that was fast—must be a smart mouse already. We may need to exclude it from the trial."

They repeated the process with the other mice. Each mouse was faster than the previous one. They finally reached the minimum of five seconds to finish the maze.

"I don't get it," said Nomie. She went back to the mouse cages, studying Alpha and the other mice. Finally, she said, "Tim, I want to retest Alpha." She retrieved Alpha and placed it in the maze.

"Five seconds," reported Tim. "You don't think they are watching each other?"

"Don't be silly, child. Oh, that was a joke. Ha ha." Nomie had visions of her grant money being terminated. Why give money to a researcher who can't manage a simple mouse maze test?

"Tim, we need to review the perception logs."

"Sure," replied Tim, peering at the server console. "Shit! Oh, jeez, Nomie, I'm sorry! I fucked up!"

"What? You mean you weren't recording? Tim,

you're fired!" She took a breath. "I'm sorry; I didn't mean that. What happened?"

"We recorded all right. Remember the feedback diagnostic I ran last night? It's still running."

"So?"

"The server shared each mouse's experience running the maze. It sent them to their nanobots."

"Ah, I see. It would be like a memory. They learned from each other."

"So, Nomie...."

"Hush! I'm listening."

She sat silently for a minute and looked over at the cages.

"It's very quiet now; there are only two mice chattering. The rest are quiet, and they're not moving." She walked over and looked at one of the quiet mice. "His eyes are not moving." She took the mouse from the cage, holding it. "Alpha, how are you?" She returned the mouse to the cage.

She went over to the end cage, where one of the active, chattering mice was. "This is Omega, the control mouse." She walked back to the other end. "This is Gamma. Tim, the implants did not take for Gamma, correct?"

"Yes, he's been excluded from the study."

"Tim, change the server interface from send and receive to receive-only. I want to see what happens when the mice are no longer getting information from the server."

"Sure," he picked up his tablet and tapped on it. "Done."

He dropped his tablet and covered his ears, "My God! What a racket!"

Nomie backed away from the cages, covering her ears. She rushed to the drug cabinet and withdrew a set of preloaded syringes. "Tim, take these and start injecting them. We need to sedate them!"

Tim took a handful and went to one end of the cages. "Tim! Put on gloves." She pulled hers on and went to the first cage. "Poor Alpha" It was screaming and grinding the cage wire. She opened the door and swiftly reached in, grabbed the mouse and injected it. Closing the door, she moved to Beta, in similar distress.

"What's going on?" said Tim, his voice shaking and barely audible over the din.

"I'll explain later! Keep going."

After sedating the last mouse, they collapsed into the chairs by the small table. Moloi cradled her head in her hands. Tim sat back. Both were stressed from the ordeal.

"Withdrawal, Tim. That's what happened."

"Withdrawal from what?"

Nomie got up and went to the sink, found a kettle, filled it with water, and switched it on. "From being connected. The poor things went from solitary creatures, only able to communicate with their chattering, to being able to see and hear everything their companions saw and heard." She filled the teapot with tea, waiting for the water to heat up. "I'm surprised they lasted this long."

"So, the maze—that was a kind of sharing, right? They learned from it," said Tim. "Then they were still connected. And they were quiet."

"Yes," said Nomie. She added water to the pot and let the tea steep. "But they were still chattering. The implants interrupted the signal from the brain to their speech organs. The signals were redirected to the server, which the other mice then received. Not only that, but signals as well for sound, sight, smell, and touch." She sighed. "I am sure it was very confusing for them."

She filled two mugs and brought one to Tim. "Then we changed the server comms," said Tim, "the implants redirected the inputs again, back to normal. That's when we heard their anguish." He sank his head, ignoring the tea. "The poor mice—this is all my fault!"

Nomie put her hand on Tim's shoulder. "We learned something today. Something we didn't expect. Great things often come from such mistakes." She sipped her tea. "The mice could not have understood what was happening to them; they could not have processed it. I'm sorry, Tim, we must euthanize them. It is for the best. We will need to examine their implants. We cannot continue the trial with them. I'll need to get a new set of mice and implants from the Phillips Foundation."

"Nomie, this is not making me feel any better," said Tim, looking at the sleeping mice.

"Oh, Tim. Do you have any idea how many mistakes I have made? Look at me now! A full-fledged PhD with funded research! You are an able assistant, and I value you."

"Okay, fine." He took another sip of the tea, then went to the drugs cabinet. He took out another set of syringes. "This is my responsibility, Nomie. I will take care of it."

Nomie watched as Tim went to each cage, removed the mouse and administered the lethal injection. The only sounds came from Omega and Epsilon.

###

The receptionist guided Nomie to a conference room. It was generic, with a long oblong table and a monitor covering one wall. A large window provided a panoramic view of the Washington and Jefferson memorials. If the Phillips Foundation can afford this view, she thought, it could certainly afford a new set of mice and nanobots.

"Please take a seat; Mrs. Phillips will join you shortly. Would you care for a cup of coffee?"

"That would be wonderful! Cream and sugar, please."

Nomie took a seat and smoothed out her dress. What a waste of time! she thought. But without mice and nanobots, there was little for her to do. The Foundation paid for the express train from Boston and the hotel. So just enjoy yourself, visit a few museums. The receptionist returned with the coffee, the same smile painted on her face.

Nomie sipped the coffee, the best she'd had in a long time. She checked her messages for any news from the mouse autopsies. Nothing. After an hour and a cold coffee, she turned to playing chess on her tablet in desperation. Once again, the Caro-Kann defense failed her. Often, the door to a neighboring office would open, and she would glance up quickly. Nothing.

Finally, a tall, middle-aged brunette woman entered. She was well-dressed and had a pleasant smile.

"My coffee is cold," said Nomie. "It's about time someone checked on me. I'll take another, with more cream this time!"

She nodded. "Certainly," she said. "I'll be right back."

She returned with the coffee. "How's this?"

Nomie took a sip. "Much better."

"It's so nice to have competent help, isn't it? Tell me, why do you continue to employ Tim Sutherland?"

Shit, thought Nomie. I should have recognized her. Get a grip. "If I fired everyone who had ever made a mistake, I would have no employees. Tell me, Mrs. Phillips, how is it you still have any employees? Or are they all temps?"

"Hah! I like you already, Dr. Moloi. Besides, you'd only have one employee. If you fired him, you'd have none. That's bad arithmetic."

Nomie smiled. "You may call me Nomie. You are in charge here after all. And Tim is quite competent."

Phillips held out her hand. "Pleased to meet you, Nomie. I'm Isolde Phillips. I run all of this. You may call me Izzy."

Nomie rose and shook her hand. "So, Izzy. Why am I here? We could have met virtually."

They both sat down. "I like to meet some people face to face—people I find interesting."

"Interesting? I'm just a low-level researcher who managed to kill off all her research subjects. Good thing

12

the Internal Review Board isn't involved!"

"Not now, anyway," said Izzy.

Nomie shifted in her seat. "What do you mean? The drugs are meant for subsequent human safety trials. If we get that far."

"I don't care about the drugs."

"But they were the whole point of the project! Cognitive-enhancing medications." Nomie looked at Izzy; her smile had grown larger. "Ah, the nanobot implants! That's what you care about!"

"Yes, it turns out your assistant is useful, after all. That mistake he made, I think it will be a very profitable one."

Nomie shook her head. "No, Izzy. The mice, they went crazy. They couldn't handle all the conflicting input!"

"Nomie, they were *mice*. Humans are not mice. They can handle it."

I came here to get mice, and I'm getting humans. Is this the way it always is with people like Phillips? I guess that's how they get to be such people, and people like me come begging.

"What do you want, Izzy?"

The door opened, and the receptionist brought in a glass of water and some pills. She left, and Izzy took the pills without comment.

"First, I want an exclusive license to produce implants

based on your design. I'd ask to buy the patent and design from you, but I think you are too intelligent to give that away."

Nomie smiled. "I'm surprised you didn't try. But you are correct; the design is my life's work. So, no, I wouldn't do that."

"I'll ask for the next best thing, then. Come work for me. I'm starting a new company. You will be the chief research officer and report directly to me. You can even bring your assistant, Jim, with you."

"Tim."

"Fine, Tim. Who gives a fuck? What you two stumbled upon, it will change the world! I want it, and you will give it to me."

"Give you what?"

Izzy leaned forward, steepling her fingers. "I've had marketing work on it. Everything needs an acronym, after all."

Nomie's head was spinning. Chief Research Officer? What do they do?

"What acronym?"

"CIPHER: Cybernetic Implant for Personalized Human Experience and Recording."

"I understand why you need an acronym."

Izzy sat back. "I like you, Nomie! You have a sense of

humor, and you are not afraid of me. Most people are."

Probably for good reason, thought Nomie.

Izzy went on, "It's what happened with your mice, isn't it? They recorded their experience navigating the maze; they all learned from it. They communicated that with each other; they experienced events through others."

"And it drove them mad. Let's not forget that."

"You keep harping on that. I guess that's why you are the scientist and I am the risk taker." She paused. "You are right to be concerned. We need to take this step by step. The first version of this will focus solely on communication. People will be able to communicate and collaborate over long distances. Better and faster than ever."

"This will require a tremendous server farm," said Nomie.

"Absolutely! And CRI will own it."

"CRI?"

"Yes, CRI. CIPHER Research Institute. Please pay attention, Nomie."

Christ, yet another acronym, thought Nomie.

"That seems fine. And the next version?"

"That will allow people to share experiences," said Izzy, "like the mice. Only this time, they won't go crazy."

"Let's hope not..."

"I know this is a lot, Nomie. I need you on this. You are not afraid to speak your mind to me. Most people would jump at this... Oh, I should show you this—your salary, moving expenses, housing, staff, and budget." She produced a tablet and passed it to Nomie.

Shit. "I can pick my staff?"

Izzy nodded.

"OK! Where do I sign?"

The New World
June 2085

Gareth tied his robe as he walked out of the bedroom into the kitchen of their small apartment. He surveyed the unholy trinity of half-empty beer bottles, totally empty wine bottles, and greasy pizza boxes scattered about the living room. It smelled like a dive bar in downtown Kalamazoo: stale beer and congealed grease. Where do I even start to clean? he asked himself. Why bother?

The college graduation celebration party had turned into a wake. Their hopes and dreams were now a corpse laid out in the small living room. Everyone had brought the FuckOffAndDie replies to their job applications. They printed them out and held a pagan ritual burning, setting off the fire alarm. That had been fun, he mused.

"Good morning, Gareth," he heard Cathy say from

behind him. He turned and saw her drying her light brown hair with a towel. Her untied robe hung loosely open, draped around her otherwise naked body. She looked around the kitchen and said, "What a mess! God, that smell!"

"Good morning. You're right, it's a disaster area—probably toxic. I don't have the will to deal with cleaning this up now."

She finished with the towel, tossing it back into the bedroom; her short dark hair was drying quickly. He liked it longer, but it was smart to cut it short for the trip to Africa. She came over and kissed him good morning.

"That was such an awful party," said Gareth. "All of us getting totally shit-faced drunk." Gareth frowned. "Except Alex, of course. He's got it made, born into the right family. CIPHER will make them rich."

"Gar, that was last night. The less I think about that, the better. Fuck the past, it's gone." She grabbed a slice of leftover pizza and tossed it into the trash. "See, just like that! This is a bright new morning. You and I, we'll figure out our future together," she said, hugging him.

Cathy grabbed his shoulder-length hair, pulling on it. "You know, pretty boy, we're going to have to cut this long blond hair. You won't be able to luxuriate in the bucket shower at camp. No twenty-minute showers there! There won't be enough water to properly clean it if you keep it this long."

"Ouch! Stop pulling," he grinned. "I know. I'll get it cut tomorrow. We're not leaving for a week." He felt the closeness of her, the scent of her hair, the softness of her skin. A morning erection made itself known. Cathy untied his robe and pulled him to her. She reached a hand around and down his back, landing on his butt, giving it a light slap.

"Hey that hurt!" he said. "What a tease, showing up half naked. Well, mostly naked." He sighed and looked at the mess in the kitchen. "Well, if you insist. I guess I'll clean the kitchen later."

"Your choice," she said. "You can follow me or stay here and clean. One way or the other, I'll get what I want, but it's more fun with you."

She offered her hand and smiled at him; it was a playful and loving smile. That and her laughter were all her, nothing hidden, nothing held back. Why can't I be like that? Gareth wondered. She was so open and spontaneous. I'm so guarded. What am I trying to protect? 'I love you', he wanted to say. He took her hand and followed her, taking off his robe and tossing it somewhere, following as she led him back into the bedroom.

They held each other afterward, Cathy resting her head on Gareth's chest. He woke from a light sleep and wondered what was next. CIPHER had ripped away their plans and ambitions. They had no prospects.

"What will we do, Cathy? We don't have jobs. Six years of classes and tests down the drain. Not to mention the loans we took out. How could everything have changed so quickly?"

"I don't know, sweetie. It's a shock, all right."

Gareth gathered some pillows from the floor that had become dislodged and propped himself up, offering some to Cathy. So many pillows tossed aside earlier. They had been in the way. Now called back into service. Cathy took some pillows and placed them behind her, sitting up next to him. She placed her hand on his. The touch calmed him.

"We're OK for now. Dad will float us until we can figure something out," said Cathy.

Gareth pulled his hand back, crossing his arms across his chest. "Cathy, I, well, that's not something I want. I like Walter. It's just that he's done so much for us already. He's even paying for our graduation vacation." He shook his head. "Why? What's the point? We didn't graduate, not really. You're supposed to graduate *to* something. We just stopped one part of life, with no next."

"We'll figure something out, Gar. We just need a little time. We're still young. It's not like we're middle-aged and have lost our jobs. They're the ones who really got screwed. They'll never get their lives back."

"I guess."

"Let's take the trip like we planned. I'll ask Dad to look into some job options for when we get back."

Gareth threw the sheets off and got out of bed. "Walter, again?" His voice shook, and his face flushed red. He searched around for his robe. *Right, I left it in the kitchen.* He gave up the search and sat on the edge of the bed. "Do I ever get to do something without Walter handing it to me? God damn it! I should have a job! I studied and worked for it, did everything I was supposed to do!"

Cathy slid over next to him and put a hand on his thigh. "It's not your fault, Gareth. I know you will get a good job. It can't hurt to take a little help, can it? We could both use a little help. I mean, look at Alex. His grandmother is setting him up at CRI. That's not a bad thing; he deserves the job. So, he used a connection to get it. Why not? We can too."

Gareth collapsed back onto the bed, staring at the ceiling. "You're right. Alex had help, so I shouldn't be so proud. Do you think Walter can help us get CIPHER implants? I mean, they're still pretty new, so that would give us a leg up looking for work."

Cathy rolled over and kissed him. "Yes, I'm sure he would. Maybe we can get something set up for after the trip." She caressed his chest, running her fingers through his blond chest hair. "What do you say?" She kissed him on his chest, moving her way down. He felt himself stiffen.

He rolled Cathy over onto her back, making his own journey down her. "I'd say yes. But I'm a little distracted at the moment."

"Doesn't look so little to me..."

Gotta Have CIPHER 1
September 2085

The nurse had left Cathy and Gareth alone in the procedure room. They decided to get their implants at the same time, and Walter had pulled a few strings to get them an appointment with Dr. Francis's CIPHER Implantation Clinic. The procedure room was nearly as plush as the waiting room. It had all the usual features: a sink, cupboards, chairs that looked like they belonged in a high-end restaurant, and a large, comfortable-looking chair.

Cathy sat down in one of the chairs while Gareth paced around the room, stopping occasionally to inspect the large chair. There were pamphlets on the counter by the sink. He picked them up and quickly set them down again.

"Gareth, are you OK?" Cathy asked.

"What? Me? Um, sure. I'm fine. Why?"

"It's just that this is what you wanted, CIPHER, and it seems like you're upset."

Gareth sat down and ran his hand through his hair. It was long again, having grown back in the three months since they had returned from Africa. He sat down in the chair next to Cathy.

"I guess that I'm just excited, that's all. I mean, what if they don't take? It happens. Maybe I'm too old."

"At twenty-five? Please, Gareth, you'll be fine. Dad's fifty, and he's had no problems. He's even on the priority list for CIPHER 2."

"Hah! Connections and money don't hurt, either," said Gareth.

"Gar, can we not talk about that now?"

He shrugged and sat down. "Sure, sorry. I really do appreciate what Walt's doing for us. I'll pay him back; this is just a loan."

"I know..." said Cathy, as the door opened and a tall, thin, middle-aged, white-coated man walked in, accompanied by a young woman wearing scrubs.

"Hi, I'm Dr. John Francis." He extended his hand to Gareth and then to Cathy. "You are Gareth and Cathy Williams?"

"Yes," said Gareth, shaking the doctor's hand.

"This is Pam. She's interning with us. Do you mind if she observes the procedure? She'll assist with the acclimation process."

"Acclimation process?" asked Gareth.

"Yes, verifying that the implant is making all the proper connections."

"Oh, I see. That's fine," said Gareth. He looked to Cathy for confirmation. She nodded her head.

"I see you are both getting CIPHER 1 today. Do you have questions about the procedure? About the implants themselves?"

Gareth looked at Cathy, then back at the doctor. "How long, I mean when will I know that the implants have taken hold? That they will work for me?"

Dr. Francis looked to his assistant and said, "Pam, would you answer the young man's question?" He went to the cupboard and retrieved two vials, inspecting the labels.

She nodded and said, "Of course. We will know within five minutes whether the process is a success. At the end of the acclimation, you will receive a CIPHER score showing the quality of the connection. Anything over 80 is good."

"Does anyone ever get a 100?" said Gareth, smiling.

"No, scores over 90 are rare. Doctor, I believe the

highest score recorded is 96?"

"Correct, Mr. Williams, would you like to go first?"

"Well, sure. What do I need to do?"

"Not much, just take a seat in the procedure chair." Dr. Francis indicated the large chair.

Gareth sat down. "You can lean back," said Pam. He reclined, and the chair moved to cradle his head and raised his feet, conforming to hold his body.

"Now, you won't feel much after I perform the injection," said Dr. Francis. "The injection itself will be a small pinprick. The nanobots that comprise the CIPHER implant will then quickly make their way to your brain. They will pass through what we call the blood-brain barrier, which is easy for nanites to do. Once there, they will assemble themselves into thousands of specialized nanobots that will integrate with the speech and auditory centers of your brain. As Pam said, we will know soon after that whether the implant is working for you. Any questions before I proceed?"

"Gareth, are you sure?" Cathy asked.

"Cathy, yes, I'm sure! Let's do this!"

Dr. Francis walked over to Gareth and injected him in the arm. He handed the vial over to Pam. "Scan this and start tracking."

"Yes, Doctor. I have scanned the vial, and we are

tracking."

After a few seconds, Gareth's eyes closed, then opened again.

"It feels odd," said Gareth. "It's like I'm hearing something, but I'm not. Did someone just say something?"

"No, Mr. Williams," said Dr. Francis. "It's the implant. The nanobots have already assembled and are connecting. Pam, what are you seeing?"

"I can confirm the connections are being made. It's only been a minute. Isn't that faster than normal?"

"Yes, but not beyond expectations. Send a test ping."

Gareth heard a voice.

Gareth, this is Pam. Are you receiving?

It sounded like Pam, thought Gareth. But I didn't see her lips move. He heard her voice again.

Just think what you would say to me. But don't say it.

OK. Pam? Is that you?

Ask your CIPHER. It will confirm my identity.

How do I ask?

Just use the wake word: cipher. It will respond. You don't really need to use the wake word, but some find it useful.

OK, thought Gareth. I've read the materials, so I should know what to do. *Cipher, identify source.*

Source is Pam Martins, CIPHER ID f8815c29-7298-4f9e-82af-5b3c21213182.

OK, that's more that I needed to know. There is one thing I'm still not clear about. How does my CIPHER know to send these thoughts to you?

Each CIPHER communication, like this, has embedded in it the CIPHER ID of the sender. Your implant sends the response using the ID. The cloud then knows who to route the response to. This all happens automatically. Your CIPHER also creates an association between my 'name' and the CIPHER ID. It knows to use that information to send me a message when you think of sending one to me.

I see, I think.

"Gareth, I need you to do one more thing. Talk to me."

But we are talking...

"Use your voice. CIPHER cannot be the only means of communication. Not everyone has or can have CIPHER. For the sake of the CIPHERless, you still need to speak with your voice and process sounds. It's important to keep that active. Try again. Maybe try to say hi to Cathy."

Try how? thought Gareth. OK, *Cathy.* No, that's right. I heard nothing. Focus on sound. "Cathy?"

"Yes, I'm here, Gareth. Are you OK?"

"OK? I feel great! You'll see soon, too! Doctor Francis, how did I do?"

Dr. Francis smiled. "You did great, Gareth. A CIPHER score of 92, which is exceptional for a person of your age. It seems that your brain is still quite plastic."

"Plastic?" said Cathy. "What do you mean?"

"It's the ability of the brain," said Dr. Francis, "to make new connections, to learn new things. When we are very young, think newborn to toddler, our brains are constantly creating connections between neurons, which is how we send and process information. CIPHER connects into that system. The more plastic your brain, the better CIPHER does."

"Hear that, Gareth?" said Cathy. "It looks like you can learn new things after all."

"With a score like this, Mr. Williams," said Dr. Francis, "I'd like to forward your information to CRI. They are very interested in people with scores over 90. They may have some opportunities for you. May I do that?"

"Sure," said Gareth, grinning. "Cathy, this is great! CRI! This could be fantastic for us! Your turn. Maybe you'll beat my score?"

"It's not a competition, Gar," said Cathy. She sat down

in the procedure chair. "OK, I'm ready."

Walter Goes Fugue
April 2087

It was late evening when Cathy and Gareth arrived at *Happy Meadows*, their clothes damp from the rain. The sanitarium was one of several recently built, designed to care for victims of a rare side effect of CIPHER 2 technology. The care facility appeared as if it had only recently opened—some lobby furniture was still in shrink wrap.

The message from Cathy's mother had been brief, without a lot of detail. Just that something had happened to Walter, and she needed to come right away. Cathy was doing her best to keep her worries at bay. Gareth tried to reassure her, but nothing he said helped.

As they entered the reception area, they witnessed a heated discussion between two women at the desk. *I recognize them,* ciphered Gareth.

Yes, so do I. My CIPHER confirms that it's Moloi and Phillips.

What are they going on about?

"Izzy," said Moloi, "I warned you about this! We are moving too fast! You are bringing out new versions with insufficient testing."

"Please, Nomie! Take a breath. You know we have been quite thorough. The FDA has approved every version."

"The FDA approval process for medical devices is historically lax!" Nomie paused. "That's why you stopped the drug trials, isn't it? Drugs are a lot more difficult to get approved. A medical device—that's easier."

Phillips noticed that Gareth and Cathy were within earshot. "Enough! We are in public. We will discuss this back at CRI. For God's sake, Nomie, please use CIPHER for comms!"

Moloi glared at Phillips and left. Phillips looked over at Gareth. "I recognize you. Are you a friend of Alex? Yes, I met you at the graduation ceremony."

"That's right, ma'am. My name's Gareth. Gareth Williams. This is my wife, Cathy."

"Hello Cathy. Ah, Gareth Williams—that is an odd name—Gareth. Welsh, correct? I'm sure I recognize it.

Ah, you work for me. And you are a friend of Alex." She smiled and followed Moloi out.

"Gareth," said Cathy, "please, can we move on!"

"What, oh sure. That's probably the last time I'll see either of them. I can't tell whether they are friends or enemies. But yes, let's see if reception knows where your parents are. Wait, I see your mother. Hi, Mary!"

Cathy's mother had just reentered the main reception, emerging from the door to the main part of the facility. She was dressed casually, which was unusual for her. She made a point of dressing well whenever she left the house. The wife of the famous Walter Mendez must always look perfect. "Cathy, there you are." She came up to them, her eyes red and puffy.

"Mother, are you all right?" said Cathy. "You look like you've been crying." She hugged her mother.

"I'm so sorry, Cathy. It's Walt; they don't know what's wrong."

"What do you mean? What happened?"

"I don't know. He was running an Experience in the library. He'd been doing that a lot since he got CIPHER 2. You know, he's so obsessive sometimes. But he'd been in for a long time and was late for our pre-dinner cocktail. When I went to get him, he was just sitting there. I shook him, and then I saw his eyes...." She shook. "I need to sit down."

"Yes, Gareth, can you ..."

"Sure." He took her arm and guided her to a nearby sofa, and she sat down. Gareth searched his pockets for a Kleenex. He couldn't find any. "I'll be back." He went to the reception. 'Experience', he thought, that's what CIPHER 2 gets you. Not just messaging but re-living an activity that someone, an Experiencer, had recorded using CIPHER 2. All the sights, smells, sounds that the person recording it felt. A great thing for shut-ins. So many Experiences to pick from, like scuba diving and parasailing—all without a risk. What a rush that would be!

"Hi, do you have some Kleenex?" said Gareth to the reception clerk. The clerk handed him a box.

"Here, Mary," said Gareth as he handed over the box.

"Has Dad seen a doctor? What do they think?"

Mary took a Kleenex and blew her nose. "Yes, so many doctors have seen him. For all the good it did! All this money and power, the best doctors, even the top people from CRI. They just don't know."

"It's not a stroke?" said Cathy.

"No, physically he's fine. But he's not responding to anything! I've talked to him, held his hand, kissed him. Nothing! His eyes ... they haven't closed since I found him. They're always darting around!"

"My God," said Cathy. "Can I see him?"

"Soon. I had to leave while they got him settled. They need to treat his eyes and set up a bed. One doctor called it Fugue. He said that he'd seen a few cases. They like the Experience so much, they never want to leave it. One of the other doctors vehemently disagreed."

"He must be right," said Gareth. "That first doctor, he's got it wrong! Walt wouldn't do that. He loves his work too much. There must be a medical reason."

I'm sure it has nothing to do with CIPHER 2 or Experiences, Gareth thought. He looked at Cathy, lines of concern and worry on her face. She thinks it does, and she knows I want it. Why not! With my CIPHER score, I'd be able to get great work and pay.

"I hope you're right, Gareth," said Mary. "If there's a physical reason, they'll find it. He'll get better."

Gotta Have CIPHER 2
November 2088

"No!" said Cathy. "I told you before, CIPHER 2 is out. No way are you getting it!"

The morning had started so well, thought Gareth. Finally, it was the weekend. The farmer's market had been fun. They had picked up some fresh bread, wine and cheese. They were all set to go to the concert in town tonight. Just the sort of thing Cathy liked. She was happy. As happy as she could be given her father's condition. There would be no better time to talk about the future.

"But, I ciphered you the ad," Gareth protested, "it won't cost anything. I talked to Alex—he works at *Multitudes* now as a CIPHER tech. He's already set up the interview. I'm sure I can get in."

"Damn you, Gareth! You always want more! How

could you even consider this? My father's lying in Fugue or something at *Happy Meadows*. You know it's because of CIPHER and Experiences!"

Gareth put the cheese in the refrigerator and unpacked the other goods on the kitchen counter. "No, I don't know that," he said, trying to inject calm and reason into his voice. "There are so many viruses out there today. It could be one of them. I'm sure he'll come out of it soon."

"I don't believe it! It's been months now! Damn you, Gareth! I was so looking forward to tonight. Isn't this enough for you? What more do you want?" Her voice was shaking. "What's wrong with the job at CRI? You're making good money. What? Do you want a bigger apartment? Do you want to buy a home? Start a family? We can do all that now. You don't need CIPHER 2. What happened to Dad could happen to you. Don't you see that?"

He finished putting the rest of the groceries away. "I feel like I'm being left behind again. The world keeps moving along; I need to move with it. Remember all our friends from college? How many of them have jobs? How many have CIPHER? All of them! Now they're getting CIPHER 2!" I lost this argument before it even started, he realized. "And yes, dammit! I want a house! I'm fucking sick of this small apartment!"

Calm down! I need to sound reasonable so that I can convince her.

"Gareth, the company you want to work for, they create Experiences. That's what put Dad into this Fugue. I can't be with you if you take this job!"

"You keep coming back to that. You don't know that's true! Even if it is, they'll figure out something—a way to make it safer and bring people like Walt back."

She shook her head. "No, I don't think so. There are more places like *Happy Meadows* being built to house and take care of these people!" she said, her voice getting louder. He could hear her stress. "It is not just a rumor! It's become its own business!"

"OK, but I'm sure it's temporary; they'll come out of it! I know they will!"

"Please, Gar, why won't you listen to me?"

He went to her to hold her, to reassure her. I know what I'm doing! This seems so right. How do I convince her? She pushed him away.

"If you do this, I'm leaving. You've backed me into a corner, goddamn you!" He could see tears forming and heard the shake in her voice. I should just drop it, he thought. But I can't; I need this. She always shuts down the discussion like this. Not this time!

"You're not serious! All the years we've been together! You won't throw that away! You can't!"

Cathy bolted to the bedroom. He heard her get a suitcase down from the closet. She's bluffing, he thought. The sound of drawers slamming open and closed came to him. How do you slam a drawer open? he mused. If anyone could, Cathy could. It's just another part of the show, the act. I'm not falling for it this time.

Cathy emerged from the bedroom, suitcase trailing behind her. "I have what I need. You can sell or donate the rest. I don't care." She sounded defeated, like she had lost some battle he didn't know was being fought.

"Cathy, please. Just sit down. You don't want to leave."

"No, I don't want to. But I can't stay here, not with you. I can't deal with the pain."

"Pain?" he asked. "What pain? Am I that bad of a person? I just want ..."

"I know, Gareth." Cathy sighed. "You are not a bad person; I'm just afraid for you. I don't think you understand what you want. What it means. Won't you just trust me?"

"I do! But you've got to let me do this!"

"I, I just can't," said Cathy, letting out a heavy breath. "I wish I could. I love you; I want to spend my life with you. But not if you keep going this way. I can't be around when...I hope that..." Unable to finish either sentence, Cathy walked out and shut the door behind her, jarring the shelf holding the mementos of their trip to Africa. The hippo and giraffe fell to the floor.

She'll be back, he thought. I'll get the new job; nothing bad will happen. She'll come back, and everything will be better. He went to the fridge and took out two beers. Gareth headed to the sofa, then turned around, returning to the fridge. He put one beer back.

Sitting down, he opened the bottle and took a drink. Cathy will be back, he thought again, trying to convince himself. He looked down at the fallen hippo and the giraffe, hoping for an answer. Patiently waiting, he took another drink.

The Protest

September 2089 - February 2090

Cathy walked through the National Gallery's outdoor Sculpture Garden and headed towards the crowd that was gathering on the grassy lawn of the National Mall. It was early morning. The air felt crisp and cool. Red and orange leaves bordered the sidewalk and appeared on the lawn as islands in a sea of people.

It was exciting, but also unnerving, to be in such a large crowd. Most people don't go out anymore. They stayed home, running CIPHER Experiences. That was always the best way to enjoy concerts and sporting events. It's what CIPHER stood for, after all—Cybernetic Implant for Personalized Human Experience and Recording. A long-winded techno-babble way to say—'I see what you see or saw and felt and heard and smelled'. All of that put together gave the user a fully immersive experience. I bet Gareth has created a few concert Experiences, thought Cathy.

As she drew nearer to the crowd, she noticed that most of the people at the rally were much older than she was. The music blasting from the sound system was age appropriate for them. Of course, she realized, there would be a lot of older people in the Isolator movement. Many were likely too old for the CIPHER implants to take hold. They were isolated by default. CIPHER came too late in their lives for them to tolerate the CIPHER implantation. Their brains were no longer 'plastic' enough to make the required connections to the nanobots.

Cathy looked around for an information table to get a better idea of the program for the rally. She found a table with someone just leaving it. A man and a woman were standing behind it. "Hi," she said to the young, slender, blond woman at the table. "This is my first time at one of these. I wonder ..."

The woman continued packing and didn't look up from the table. "Sorry, we were just packing up."

"Oh, I see. I'll try another table."

"Hey! That's okay. We can hang around for a bit," said the man. He was good-looking, with short, dark hair.

"Alright, Rick." The woman looked up from the table

at Cathy, her vibrant green eyes making contact with Cathy's inquiring gaze. "You're young!" Rick stifled a laugh.

"Well, yes. Is that a problem?" Cathy asked, smiling.

"No, no, of course not," she replied, stumbling over her words. "Stop laughing, Rick! It's just that, well, most people here are older."

"You're not so old yourself," said Cathy.

"Good to hear," she replied as she and her partner finished packing the materials into boxes. "Hey, there's not much going on for a while, just some warm-up speeches. It's great to meet someone closer to our age. I'd love to know more about you and what drew you to the Isolator movement."

"Sure! I guess we can start with our names. I'm Cathy." She held out her hand. Such an old gesture, thought Cathy, but I need to feel contact with someone. God, I'm getting desperate for human connection. Is that why I'm here? The woman took her hand, shaking it lightly. Suddenly, Cathy felt the connection she had been seeking since she had left Gareth.

"Sam, short for Samantha, of course. Nice to meet you." She released Cathy's hand.

"Can I help you with the boxes?" Cathy asked. Why did I offer that? I don't even know them. It doesn't hurt to offer, I guess."

Rick spoke up. "It's okay, I'll take them. I need to help set up for the big speech later." He kissed Sam on the cheek. "I'll catch you later." He placed the boxes on a hand-truck and disappeared into the crowd.

"It looks like I have some free time," said Sam. "How about you? I know a quiet café off Dupont Circle. Care to join me for a cup of coffee? I'm kind of addicted to it."

Why not? thought Cathy. There was something really likable about her. Well, not only likable, but the kind of person who you know you want to be with. "Sure, lead on."

Sam guided her out of the crowd, and they took a taxi to the café. The sidewalk tables were mostly empty due to the cool fall weather. They sat down, and Sam ordered cappuccinos for them.

"There are just so many ways to enjoy caffeine," said Sam. "Life would be miserable without it, don't you think?"

"Can't argue with that," said Cathy.

"Tell me, if you don't mind my asking. Why join the Isolators?"

"Well, I'm no Ludd. I don't think violence solves anything."

"Of course not! But I mean why not get CIPHER like

everyone else your age and be happy? Lose yourself in Experiences and all that?"

Cathy took a breath. Do I want to tell? she wondered. Can I tell her? I've told no one except Gareth. And he didn't understand. Why would I tell a stranger, someone I've just met? Maybe that's why. We have no history, not yet.

Sam waited quietly for answers, her body language telling her to take her time. She's so patient. Sam's green eyes were like a well she could pour her worries and disappointments into. Her whole body invited her to talk, to unburden herself. I can't tell her yet—not the real reason.

Cathy played with the ring on her finger.

"I noticed that," said Sam, nodding at the ring. "You're married. Is he an Isolator, too?"

Cathy laughed. "Oh, no. Not at all. He went all in on CIPHER. Still is."

"I see."

"No, it's not just that, not just CIPHER. I can't blame him for being ambitious. It was such a blow when we graduated. CIPHER changed everything. Our education was rendered obsolete overnight. I get it; he wanted a job, so he needed CIPHER."

"That sounds reasonable."

"Sure. It was. I got it, too: CIPHER 1." Cathy shrugged. "He changed after getting his. I can't say how exactly. We didn't talk like we used to. He pestered me about his getting CIPHER 2. I told him I didn't think it was a good idea. He didn't need it. CIPHER 1 was enough. Gareth, that's his name, he didn't listen. He wanted a job as an Experiencer." She looked back at Sam, nearly spitting the last word out.

Sam's eyes opened wider. "An Experiencer? Really..."

"Yes. And he's *really* good at it. At least, that's what I've heard from Alex. Sorry, Alex is an old friend of mine and Gareth." Cathy spat out a laugh. "Alex is Isolde Phillips' grandson. What a coincidence."

Sam sipped her coffee and leaned in closer.

"But I couldn't take it," Cathy continued. "I left. Since then, I guess I've been looking for something to connect with. Really connect, not just ciphering people. I'm looking for what Gareth and I used to have." Cathy took a breath. Sam was an attractive young woman. It had been such a long time. Should I take a chance? "Like with you now. Does that seem crazy?"

Sam smiled. It was an open, inviting smile, confirming Cathy's hopes. "No, not at all. Honestly, Rick and I feel the same way." The smile faded, and she looked somewhere over Cathy's right shoulder—at a void, at an absence. "We had such a strong connection once...."

"What is it with you two? What made you join the Isolators?"

Sam shook her head and said, "Other than what you mentioned with Gareth. There are worse things. Rick and I—we had a lover—Ruth. She had a bad Experience. I'm sure that Gareth creates quality Experiences. But Ruth ran one she found on the Moloi dark cloud. It didn't go well."

Fugue? Is that what she means? Sam looked back at Cathy. She gave a light nod, a curt acknowledgment. "I'm so sorry," said Cathy.

"Wow," said Sam. Sam took another sip of her cappuccino. "Sorry, this got heavy fast. Look, I enjoy talking with you. It's like you said, we are really connecting. I need to get back to the protest. Can you come along? We can get together with Rick afterwards."

For once, the regret she had over leaving Gareth subsided. I like Sam. "Yes, that would be great!"

Snow. Cathy recalled Grandpa talking about 'Snowmageddon'. Apparently, it snowed so much that the city shut down for three days. How could snow shut anything down? It hardly snows in DC now.

Cathy gathered her cardigan around her and sipped her coffee. Gazing out at Sam's backyard, Cathy thought the flakes looked so delicate—not meant to survive long. They melted as soon as they made fleeting contact with the too warm ground.

"Cathy, pay attention! We have a lot of material to put together," said Rick. He was in the kitchen working with Sam, trying to find the best wording to attract new recruits. Sam smiled at Cathy. "She's fine, Rick. Let her enjoy the beauty of the moment."

It seemed as though Rick spent a lot of time at Sam's house. Cathy felt the emanations of jealousy at that. But she reminded herself that they were ex-lovers, now friends; there was both more and less to their relationship. The shared loss Sam mentioned before was an anchor for them—holding them together and weighing them down.

"Right," called Rick from the dining room, "you two enjoy the beautiful moment while I do all the work. Typical."

"OK," said Cathy, "if you don't need me."

"That's not what I... Oh, whatever."

Sam joined Cathy by the large window looking out at the backyard. She put her arm around Cathy's waist. Cathy sighed and leaned her head on Sam's shoulder. "The last time I saw snow was with Gareth. We had been on a hiking trip in Scotland just before graduation. It was in the Highlands. Such an austere, beautiful place."

"You still miss him, don't you?"

Cathy turned to Sam. "Yes, I guess I do. Or the way he used to be; the way we used to be. He was so happy to see new places, so happy to be with me." Cathy paused. "There is no going back, is there? The CIPHER genie is out of the bottle. Each new version supposedly bringing people together, but not really in any direct way; just still driving them apart. And Gareth, he's a part of that."

"Hey, don't be so harsh. He's just making a living."

"Hah, more than that. I've heard he's one of the best at *Multitudes.* He's in demand."

"Good for him. You know, Cathy, there has been good. CIPHER 1 allows us to share information and communicate better. CIPHER 2 letting us relive another person's experience. Who knows what the next version might do?"

"Wow! I thought you were an Isolator. You sound like you think CIPHER's great."

Sam chuckled. "Don't get me wrong. I agree with you. I can't deny that CIPHER could be good. But with the way it's become such a big part of our lives, and controlled entirely by CRI, I think *that's* wrong." She shook her head. "With CRI in control, I can't see anyway that

CIPHER will be a good thing."

"Really," Rick called from the dining room again. "I could use a little help." He paused. "Maybe what you said about CIPHER Research Institute having a monopoly—we can work with that. 'CRI is not your friend' or something like that."

"That's kind of clunky, Rick. You really do need our help." Sam winked at Cathy and kissed her on the cheek. The kiss melted there, like the snowflakes on the ground. Like them, it held an inviting promise—or a lingering memory. Cathy looked at Sam, her eyes asking. Sam answered, pulling her in for a kiss.

"We'll be right there," Sam called to Rick.

It was called Izzy's Joint. Sam said it was a great place to recruit Isolators. The bar was loud and frenetic. So much talking and so much laughing, thought Cathy. It was like being thrown back five years in time, before CIPHER. For the customers here, the CIPHERless, this was true. They still lived in that time, before the world changed on them. Sam guided her to a table off to one side, dodging servers and waitstaff. There was no ciphering orders here. She saw monitors hanging over the bar, televising a soccer game.

"Why," asked Cathy over the din, "why is it called 'Izzy's Joint'—some kind of joke?"

Sam shook her head. "No, not a joke. It's run by the Phillips Foundation. Did you notice the CIPHER clinic across the street?"

Cathy nodded. "Yes, kind of an odd placement for this bar."

A server came by, and Sam ordered two glasses of wine. "Not a coincidence. Phillips makes money from every CIPHER implant that works and makes money from the people the CIPHER doesn't work for. Do you notice the average age here? Over forty, at least. These are the ones that either tried the implantation and failed, or didn't qualify."

"But why come here? There are still a lot of other bars."

"Sure, there are, but they cater to people with CIPHER. You order using CIPHER, you watch sports with CIPHER. You hardly talk. The CIPHERless don't fit in. OK, you can still order from a human. But you stick out. Everyone knows you're a failure or soon to be extinct."

"Sam, that's cruel."

"No," said Sam as she accepted the wine from the

server. "It's just the truth. The people here need a place to go where they aren't reminded of that truth. They go to places like this to feel normal again, and we Isolators come here to recruit."

Sam removed a large envelope from her backpack and took out a piece of paper. "This is recruiting information for New Nottingham."

Cathy took a sip of the wine. "New Nottingham?" asked Cathy.

"Yes, we Isolators have built a habitat on Mars, and it's almost ready for immigrants. It can be a new home for the CIPHERless. Many of the people have useful skills, skills that we can use, and they'll fit in. No CIPHER, no Moloi cloud. It will be like it was."

"OK," Cathy said as she stood up from the table. "Hand me a couple of those, and I'll recruit us some CIPHERless."

"Cathy," Sam started to say.

She felt a hand on her shoulder. Cathy turned around and saw a middle-aged man—bald and slightly overweight, not much taller than her. He held a half-empty drink in his other hand.

"What did you say?" he asked.

"Nothing, really. I just want to talk to some people here..."

"The *word* you used—CIPHERless. You mean me, right? Not like you, pretty young thing, I'm sure you're not *CIPHERless.* What are you doing here? Seeing how the less fortunate live?"

"No, no, not like that." Cathy could smell the whiskey on his breath and noticed his bloodshot eyes. "I didn't mean anything by it, really. I want to help. There's this new habi…"

He grabbed Cathy by the wrist, squeezing it.

"Let go!" she said. This drunk is going to hurt me, Cathy thought. She tried to push him away.

"You heard her!" said Sam. She'd come around the table and was standing next to him.

"Shut up! I heard you too. Talking about us! CIPHERless! You pretend to want to help us! You're the same as everyone else! Have you come here to look at us specimens? Well, have a look! We are the last of our kind! Soon to be extinct, you said!"

He squeezed Cathy's wrist harder. She closed her eyes at the pain. "Please! Let go!" She heard a gasp, and her wrist was free. She opened her eyes and saw the man on the floor, his drink spilled next to him. People were standing around him, Sam looking down.

"You bitch! What the fuck did you do?"

"Never touch her," said Sam, her voice calm and level.

"CIPHER or no CIPHER, you are a bully. There have always been bullies."

He started to get up. Others stood between him and Cathy and Sam. One of them said, "Frank, settle down. I'm sure they meant no offense, and you are in no shape to keep after this." Turning to Sam, he smiled and said, "That was a nice move. You'll have to teach me how to do that."

"Come to New Nottingham and maybe I'll show you," said Sam. "But leave Frank behind." She handed him one of the recruiting sheets. Sam grabbed her backpack. "Come on, Cathy, I think we should go."

Cathy massaged her wrist, wondering what had happened. Sam reached her hand out and smiled. "Let's get you back to my place; we'll put some arnica gel on that." Cathy took her hand and followed her out.

Sam fixed Cathy a bourbon and water with ice when they got back to her place. It was early evening, and Cathy sat on the sofa in the sunroom, watching the sunset.

"I'll be right back with the arnica," said Sam.

Cathy wondered how she could have been so insensitive to the people at Izzy's Place. She should know better. CIPHERless is not a word she should say so casually. She took a sip of the drink, then held it on her wrist. The cold soothed the pain.

"Here," said Sam, handing her the tube of gel. She sat down on the sofa next to Cathy. "Put some on and rub it in. It will keep it from bruising."

"How did you take that guy down?"

"Tai Chi."

"Really," said Cathy. "You'll need to teach me."

"Well, that and some Aikido. But sure thing!" She placed her hand on Cathy's knee. Sam felt the comfort of her touch. "How's your wrist doing?"

"Much better. The drink helps." She sighed and rested her head on Sam's shoulder. "I feel like such an idiot! Getting into a bar fight, of all things! And then you have to step in and rescue me!"

"My pleasure, ma'am," said Sam. She smiled and caressed Cathy's hair. "You did nothing wrong. The man was drunk and was looking for a way to take out his anger. You were just a convenient target."

Cathy set her drink down and let Sam hold her. She felt safe with Sam. *Would Gareth have fought for me? Maybe. He'd try to talk it out first. Not Sam, she takes the battle to the enemy—my enemy is Sam's enemy.* Cathy felt herself relaxing in Sam's arms. The early trouble faded, and Cathy eased closer to Sam.

###

55

Cathy nestled up next to Sam, laying her head on Sam's shoulder. She cradled Cathy's head. Making love to Sam had released so much tension from her body. The fight at the bar was a distant memory. The tension, she knew, came from Gareth. It had been building the more she thought of him and his work at *Multitudes,* the more it felt like a betrayal. She had been full of memories of her father and dread for Gareth for the past few weeks.

Sam had been patient, listening to her worries—often over dinner. Rick came by less and less often, allowing Sam and Cathy to enjoy more time alone with each other.

"That was great," whispered Cathy.

"Glad to hear it," Sam said.

"I mean it."

"Did I help you forget about Gareth?"

Cathy sat up. Why did she have to mention him? It was going so well. "I had until you brought him up."

"Sorry, I can't help myself sometimes. Rick says that I spend too much time comparing lovers."

"Wow, now there are suddenly two more people in this bed. Isn't one enough for you?" Cathy asked.

Sam lightly kissed her breast. Cathy felt the electricity as Sam then licked her nipple. Cathy looked up at her and smiled. "It is, if it's you," Sam breathed.

Cathy rolled over and held Sam's arms down by the wrists. She lingered there, lost in Sam's eyes, before kissing her, their tongues mingling. Sam smiled back.

Cathy rolled onto her back and stared at the ceiling. "OK, I guess I still miss Gareth. You *are* helping to make that feel less. He had become so complicated. I know he loved me; he said as much, repeatedly. He was sweet, in his way—but so tentative. Not like you. I always had to initiate sex. I didn't mind at first. He was a tender lover and sweet. It didn't hurt that he was easy on the eyes."

"That doesn't sound so bad," said Sam, rolling over and kissing Cathy's nipples. "I hate pushy lovers." She paused and grinned. "I'm not pushy, am I?"

Cathy smiled. "Just a little, but in a good way."

Sam propped herself on her elbow. "You know, sometimes, the best way to get over someone is to talk about it. Exorcise the demon, so to speak."

"He was no demon." Cathy pushed the covers aside and got out of bed, looking for and finding her robe. She sat down in one of the two chairs by the window, listening to the birds singing outside. "No, Gareth wasn't pushy. Not in how we were together. In fact, he was always trying to figure out what I wanted—when making love, when going out." She smiled. "Not like you. You know what you want, and you take it."

"Most women would like that, being catered to." Sam said as she put on her robe and sat in the chair next to Cathy. She reached out and placed her hand on Cathy's.

"Maybe I did. Maybe things would have been all right if it hadn't been for CIPHER. And now, CIPHER 2."

They sat silently for a while, enjoying the peaceful sounds of Sam's backyard. "At the risk of sounding pushy," Sam said, "I think you should move in with me. At least stay here for a bit. That would help you get over Gareth."

Why not? Wondered Cathy. "You think so?" she asked. Cathy heard the tremor in her own voice. Yes, talking things over with Sam could help. I need to move on from Gareth. Then, well, we'll see. "Yes," she heard herself say.

Blissful Moments

February 2090

After Cathy left, Gareth had settled into life on his own. He took the job at *Multitudes* and he got what he had wanted—the CIPHER 2 implants. The implants that had driven Cathy away. She would come back, he was certain of it, once he built a successful career. Walt would come out of his coma, and everything would be good again. He was sure of it.

In the meantime, he kept busy, training to become an Experiencer. At first, he was uncomfortable with the idea of other people reliving things he had "experienced". What if they didn't like being Gareth? His instructor said it wasn't like that. People would see, hear, taste, touch everything Gareth did, but it would filter through their emotions and feelings. The Experiencer is an empty vessel, he had said, a conduit to an Experience the user might not otherwise have.

Gareth quickly got the hang of it. It was easy following the parameters of Experience creation, sublimating his own desires and wishes to the needs of the Experience. That was fine with Gareth. His wishes had led Cathy to walk out on him. Perhaps it was best not to want anything.

Tonight, the instructor said Gareth should run an Experience: *Blissful Moments*. He should pay attention to how the creator did not intrude on the Experience. Gareth decided to try it before dinner. Sounds from the upstairs apartment already disturbed his evening. This would be a good distraction. He sat in the Experiencer chair that *Multitudes* had provided him with. There was barely space for it in his small living room next to the sofa.

Cipher, sent Gareth, *start Blissful Moments experience. Blissful Moments* had a catalog of places and seasons. Gareth's CIPHER read the catalog and picked a time and a place for maximum effect. CIPHER's nanobots efficiently rerouted the input to Gareth's brain from his senses to the recorded Experience. He was still Gareth, but in a way, he wasn't. His apartment disappeared, and he was sitting at a beachside table. The sounds from upstairs had ended abruptly, and instead he heard the gentle lapping of waves onto a shore. He was calmer now that the menagerie of sounds and smells of the apartment building had receded.

Gareth felt the breeze from the ocean and the warm sun on his skin. He looked out over the horizon, the sun still well above the ocean. The combined effect soothed him. He reached out for the drink on the table. It wasn't him, but the Experiencer reaching out for it. Taking a drink, he tasted the cool sweetness of it. Rum and Coke? thought Gareth. Yes.

He looked over to his companion and saw her smile. She was wearing a two-piece bikini with a colorful fabric wrap. Her face was youthful, and she had bright blue eyes and blond hair. "What do you think?" she said. "They make the best drinks here. The bartender is an old friend of mine."

"Delicious," he heard himself say.

"Did you enjoy dinner?" she asked.

The taste of the meal was fresh in the Experiencer's memory—the pan-seared Ahi Tuna. Gareth didn't care for fish, but the Experiencer did, and Gareth's perceptions channeled that pleasant aftertaste to him.

"Yes, very much." If I could only stay here. No pressure, nothing to worry about. The Experiencer looked at his companion once more, and Gareth felt how comfortable they were together. That they had known each other for a long time. Maybe they were a couple? Some Experiencers work as a team, well-suited to creating this kind of Experience.

The scene shifted; he was no longer sitting by the beach.

He walked along the beach now, holding her hand. The waves, even calmer now, reached out to them, washing over his bare feet, then pulling away. The water felt cool on his skin. He looked out at the setting sun, just above the horizon. Gareth had heard of the "green flash" phenomenon. The Experiencer was waiting for it. Perhaps he was anticipating it. Gareth felt his own anticipation of it. He had never been to Hawaii, so it would be wonderful to see it. The Experiencer looked back at his companion. They paused and shared a kiss. It was sweet and soft, with a taste of their after-dinner drinks.

"Any time now," she said after an embrace. They turned and watched as the sun continued its descent over the ocean. Then suddenly, they saw it: the green flash as the sun set.

Another change of scene.

So many fish! He was underwater, feet kicking slowly, schools of vibrantly colored yellow fish swimming around him. Gareth didn't know what they were, but they were beautiful. They swam around coral that was shaped like deer antlers. The water felt cool on his skin. He looked over and saw a woman swimmer, likely the same woman from earlier. He rose up and took in more air with the snorkel. He sank down again, looking for more…

Gareth, sent **CIPHER**, *I have a priority message from Alex Phillips.*

The Experience ended. Gareth found himself once again in the apartment. The message Alex sent via **CIPHER** had taken him out of the Experience.

Alex! What the hell? *Alex, why are you bothering me!* Gareth struggled to orient himself in time and space. It was dark, and his stomach was aching.

Cipher, sent Gareth, *turn on the living room lights.*

He stood up from the chair, his legs unsteady. Then the pain hit, doubling him over. His full bladder urged him to the bathroom. God, I'm going to burst!

Sorry, Gareth, replied Alex. *I'm worried, you missed today's training session. Is everything OK?*

Gimme a minute!

Gareth barely made it. What a mess! He left his soiled

clothes in the bathtub and went to the bedroom to change into a fresh pair of underwear. Shaking, he sat down on the bed and put his head in his hands. How did I let this happen? If it hadn't been for Alex...

Gar, sent Alex. *Is everything all right?*

Yeah, I'm fine now. Sorry I snapped at you. Today's session? What do you mean? Missed?

His empty stomach growled at him for attention now. The memory of the Ahi Tuna was insufficient to soothe his stomach. How long have I been sitting? He wondered. *Cipher, what time is it?* The response came, *Eleven AM, Gareth.*

What? I've missed all last night and this morning! I was in the Experience the whole time? No wonder. He struggled up from the bed and returned to the kitchen to pour a glass of water. He drank the glass down and poured another. But I only ran a couple of scenes! No, that's not right, I repeated them several times. Each time, I felt happier. That's the point of *Blissful Moments*, after all. If Alex hadn't ciphered me...

Sorry, Alex. I guess I must have come down with something....

It's OK, Gareth. I made an excuse for you. You are still on probation, you know.

Sure, sure. Thanks, Alex. Tell them I'm feeling better

and will be in tomorrow.

No problem, see you then, Gar.

He searched the refrigerator for something to eat and found half a sandwich from yesterday's lunch. He devoured it, washing it down with more water. I need to be more careful with this. In the future, I will set a timer for CIPHER to end the Experience.

Is that what happened to Walt? Is he just running an Experience over and over again? I'm sure I would have come out of it, eventually. Hunger, whatever, would have forced it. What happened to Walt must be something else. Walt was happy and successful, with a family he cared for. He would have come back to them if he could have. Something is preventing him.

Gareth stretched and yawned. He could smell the stench of himself now. Disgusted, he stripped and gathered his clothes, throwing them into the washing machine. He stepped into the shower, turning the water on. The hot spray washed off the accumulated odors of the last sixteen hours. It's a miracle I didn't shit myself.

Moloi has Concerns
March 2090

Isolde's butler, servant, bodyguard, whatever, led Nomie through Izzy's house to her study. He certainly looked like a bodyguard, she thought. After what happened to my lab, I should see about getting one. Perhaps he could recommend someone? He announced Nomie's arrival and left.

She saw Isolde Phillips seated in an overstuffed leather chair. The burning logs in the fireplace cast a flickering golden glow on the books assembled in the cases surrounding the room. Izzy had been keeping her rooms dark of late. The better to keep hidden, maybe? It's part and parcel of Izzy's rising paranoia. The attack on my lab probably is not helping.

"OK, I'm here. What is so important that we couldn't

just talk at the office tomorrow?"

"I'm never going back to CRI," Izzy said from the plush easy chair, drink in hand. She sighed, "The board forced me out. They gave me a nice package, of course. I have had my eye on an interplanetary yacht for some time. I think that I will buy it now."

Forced out? CRI is her dream, her baby—and they've forced her out? And all she's talking about is a spaceship?

"Izzy! They can't do that! You must fight them! How can I help?"

"Honestly, Nomie, it doesn't matter. CRI has become too dangerous for me. For us, really. Forgive me, I never told you how sorry I was when I heard about your lab. But that's the point; the Ludds have lost all restraint. Ludds— what a stupid name!"

"Yes, I know. But they have a point. Ludds— Luddites—I get it. CIPHER tech disrupted their lives. They want things to go back to the way they were. So, destroy the technology, and then everything will go back to the way it was."

Izzy smirked and said, "Nomie, I never took you for one to fall for such things."

"Of course not! It's magical thinking. The genie is out of the bottle. Or maybe we opened Pandora's box, releasing a new set of troubles into the world. But, CRI, we are making things worse. We are moving too fast, Izzy. This problem, the Fugue, or whatever it is. We released CIPHER 2 too soon; we did not test it sufficiently."

"No amount of testing can compensate for human weakness. We have done nothing wrong! If people are unhappy, they can join the Isolators and go to Mars! Let the rest of us reap the benefits of CIPHER!"

Izzy stood and went to the liquor cabinet. "I'm sorry, Nomie. I've been a poor host. Single malt? Neat?"

Nomie sat down in a chair by the fireplace, watching the flames dance. "Sure. Thanks, Izzy."

She poured two glasses and handed one to Nomie. She sat down in the chair across from Nomie. "Here you go. Next time, it won't be a lab; it will be you or me. You know they plan to execute us." She took a sip. "And they plan to hack our CIPHERs, too. That would be worse, much worse. Can you imagine what they could do? We are too vulnerable."

Nomie took a long sip, tasting the warm peat. She had never drunk alcohol before meeting Izzy and starting CRI. Still, after today, it is helping to calm her. Unfortunately, Nomie thought, it has the opposite effect on Izzy. It winds her up and feeds her paranoia.

"We must protect ourselves," Isolde continued. "We can continue to harden our CIPHERs to prevent such attacks. But that won't be enough; eventually, an attack will succeed. Then what? It could scramble our brains, do irreparable damage."

"I know it's a risk," said Nomie. *I need to partially agree with the premise, then maybe I can convince her of how small a risk there is.* "Our CIPHERs have redundancies built in. You know that. It can repair most any damage."

"Not good enough! We need a backup. We need to back ourselves up to the cloud."

Not this again! These attacks have given her an excuse, another justification to push for digital ascension. She just will not let this go.

"That's why I asked you here. If you don't mind, I've asked Alex to join us."

"Hello, Nomie," said Alex as he entered the study, looking disheveled as ever. He had not inherited Isolde's sense of fashion and decorum. "I was sorry to hear about the lab. I saw Tim just this morning. They are making good progress in cleaning it up."

"Hello Alex, thank you. I am glad to hear that. It is good to see you."

"My grandson is not here on a social call, Nomie. As I said, we need a way to upload ourselves to the cloud. With some help from Alex, I have created a program to do just that."

"But, Izzy," said Nomie, "you know that's not the same as you—it's not a complete transfer. It won't really be you. No endocrine system, no emotions: no love, no anger. I suspect you will miss anger the most." Izzy values her little explosions, the way they strike fear into her opponents, and sometimes her friends.

"That's what this program will fix," she insists. "It will learn how to emulate all of that. Just look at the code, please. You and Alex are the only ones I trust. That is why you are here. I want you to check the code."

"I'm not a programmer, you know that!"

"False modesty! You are a fine programmer; you just don't want anyone to know it!" Izzy smiled.

She is in one of her moods, Nomie realizes. She's not about to take no for an answer. If she is resorting to flattery, she'll stop at nothing. Threats will be next. "OK, send me the code, Alex."

Nomie closed her eyes. She let her CIPHER create a virtual environment complete with a monitor to review the code. It had taken her some time to get used to reviewing code this way. It was now nearly second nature. Izzy's cozy library disappeared from her senses, replaced with a simple desk and monitor. She could review the code the way she was used to, before CIPHER.

Younger people like Alex could interact with the code directly with CIPHER. Nomie's virtual setup was the next best thing. She created a virtual CIPHER system, firewalled from her own, and loaded the code. After running the associated unit and integration tests, she ran it in the virtual CIPHER. As far as she could tell, the code worked as promised. Nomie shut down the virtual environment, and her senses returned to the library.

"Well?" said Izzy. She had poured herself another drink and was evidently waiting for Nomie's return. "Satisfied?"

"It looks correct. I've run all the tests I can. But, Izzy, I really want another set of eyes on this. May I send it to Tim? He's an excellent coder and can work with the code much more effectively that I."

"No! No one else! This code never leaves this room. Nomie, wipe it from your CIPHER!"

"OK, OK—done! I understand the concern about the Ludds, but Izzy, you are jumping at shadows. You know Tim; you can trust him. He's one of us. He's been with me from the beginning, you know that."

"Tim's a lab rat! For God's sake—he's the one that messed up your experiment!"

"That fateful accident is why we have CIPHER today," said Nomie. "You should thank him."

"No, I do not thank incompetence!" She took another drink of her Scotch, composing herself. "Sorry, Nomie, I didn't mean that. I like and respect Tim, of course. I'm just not in a place where I can trust anyone else. There's too much at stake."

"Fine. The style isn't familiar. I recognize the style of most of the programmers. They all have a unique style; this is different, a cobbled-together mix—mongrel code. Where did you get this?"

"It doesn't matter! Will it work?"

"I think so. We need to run a simulation on a physical CIPHER setup first."

"Why?" she says, impatience growing in her voice. "What would that tell us? It needs to run on a human-integrated CIPHER. So, it has to be me. I'm running it."

"Izzy, wait!" Nomie said. I'm too late, she realized. Izzy's gone slack in the chair, her eyes losing focus. She is running the code. "Alex, what server is she connected to? I want to monitor it."

"Yes, sure. I didn't think she'd run it so quickly." He frowned as he connected his CIPHER to the server. "This isn't doing what I thought. Well, it is, but it is doing something else too. There's some kind of crosstalk back to her CIPHER. Maybe comparison checks?"

"Alex, sever the connection now!"

"Done, but you better have a good reason."

Izzy's eyes opened. She glared at Alex. "What the hell! The program just aborted. What happened?"

"I told Alex to cut the server connection. I had a bad feeling about what was happening. We should look at the logs."

"Jesus!" exclaimed Alex, turning pale. "This could have been terrible. Nomie was right. The program was downloading a virus from the dark cloud: a Ludd virus. It would have corrupted your CIPHER and put you into Fugue."

"Where did you get the code, Izzy?" Nomie asked.

"Like I said, it's mine. Well, mostly. I added some pieces I found from other programmers..." She frowned. "I should have known better! But this proves my point." She rose out of the chair and set down her glass. Her hand was shaking. Or was it a tremor? wondered Nomie. "Don't you see? They're after us, and they nearly succeeded. We need to protect ourselves. Just as I was saying."

"Izzy this was damned close; you must stop this obsession."

Izzy sat back down and rested her head in her hands. "I can't. I have no choice." She looked at Nomie. "I'm dying."

"What? What do you mean, dying? You look fine to me!"

"Not me, not so much. I tried an earlier version of the CIPHER 3 beta—with some enhancements. It's why CRI kicked me out."

"Alex," said Nomie. "Do you know about this?"

Alex remained silent, nodding his head, then inspecting a spot on the floor.

Nomie sighed and took a sip of the scotch. This is classic Izzy. Always pushing the boundaries. "What can I do? How can I help?"

"I'm sorry, Nomie. I shouldn't have said anything. There's still plenty of time yet. Plenty of time for me to figure out a solution. You're right, I suppose. Simply creating a copy of myself in the cloud isn't enough. I need CIPHER 3. I'll just need to wait."

Isolde finished her Scotch. She stared at Nomie. "You need to protect yourself. These Ludds, you've seen how serious they are. The attack on your lab is a warning. You need to find somewhere safe. Where they can't reach you."

Nomie laughed. "Right, like you said. There is nowhere safe. It's not like I'm going to run off to Mars!"

Izzy poured another glass and smiled. "Let me think on that."

The Assignment
June 2093

The voice in Gareth's head interrupted his slumber. Well, not a voice, really. It was a message from a chorus of a million nanobots. They comprised the web of connections the CIPHER implant made to the sensory processing centers in his brain: gatekeepers to what Gareth saw, heard, smelled, tasted and felt. The ones integrated into his auditory processing centers had spoken to him: *Gareth, time to wake up. It's been one year. Time to move on.*

What? Gareth thought. Why is CIPHER telling me that? Oh, I remember now. My friends convinced me to set a deadline. Give it a year, they said. If Cathy's not back, then she's never coming back. Set a reminder so you'll know it's time. Maybe they were right. It really is time to wake up—in more ways than one.

He got out of bed and made his way to the kitchen. There was still some coffee left in the pot from the day before. He poured it into the instahot mug. Taking a sip, Gareth went to his desk and searched for the document mixed in with the pile of papers, junk mostly. He found the envelope marked "Divorce Papers".

Amazing, he thought, in the time of CIPHER there was still a place for paper. He could just cipher-sign the cloud version. But Gareth needed the physical version to make it real. Now and then, he would pick it up and consider opening it. He would quickly set it down again and let it get covered over again until the next time. The prospect of that reality was a barrier for him. For now, they are just separated. He still had hope. Cathy had moved on; Gareth wasn't ready yet. He put the envelope back on the desk—until the next time.

He returned to the bedroom and changed into his running shorts and shirt. A quick morning run will help clear my mind, he thought. Exorcise the memory of Cathy with a bit of exercise. It was early, and few people were out and about. He saw Seth coming into the apartment building. He nodded hello.

"Hi Gareth. Beautiful morning for a run!"

"It sure looks like it. How was your shift at *Happy*

Meadows?"

"Quiet, as usual. Fugue victims are always quiet. Not a bad gig, a little eerie with all the quiet. No visitors after six PM, you know. On the plus side, I've got lots of time to read. No offense to your occupation, man, but I'm glad that the implants never took hold for me. I might have been another resident there."

"No offense taken. We all just do the best we can with what we're given, right? Catch you later, Seth!" said Gareth as he started his run.

At fifty years old, Seth Morrison had been too old for the CIPHER implants to make the proper connections in the brain. He was now one of the CIPHERless. At least he had found work; there are still jobs that don't require CIPHER. Gareth's thoughts returned to the task at hand, and he reviewed the assignment as he ran. As with the other assignments on this contract, it was quite specific in some ways but vague in others. Just drink a cup of coffee at a café and read a newspaper.

He returned to the apartment with plenty of time to spare. After kicking off his shoes, Gareth headed to the shower. *I need to be at the café in an hour. The contracts to create Experiences are the only thing keeping me going. That and the occasional night at the local bar. It's ironic that Cathy left me on account of my taking this job; now, it* is of the few things I have.

Drying off after the shower, he assembled his clothing for the assignment. Cathy had good taste in clothes; she usually picked them out for him. Gareth had little patience for shopping and always agreed with her choices. They still fit, saving him the trouble of finding anything new. Fortunately, she had arranged the closet so that he could easily pick out what he needed for the day. It was even easier now that her clothes were now gone.

He dressed and went out to the living room, where he saw the copy of the Washington Post on the kitchen table. The publication date showed today: Wednesday, June 17th, 2093. It had been delivered yesterday, specially printed for the assignment. He picked it up and made his way out of the small apartment to the metro stop next door.

It was a quick trip to Dupont Circle. He could hear music from the street musicians as he exited the train. Emerging onto the street from the station, he saw it was market day; the area was closed off to traffic. The morning had warmed up with a light breeze. Gareth saw market stalls displaying farm produce, cheeses, wines, and MiXes. There was a MiXe vendor on the way to the café.

As he walked by the stand, the vendor called out to him. "Good morning, sir! Can I interest you in a tailored

Micro Experience, a MiXe? Guaranteed to stimulate your nervous and cannabinoid systems with unique, targeted blends of sounds and smells. Can't sleep? *Serenity* will help with soothing ocean sounds and scents of lavender, rose, and jasmine. Need to concentrate? *Laser* will help with white noise and scents of peppermint and sage. All proven to be clinically safe and effective!"

I have some time, Gareth thought. I really need help with sleeping. He checked his CIPHER to verify the vendor's credentials. Hmm, a subsidiary of CIPHER Research Institute—seems legit.

The vendor pressed on. "And for a young man like you—I'm sure you have no problems in that department—but maybe you want to take it up a notch?" he said with a grin. "We have *SexyBeast*, another proprietary blend. I'm not at liberty to divulge the ingredients, still CRI approved. It will enhance any sexual encounter. You simply tell *SexyBeast* your preferences: Partner/No Partner, Straight, Bi, Gay, Top or Bottom and intensity. *SexyBeast* does the rest."

"I'm pretty sure I don't ..." Gareth said.

"But wait, if you find a willing partner, they get it free for the encounter, as many partners at a time as you can manage! Just imagine what that would be like! What do you think?"

Gareth checked the time; five minutes until the assignment. What would be the harm? And they are CRI-approved. "OK, sold. Cipher all three to me on my account."

"Certainly, you won't be disappointed: thirty-day money-back guarantee!"

Gareth continued to the café and found a table providing a good view of the street scene and ordered the Americano the client had specified. As requested, Gareth opened the Washington Post and sipped his coffee. It had a slightly acidic taste, a hint of chocolate, and a rich, roasted aroma. The mug fit nicely in his hand. He felt the heat warming it in the cool morning air.

Reading the newspaper was part of the Experience; the actual feel of the newspaper in his hands. Almost no one reads a physical paper anymore. The customer must have wanted a nostalgic experience.

Unlike Seth, he seldom had to read like this. Since he had taken the job at *Multitudes,* he could access news anytime he wanted. It was all available in the Moloi Cloud. *Multitudes* paid for the upgraded CIPHER implants as they were a requirement for his work, to allow for the recording of Experiences such as this. They deducted the cost from his salary, of course.

The lead story in the newspaper concerned the

Isolator movement and the progress of their habitat on Mars. The test spin was complete, and they now had Earth-standard gravity. It was ready for the engineers and other workers to arrive and prepare for the first wave of inhabitants. They could then create their own world isolated from Moloi technology.

Like many boys, Gareth had dreamed of going to Mars someday. It was a fantasy, maybe in the distant future. CIPHER sped up progress on so many different fronts: space travel, habitat design, even a space elevator to reach low-earth orbit. All of that made New Nottingham, the Isolators' habitat, possible.

He couldn't understand the Isolators, why they resisted CIPHER-tech. At least they were a peaceful group. Not like the Ludds. The sidebar to the story mentioned the recent hack attack on CRI by the Ludd splinter group. Gareth shook his head, imagining the harm such an attack might cause for CIPHER users. Especially those running Experiences. The risk of Fugue unnerved him.

There were a couple of other sidebars recounting the history of CIPHER, as well as attention-grabbing speculations on the current lives of Doctor Moloi and Isolde Phillips, two of the key figures of CIPHER. Moloi was still a recluse, whereabouts unknown. That was wise after the Ludds threatened to kidnap her and execute her for crimes against humanity. Isolde Phillips is cruising around on her own space yacht. That should keep her safe. The Ludds have placed a bounty on her as well: dead or alive.

Gareth looked up from the newspaper and surveyed the café. There were six small tables arranged on the sidewalk. Gareth noticed a young man and woman sitting two tables over. The woman seemed familiar, but Gareth couldn't place her. An old friend of Cathy's, maybe? No, maybe just one of those faces. Pretty, thought Gareth. He couldn't help overhearing their conversation. In any case, *Multitudes* had no restrictions against eavesdropping. The more background Gareth could gather, the more the editors would have to work with. They could excise anything they deemed not worthwhile.

"Why did you ask me to come out here with you?" Gareth heard the young man say. "I can't stay long. I've got to get back to work. But you're just sitting there. You haven't said a word!" He seemed to be the typical Washington DC professional: well-dressed, wearing a suit and tie. Unlike him, she dressed casually and wore a wide-brimmed hat and sunglasses. Images of birds flying in complex patterns decorated her dress. Long blond hair fell lightly around her shoulders.

"It's a pleasant morning. Loosen your tie, take off your jacket! Relax and enjoy it. Feel that wonderful sun, just beginning to warm things up! No one's going to miss you at work," she responded.

That's cold, Gareth thought. Is she deliberately trying to antagonize her friend? He could see her face from where he was sitting, and, despite the sunglasses, Gareth felt she was watching him.

Gareth went back to his newspaper and tried to ignore them. He reminded himself that the assignment was simply to sit at the café, read the paper, and enjoy the coffee, not to watch pretty girls or get involved in someone else's business.

"That's it! You tell me to relax and enjoy the sunshine, then you insult my job!" the young man said. "I've had enough of this. Every place we go, you find some way to insult me, some way to belittle me!" He gestured wildly, spilling his coffee. "I am fucking tired of these head games you keep playing! I'm out of here. My job's stressful enough. I don't need a complicated girlfriend. Good luck finding someone who'll put up with you and your drama."

She sat quietly and didn't respond, looking past him. She is watching me, thought Gareth. This is going to blow the assignment. He raised the newspaper to block her view. Even above the sound of the street market, he could hear a metal chair scraping back along the sidewalk. He couldn't help himself; he looked up. The man had gone, and the girl was now sitting at his table.

Damn, this assignment's blown. We'll need a total do-over, he thought. He sent to his implant, *Cipher stop recording.*

"My name's Sam. You were watching me." Gareth was waiting for confirmation that the recording had stopped, but she continued talking. "I'm glad he left, and you should stop pretending to read the paper. Where did you even find one?" She had removed the sunglasses, and he noticed her green eyes. No, he thought, I'm sure I don't know her. Too bad. Still, there was no confirmation from CIPHER that the recording had stopped.

"Sorry," he replied. "I couldn't help noticing the commotion."

"Yes, well, trust me, he's no loss." Her eyes focused on him, and she spoke more softly now. "You're an Experiencer." She stated it as a fact, not a question.

"It shouldn't be that obvious. It's kind of embarrassing that you caught on." Why haven't I heard the confirmation from CIPHER yet? he wondered. Am I so distracted by her I didn't notice? "What gave me away?"

"No one reads anymore, let allow an actual paper newspaper. That means your client wants that feeling.

Probably some old guy wanting to relive his youth."

She backed away from the table and stood up to go. As she walked away, he heard her say, "Also, because we've met before. I already know what you do."

Recording stopped, Cipher responded.

Finally! Why had it taken so long to stop recording? This shouldn't happen. Gareth pushed back from the table. The Experience recording should have stopped immediately. I know I've never met her before. I'd remember her. Still, there was something about her, very pretty. Never mind, just wishful thinking. I'll need to talk to Alex about that glitch during my next tech review. *Cipher, pay the bill and tip twenty percent.* Nice dress, too. It complemented her green eyes perfectly.

Tech Review

June 2093

The morning air was cool, but the light jacket kept Gareth warm enough—that and the coffee from the corner shop. *Multitudes* was only a few blocks from the metro stop, so he walked. It was still early, and few people were out on the broad sidewalk; he only had to dodge the occasional scooter and delivery bot.

I need some time to get my head back together before meeting with Alex, he thought. The CIPHER recording "glitch" at the café had come up during the routine review of the Experience. Alex insisted Gareth come in, so he could investigate it. That meant another session with the CIPHER monitor. Gareth wasn't looking forward to it, disliking the way the machine invaded his privacy. Alex assured him it only examined the CIPHER logs and ran validation checks on the nanobots. It wasn't a mind-reader.

Gareth arrived outside *Multitudes*. The walk had done the trick, he thought, feeling better. What happened at the café wasn't a big deal. Now Alex can check his CIPHER and find the cause of the glitch, and that will be that. He had resigned himself to being hooked up to the monitor. Gareth finished the coffee and tossed the cup into the recycler.

He entered the building; his CIPHER provided all the required access codes. There was still the requisite physical security check. The guards were politely efficient. This check was new after the recent spate of Ludd attacks on CRI and Experience companies, resulting in a few deaths. That was bad enough, but the real target is the Moloi cloud. The Ludds are always trying to hack it. They could do a lot of damage there. There's even a rumor that the Fugue is really a Ludd virus. Not likely, Gareth thought, but it was a scary possibility.

After the check, Gareth headed to Alex's office in the basement. Alex could have had an office with a window, but he seemed to like it down here. Maybe he felt safer in the basement, Gareth realized.

"Hey Alex," Gareth announced as he walked in. He noticed again Alex's lack of personal items. There was just a simple desk and the examination chair and equipment. All that was required for his job and little else. The only exceptions were two 3D photo displays. One was of Alex with Gareth and Cathy at their wedding. Alex was grinning, so excited that he was part of the wedding party. The other photo was of his grandmother, Isolde Phillips. Gareth usually found it amusing that they were all somehow joined in Alex's world. Today, it occurred to him that it was a little creepy as well. As if Isolde were the center of this little solar system and he and Cathy were in her orbit. I guess as the founder of CRI, they kind of were. Everyone is in her orbit.

"Hey, Gar, good to see you."

"You too! How have you been, buddy?"

He looked up. "Me? I'm doing fine, thanks. I'm sorry, we haven't talked much lately. Have you heard anything from Cathy?"

"No. Look, Alex, I know you miss her too. But this job—something about it anyway—it just isn't going to work out with her anymore. If I hear from her, I'll let you know."

"Too bad," Alex said. "She was nice. You didn't deserve her, anyway."

"Alex, enough already," said Gareth with a sigh. Alex had never gotten over his crush on Cathy, Gareth knew.

But Cathy also couldn't forgive him for recruiting Gareth to *Multitudes.* Alex had thought that might give him a chance with her, in some odd, hopeful way of thinking. He had told Gareth as much over too many drinks. It had backfired so badly for them both. I can't blame him, really. Now, we share a loss.

"OK, I shouldn't have pushed. I'm sorry."

"Don't worry about it, Alex. Let's get down to business."

"Sure, thanks. Take a seat over there." Alex pointed to the chair next to his desk. Gareth frowned. It's just a chair, he thought. But it wasn't, really. There were cables running to a CIPHER monitor on Alex's desk. The cables were Near Field, NF, enhancers used to connect to the occupant's CIPHER. Even with all of Alex's assurances, he still thought of it as the 'Inquisitor'. Gareth felt that sitting in it was tantamount to undergoing an especially invasive interrogation; one where he couldn't hide anything. Techs like Alex can connect to his CIPHER and read the CIPHER logs, inspect the nanobots. Not a mind reader, but damned close.

"What, no questions about my sex life?" Alex shook his head and pointed at the chair. "Really?" He tried another tactic, appealing the Alex's inner geek. "Any thoughts on the latest CIPHER innovation? You were so stoked about the CIPHER 3 beta last week. By the way, how's your grandmother doing? I've been hearing some odd stuff."

"Yeah, right. Sorry, Gareth, just have a lot on my mind. But Granny's fine. Don't believe everything you hear. In fact, she's working on something big." Alex drummed his fingers on his desk. "Stop stalling, will you? I know you hate this, but it needs to be done. It's in your employment contract with Multitudes. You know you can trust me, right? So, can you just please sit down? We have some work to do. We have to investigate that CIPHER glitch from your last assignment. It needs to be identified and fixed before you go out again. You know this."

Gareth gave in and sat down in the chair. *I shouldn't have asked about Isolde*, Gareth thought. *Maybe the rumors of illness are true? Alex* has *been distracted lately. Something is bothering him. But after everything that happened at college, they could never really be close friends. Alex would never confide in him. Cathy was right; men are bullies. Maybe over time he will forgive him.*

"You know the procedure. I'll be accessing your CIPHER using NF and performing a diagnostic check. I will only look at the few minutes before and after it happened. I'm not allowed to access anything else in your memory. We'll pin down that glitch and get it fixed."

"Sure, also, I've been having a lot of headaches lately," Gareth said as he sat down. "Do you think they could be related?"

"Beats me. I'm just a simple **CIPHER** tech," Alex said. He paused for a moment and added, "I'll think about it."

"Uh, right," said Gareth. "OK, let's get this over with."

Connection initiated by Alex Phillips, Gareth's cipher announced, Multitudes Chief CIPHER Technician. CIPHER ID verified and administrative access granted.

Open access to nanobot storage, instructed Alex. Replay Experience ID 5c034b8e-b63f-43c5-a189-a29959d93d1a.

Gareth's **CIPHER** ran the Experience, and he watched it play from the point of him drinking the Americano. He saw the girl walk up to him. Sam, that was her name. Shortly after that, Gareth instructed **CIPHER** to stop recording. Normally, **CIPHER** responded immediately; he was surprised when it hadn't. That was the glitch. Alex ran the Experience back to before she walked up, to when Gareth had heard the chair scraping back. Alex stopped it there.

Create marker A, Alex commanded. Resume.

Why is Alex creating the marker there, Gareth wondered.

Alex, shouldn't you have marked when I told CIPHER to stop recording?

Who's the CIPHER tech here, you or me? I need to get clean margins around it if I'm going to fix it. Relax, I know what I'm doing.

The Experience continued to where Sam said, "Also because, we've met before."

Create marker B here, Alex instructed. Examine short term memory for corresponding time frame and identify the neurons storing memory.

Alex, what are you doing? Is that necessary? This doesn't seem right, Gareth thought.

Yes, absolutely. There is likely some cross feed. That's where I'll find the glitch. This is all by the book.

Correspondence found.

Copy from Marker A to B to CIPHER secure storage and delete from Marker A to B and corresponding short-term memory neurons.

Alex, wait, you can't do that! Cipher abort, delete Admin access for Alex Phillips!

I must get out of this chair, Gareth thought! Why can't I move?

Sorry, I cannot comply, replied Gareth's cipher.

Damn it, Alex, I'm going to report you! What have you done? Why can't I move? You can't go around deleting things from my brain. Stop this!

I can't, Gareth. I have to do this. This is important. Someday you'll understand, if you remember.

Understand? Remember? What the fuck do you mean?

This is bigger than you and me. I'm helping someone important. I have to protect her from the Ludds. They want to kill her.

What does that have to do with this? I'm not your enemy, Alex! I'm your friend! Please! Stop this!

Don't worry, you'll be OK. You're always going to be OK. People like you always are. But you might have some vivid dreams tonight. Don't worry, Gareth. Cipher, delete the record of this session from short-term memory.

###

"So, when do we start?" asked Gareth.

"Just finished," replied Alex.

"But I don't remember you doing anything after getting administrative access."

"Yes, sorry about that. I needed to put you under to find the glitch. I should have mentioned that. Anyway, I found it and it was an easy fix."

"Alex, I don't mean to sound upset. You really need

to tell people what you're doing. I never would have consented. You're poking around my fucking head! I deserve to be present and alert when you do that! That's standard protocol!" Gareth jumped out of the chair and crossed over to Alex's desk. Alex was still sitting there, and Gareth loomed over him. Alex flinched and put up his hands defensively.

"Gareth, please! It's my job, don't..."

I'm doing it again, Gareth thought, bullying him. He sat back down. I know better. How many times did Cathy scold me for intimidating Alex? I'm not a big guy, but Alex is meek. I'm not mean. I need to calm down. Alex was just doing his job. I forgot how easily he gets frightened.

"I'm sorry, Alex. Forgive me? It's just that you should have said something."

"Look, I'm sorry. But in cases like this, I have authority." Alex was staring down at his desk now, avoiding looking at Gareth.

I've scared him, Gareth thought. But Alex usually recovers quickly. He still seems upset, but is it just my outburst? He knows I'd never hurt him. All bark, no bite— that's me.

"It's in your contract." Alex continued. "I can cipher the clause to you, if you don't believe me. Anyway, you

94

know me; I get carried away sometimes. Really, it was an easy fix. Friends?"

"Sure, Alex—friends. Always."

"I will need to follow up with you tomorrow to verify. I'll try not to cipher you too early. Oh, and I have something for your headaches. A peace offering." Alex ciphered him a MiXe.

Gareth inspected it. It was called *EmpHance*. "I've never heard of this. What is it?"

"It's used to treat PTSD and some other disorders, but **CRI** research says it'll help with the **CIPHER** related headaches you Experiencers get. Set to level one, to begin with, then titrate daily up one to level five. I'm sure it'll help."

"OK, and **CRI**, that reminds me. Don't we have an appointment with them next week? I'll be getting the **CIPHER** 3 beta?"

"Right," Alex replied. He'd recovered and was looking at Gareth again, smiling as if nothing had happened. "Your next assignment requires it. You're lucky to be the first Experiencer to get it! It'll add a whole new layer to the Experiences you create."

"What have you heard about the Beta?" Gareth asked, glad that the altercation was behind them.

"Same as you, I imagine. You're among the first to get

it, which is really a great opportunity for you. The client must have a lot of pull." Alex frowned, nodding at the 3D of his grandmother, before continuing. "Since she was forced out of CRI, I have no one to feed me any advance info on this sort of thing."

"Yes, I was sorry to hear that. But on the bright side, because of the assignment, you'll be one of the few CIPHER techs to get a look at it." Gareth headed for the door. Turning, he added, "And thanks for fixing the glitch, I mean it. I'll see you at CRI."

I'm still angry with Alex, he realized. He should have told me what he was doing. CIPHER glitches, headaches, and now this. I've nearly lost my only friend, as well.

Gareth walked out of *Multitudes* and thought about what to do next. It was still morning, and he did not want to head back to the apartment. The zoo, maybe. No, I don't think so. Too many caged animals. I'm so lost without an assignment. I should check in on Seth. See how he's doing after last night.

Odd that Seth was the only person he could really talk to.

A Fateful Decision
June 2093

Morning light filtered through the bedroom window blinds, finding its way to Cathy. She woke up, feeling the morning sun on her eyelids. It is so peaceful here, she mused, such a pleasant contrast to the apartment she and Gareth had shared. The apartment had been small but cozy in its way. That coziness soon gave way to suffocation once Gareth began talking about working for *Multitudes* and getting CIPHER 2. There had been nowhere to hide from the collision of Gareth's wants and her fears. She had to leave.

Sam's place was an open haven surrounded by green space and trees. Cathy enjoyed waking up to chirping birds. She appreciated watching them in the morning as they flew among the various feeders Sam had set up. It was much like the home she had grown up in. Sam had surprised her when she had asked her to move in. Cathy didn't hesitate and said yes right away. After all, she had been spending most of her time here.

She looked over at Sam—still sound asleep, lightly snoring. Sam was not a morning person. Cathy rose silently from the bed, picking up her robe as she made her way out of the bedroom. She closed the door softly behind her.

Why do we need to leave? Cathy wondered as she put the coffee together. The contrast with her previous life was so dramatic. That life had been a wreck when she met Sam. First, the thing with her father. How could he just go away like that? Where did he go that was so much better than being with his family and his work? Then Gareth insisted on going to work at *Multitudes* and getting the CIPHER 2 implants. He knew how opposed she was after what had happened to her father. But he went ahead anyway!

Now, they are both gone from my life. One at *Happy Meadows*, the other off somewhere creating an Experience for fans to buy and consume.

Sam helped her forget Gareth and her father. Not so much forget but assign them their proper places in the past. She was such a good fit for Cathy, emotionally and sexually. They would be in the middle of talking about the day when something would click—a smile, a fleeting touch—and they would fall into bed. They learned how to pleasure each other, and Sam had a surprising collection of toys.

Last night they'd had "goodbye for now" sex. At the end, Sam held her. They were supposed to go to New Nottingham together, but something had come up, and Sam's trip was delayed. It was too expensive to change Cathy's ticket as well, so Cathy would head out first.

Again, she heard birds chirping as they flew around the feeders. Sam loved birds and made her yard a sanctuary for them with the feeders and carefully selected pollinator plants. Cathy thought it odd that Sam was willing to leave them behind. What kind of birds would there someday be on Mars?

Sound from the bedroom took Cathy out of her reverie. The coffee maker signaled it had finished brewing, so she poured herself a cup. Sam opened the bedroom door, emerging into the kitchen. "Good morning!"

"What's good about it?" groused Sam. "Damn sunshine and chirping birds."

Yes, not a morning person, thought Cathy. She hugged Sam and said, "How about a cup of coffee?" The coffee had finished brewing. She poured two mugs and added milk to Sam's.

Sam hugged her back and said, "I'd kill for one, thanks."

This is so beautiful here, Cathy thought. "Tell me again, why are we leaving this for an arid, inhospitable planet? I love it here. I think I'm in love with you, too."

"Wait a minute, that's too much love before I've even had my first cup of coffee."

"There's that, too. I don't think they grow coffee plants on Mars."

"I'll make sure it goes to the top of the list when we get there." Sam took a sip of the coffee. She looked at Cathy, her stare penetrating her defenses. "Cathy, you know we have to go. We have to create a new world without CIPHER. You need to leave your misery behind and start fresh."

"I know," sighed Cathy. "It's just that there are moments. Moments like this morning, which I wish could last forever. Being with you on a nice day after a great night. The sound of the birds, the smell of the coffee."

"I know. Believe me, I feel that too. There have been moments for me too ...," Sam paused then. She is nearly always present with me, Cathy thought. But sometimes, like now, she seems to be elsewhere.

"What is it, Sam? You've got that look again. What

are you thinking?”

“Sorry, it’s nothing. I wish this could last forever too, I guess. But we’ve already made up our minds. There’s a new world we can build and we must build it. Not just for us, but for the ones we’ve lost: your father and my Ruth.”

“It’s still painful, isn’t it? You hardly ever talk about her.”

“I’m not ready yet. I’ve reached closure with what happened, and I’ve said my goodbyes. I think you should do the same.”

“I’ve already said goodbye to Gareth. There is certainly closure there, and I never want to see him again.” Except I do, thought Cathy. I still love him. How would he get on without someone guiding him? He really was a child, but there’s no way I can get him off the road he is on. Sam’s right, we have to go. There’s too much pain and unhappiness here.

“That’s not what I meant. I think you know that. You need to say goodbye to your father.”

“No!” Cathy nearly spilled her coffee as the anger and disappointment came raging back. “God, this started out to be such a pleasant morning. Why did you have to ruin it?”

“I’m sorry,” said Sam quietly. “But this will be your last chance to see him. You need to go to *Happy*

Meadows. I'll go with you."

"What's the point? His body's there, sure. But you know his mind is on permanent holiday, reliving some Experience over and over. Why do I want to go to a place with room after room of Fugue victims?" Cathy's voice grew louder as she rejected Sam's suggestion.

"Yes, he's in Fugue. But no one really understands what's going on with that. I know what 'they' say. That the victims get lost in an Experience and just never come back—as if it were a conscious choice. Maybe it isn't. CIPHER hasn't been around that long; it could be a defect. It may have been nothing he did or anything he could control."

"He could if he tried! I'm convinced of it. But he's weak, like Gareth. He doesn't want to come back to us."

"You don't mean that," corrected Sam. "It's anger and grief talking. Believe me, I understand that. If you don't do this before you go, it will create a knot of regret inside you that you'll never be able to untangle."

"Why do you care so much? He's my father; it's my life."

Sam reached out and held Cathy's hand. "Yes, he is your father. But this is our life. I don't want there to be any regrets, any unfinished business when we leave. Can you do this for us?"

Cathy thought about what Sam had said. It's not just for me, she realized. Sam needs it too; our relationship needs it. She's afraid that I'll blame her for taking me to Mars, away from my father. Closure, right? It never works that way, really. How many times can I say goodbye?

"All right," Cathy gave in. "I'll go."

Happy Meadows
June 2093

It was nearly time for Cathy to begin the long journey to New Nottingham. Sam helped her pack the single duffel bag she could take with her. It was limited to twenty kilos. Other than what she had left behind with Gareth, she either sold or donated everything else.

Cathy had said goodbye to her mother last week. They were never close. Mary had wished her luck and hoped that she and Sam would be happy together. Just one more thing to take care of. Cathy and Sam stopped for breakfast, then drove on to *Happy Meadows*—where her father was housed.

What am I doing here? wondered Cathy. This was the last place she wanted to visit, but Sam had insisted that they go. She understood what Sam was telling her, but still could barely bring herself to make the journey.

Her mother visited him weekly and would inform Cathy of any changes in his condition. Of course, there weren't any changes. No one ever came out of Fugue. Her father was fortunate they could afford a private sanitarium. The public facilities subsidized by the Phillips Foundation were nice enough, but they still seemed like warehouses to her. So many Fugue victims laid out on their beds like plants in a nursery, watered and pruned daily.

They entered the main reception area. It was a large space populated with potted plants, comfortable-looking chairs, and a desk at one end. The soothing music and soft lighting did nothing to lighten her mood. "I don't know why I let you talk me into this. He won't even know I'm here," Cathy hissed.

"You don't know that for sure," Sam replied softly, reaching for Cathy's hand. "I've heard about research into brain activity changes, brain wave changes, when friends and family visit Fugue victims. They say that the changes show a less intense Fugue experience. It's like the visits allow the outside world to make its way in. The hope is that with more interaction, there is a greater possibility that they will come out of it."

"How do you know so much suddenly?"

"Remember," said Sam, "my friend Ruth is in Fugue,

too. I am interested. I have to hope that she can come out of it someday."

"Sorry, I didn't think...No, I don't buy it! I'm happy that you have hope for Ruth. I'm a realist. People are in Fugue because they are happier there; they want to be there," Cathy countered, withdrawing her hand. Bitterness had crept into her voice. This is why I didn't want to come here, she realized. I don't want to feel this way. I can't stop blaming him for what happened. That's why I left Gareth. Maybe someday he'll be in one of these places. I don't want to be around when that happens. I just don't have the hope that Sam has.

"It'll be okay, Cathy. Whatever you think about why this happened to him, you don't want to start your life in New Nottingham without having said goodbye. Trust me, it will eat at you. I made my farewells to Ruth."

"And do you feel better now?"

"Yes, I do. It's different for me, though. Someday I will tell you more about Ruth. But let's get this visit going," Sam said and walked up to the desk. Cathy sighed and followed. "Hi, we're here to see Walter Mendez. I'm Samantha Brown; this is his daughter, Cathy Mendez. We should be on the visitor list."

"Ah, yes," the woman at the desk acknowledged as she consulted a list. "I see you here. Doctor Robbins is with him right now. Your father is enrolled in a Phillips Foundation trial. The Doctor has been spending a good deal of time with him. This will be an excellent opportunity for you to chat about it, should you have questions."

"Trial?" asked Cathy. "I wasn't aware of any trial. Why wasn't I consulted?"

"I see his wife approved it, and she has medical power of attorney. I can cipher the signed documents to you if you like."

"No, I'm sure it's in order. I'm just surprised. What's the trial?"

"Doctor Robbins can tell you all about it. He's still with your father in Room 312. Here are your visitor badges. You should be able to see the doctor there."

They took the badges and headed to the elevator. "Sam, why didn't Mom tell me about this?"

"I don't know, but since I've known you, you have shown no desire to be involved in your father's care."

"Fair enough, but she could have kept me in the loop. After all, I just spoke to her last week."

The elevator stopped on the third floor, and they followed the signs to 312. They passed by room after room of patients lying motionless on their beds. As they approached 312, they saw a man standing with a younger man at her father's bedside. They were both wearing white coats. Amazing how some things never change in medicine, Cathy thought. You can still identify the doctors. Her father was hooked up to some kind of monitor, wires running from a fabric ring around the crown of his head. She stopped at the threshold of the room, unable to enter.

"Cathy, are you okay?" Sam asked.

"Damn you!" Cathy said, her voice barely audible. She shuddered, revolted by the sight. "I told you I didn't want to come. Now this is the image I'll be left with. I'll always remember him connected to machines, the object of research."

"Take a breath. You'll be fine."

"Oh, hi. Are you friends of Mr. Mendez?" the older man asked. "I'm Doctor Robbins. Please come in."

Sam walked into the room. Cathy sighed and followed, walking past her to the foot of the bed. Her father was propped up, his gray hair neatly combed. It looked as if it had been recently cut. The blue eyes were open, as they had been since the Fugue began, requiring frequent application of eye drops. What was he seeing? she wondered. They seemed to be focused on something on his lap. But there was nothing there.

"I'm his daughter, Cathy. This is my friend, Sam. How

is he?" she managed to ask.

"He's doing well," replied Doctor Robbins. "They've been able to keep him well-nourished."

"What is the monitor for?" asked Cathy.

"We are recording his brainwaves. It's part of the study funded by the Phillips Foundation. The foundation is at the forefront of Fugue research."

"Study," Cathy asked. "What kind of study?"

"We what to know what's going on with people in Fugue. Are they conscious? Do they ever sleep? Humans can't survive without sleep. Yet, Fugue victims never close their eyes, and they have unusual eye movements, which we call nystagmus. This is a symptom of some other conditions, usually caused by trauma to the inner ear. That is not the case here. It seems that they are seeing something, but what?"

Cathy had expected Sam to take an interest in the conversation. She had been going on about brainwaves earlier. But now she doesn't seem to be paying attention. It's like she's preoccupied with something else. "What are the different waveforms on the monitor?" Cathy asked.

"That's what we are tracking. There are four basic brain waves: alpha, beta, delta, and theta. Each corresponds to a different kind of brain activity. Alpha is a relaxed mind, as in meditation. Beta is an active mental state, focused on a conversation or an activity. When we daydream, we're in a theta state. It's a time when we are most creative and get some of our best ideas. Delta is the last state; when our brain has mostly shut down as in a deep sleep."

"What does this have to do with Fugue?" asked Cathy.

"It has to do with what we see on the monitor and what we expect to see. There is a reason we do this study in private facilities like *Happy Meadows*. Here, people like your father are in private rooms, separated from others. There's no near field—or NF for short—CIPHER interference leaking in from other patients. You see, CIPHER nanobots are a little permissive when it comes to making connections. They sometimes make momentary connections with other CIPHER nanobots. It's generally not a problem, but we want to eliminate it in our studies. Public facilities house four or more patients in the same room, so we get a lot of NF interference. At *Happy Meadows,* the patients are far enough apart that interference is not a factor. We can get a proper baseline."

"What do the brain waves tell you?" she asked. Cathy heard a faint sound from Sam behind her.

"It's fascinating!" the Doctor continued, talking faster, happy to have an audience. "People who were in creative professions, writers and artists, for example, spend a lot of time in theta, the daydreaming state. People like your father, he was an engineer, right? They spend a lot of time in beta. It's as if in Fugue, they are making maximum use of their potential."

"Doctor," interrupted the assistant, "she doesn't look well."

Cathy turned just in time to see Sam collapse to the floor. Doctor Robbins hurried over to her, looking into her eyes. "She has nystagmus! Harris, quick, call for a gurney and get the FAR! We need to get her out of here, away from his NF range. She's going into Fugue!" Orderlies arrived quickly with a gurney, and Robbins helped them lift Sam onto it. As they rushed to the elevator, Cathy tried to keep panic from taking over.

"What happened to her?" asked Cathy, as they entered the elevator.

"She'll be fine," reassured Robbins. "But we need to act quickly. Thank God we've got the proper equipment on hand. Harris, you have it, right?"

"Yes, Doctor," replied the assistant.

The elevator reached the fourth floor, and they rushed to a room not far down the hall. They quickly hooked Sam up to a monitor, her eyes still open. Fugue, the doctor had said. Sam is going into Fugue? she thought. Her eyes, like her father's, were spinning madly around.

Robbins and his assistant set up a device he had called FAR. Cathy had never heard of it before. "Strange, even out of NF range, she still seems connected to Mendez's CIPHER. Harris set for level one and initiate." After a minute, Robbins called for level two, then three. As Robbins monitored the device, Cathy noticed Sam's eyes move from left to right, as if tracking a moving object. Then her pupils contracted, then they opened wide, finally returning to normal. She blinked a few times. "OK, Harris, shut it down."

Doctor Robbins looked at the monitor and checked Sam's eyes. They were closed. "She's okay now. Brain waves are returning to normal. That was a close call. The lack of eye focus is a giveaway for Fugue. We were lucky to have gotten to her so quickly, and that we had a FAR device at hand. It only works if a person has just fallen into a Fugue. Fugue Arrest and Reversal produces a variety of visual and auditory stimuli via the victim's CIPHER implants. The sounds, music, and changes in lighting essentially distract them from whatever they are experiencing in Fugue and reset the nanobots. We have about a fifty percent chance of bringing them out—if we can get to them in time. Still, this is odd. There are only a few cases like this that I know of."

"What do you mean? A few cases like what?" Cathy

asked.

"As I said earlier, the **CIPHER** Near Field is leaky. It will sometimes try to connect to other **CIPHER**'s in range. This is more of a problem for people with **CIPHER** 2, like your friend. You have just **CIPHER** 1, correct?"

"Yes, but what happened to her?"

Sam was waking up, her eyes focusing and finding Cathy.

"Sam, are you OK?" Cathy asked.

"Yes, I think so. That was weird, like a dream..."

"You nearly went into a full Fugue," said the Doctor. "We got you out of Mr. Mendez's NF range, and we introduced artificial stimuli. We pulled you out just in time. Miss Brown, do you know where you are?"

"Of course, I'm at *Happy Meadows* with my friend Cathy—visiting her father."

"You had what we call NF Fugue exposure. Do you remember anything? Your beta waves were very active. As if you were talking to someone."

"I don't remember that," replied Sam, hesitation in her voice.

"I'd like to see you at my office. I'll cipher you my details. This is not a common occurrence. There have only been a few documented cases. Usually, they involve a MiXe known as *EmpHance*. It seems to make people more susceptible to this sort of thing. Are you using any MiXes?”

“No.”

Doctor Robbins did not seem convinced, thought Cathy. He disconnected the monitors. After a puzzled glance at Sam, he and his assistant left the room.

“OK, Sam. I can tell that you’re hiding something. Do you remember anything? I need to know what it was like. What did you see? I need to know what my father might be experiencing.”

“OK, but I need a drink. Let’s get out of here. There’s a bar down the street.”

###

Like most bars post-CIPHER, it was pretty empty. Pop songs played over a sound system. A few people sat at the bar, nursing a midday drink. Cathy mostly avoided bars. They were depressing now. Not the fun places she remembered from college. They settled into a booth where they could have a little privacy. Cathy ordered a glass of wine, and Sam a scotch.

“OK, you’ve got to tell me what you saw,” said Cathy.

“Sometimes, I wish you had CIPHER 2. I could share this with you as an Experience.”

114

"No, I don't think so. You're not Gareth, you're not an Experiencer. Thank God for that."

"All right, I know. I'll try to tell you what happened." Sam closed her eyes briefly. "I don't remember falling, but the room faded away, and I felt a little vertigo. It passed, and I found myself on a city street. It was no place that I recognized. I was on a street, like in an old European town, with cobblestone sidewalks on either side. It was early evening, and streetlights flickered as they came on. The street was deserted."

"There were shops on both sides of the street. On one side, I saw what seemed to be galleries, artwork displayed in the windows. I glanced at a few, mostly paintings of a queen or empress, I guess. She was usually surrounded by men and women bowing to her."

"The other side of the street looked like electronics and repair shops. There were all kinds of gadgets I didn't recognize. I felt drawn to the repair shops. As I looked more closely, they all looked the same, just different signs over the door. I notice one sign: 'Mendez Engineering, a Phillips company.' Of course, I recognized your name. The other signs had different names, but they were all Phillips companies."

"I was curious, so I walked up to the shop and entered. A bell sounded as I went through the door. It was a small, dusty, dingy space. There was a workbench, with a solitary light illuminating a spherical object and an older man. He was your father, sitting behind the workbench and adjusting dials on the object. He looked up at the sound of the bell and asked, 'Hello? Do I know you?' I said, 'No, but I'm a friend of your daughter'. He smiled and said, 'that's good.'"

"'What are you working on?' I asked."

"'There are too many walls around here,' he said. 'They must come down! I have to finish this.' He gestured at another larger object on the floor next to the workbench. He said he needed help. 'Too many walls', he said again and returned to tinkering with the object. 'What is that?' I asked, nodding at the larger object."

"It's weird, but I heard music around then, like a Bach Fugue. Funny, I know—hearing a Fugue in a Fugue. But that was what I heard. I couldn't help but listen to it: the repeating, escalating themes. It was distracting."

"He said that it was a quantum drive, or it would be. Walter went on about how Mrs. Phillips wanted the drive, needed it. He had to finish it. It would get a ship from Earth to Mars in two days, much faster than fusion drives used now."

"The music continued. And the room got very bright. I had to close my eyes until the light returned to normal.

When I opened my eyes, I saw he was working with the device again, and the wall adjoining the next shop faded. Then became solid again. He cursed."

"'I don't have enough time', he said. 'I have to get this to function before it's too late. You don't work for Phillips, do you? She's not to know about this. Please don't tell her. No, I'm sure you won't. It's a special program, you see. Phillips controls everything here. We need to take it from her, make this our place—not hers'."

"He set the tool down on the bench, and said, 'I've noticed the change in light and music, too. Someone is trying to get you back, away from here. They are punching small holes in this world Phillips created. Eventually, there will be a hole big enough for you to get out. Could that work?' He paused, picking up a small statue of a horse. I hadn't noticed it before."

Sam took another sip of her drink before continuing. "'It's like that game. The one where players fight to control a Moloi cloud,' he said. 'We can't create a hole to get out. Perhaps we can create a hole to bring something in. Vincent, in the shop next door. He understands all this better than I do. There must be a way to get control!' He became agitated and walked around the workbench to me. He grabbed me and shook me. 'You must help us! I need to talk to Vincent!' he said."

"I tried to tell him I didn't know how to help. I heard the music getting louder, and then it got very dark and I couldn't see a thing. It got brighter and, just as I could see again, he faded away, followed by the shop. I woke up and saw you."

Cathy frowned. "That's it? I don't know what to think. It sounds terrible."

"I'm sorry, Cathy. That's what I saw. I don't know if any of it was real. It was probably my imagination. I mean a quantum drive, a star drive? And that horse? What does it all mean? I'm sure that I imagined the whole thing."

Did Sam see her father? Cathy wondered. None of it made sense. It sounded like a dream. But then she remembered what Doctor Robbins had said about Sam's brain waves. Beta, that's not a dream state.

"Maybe you saw my father," said Cathy. "I just don't know. And I don't know what would be worse either. Your vision of him slaving away in some virtual shop or lost in some happy Experience. The more I think about it, the more it must have been a dream. Just before you fell into Fugue, you were looking at my father, and we were discussing the Phillips trial. Both appeared to you in Fugue, my father and him talking about Phillips. It was the power of suggestion. That's it. I don't believe that there are virtual cities populated with Fugue victims." God, I hope not, Cathy thought. She suddenly felt exhausted. The only thing I can think of doing, she thought, is run and leave this all behind. "I've got to get out of here."

"OK, I'll settle the bill."

"No, not the bar. I think I'll have a scotch too now. I just, I just can't wait to get to Mars. Away from Fugues, away from CIPHER and all the craziness."

"I understand," said Sam as she ordered the next round. "Sorry you didn't have the best farewell with your father. I shouldn't have told you what I saw. I'm sure that you're right, it was a dream. And I shouldn't have made you go to *Happy Meadows*. I was hoping you would get some closure before we left for New Nottingham."

Cathy finished her drink as the new round arrived. "It's OK. I know you meant well. I wish you could go with me now."

"So do I, but I'll be along on the next trip. Rick will be with you."

"I know Rick's a good guy, but he's really your friend, not mine. It's obvious you have history. Something happened to you two. What happened to Ruth? You never talk about it. It must have been painful."

"Someday, I will. But I can't yet. Maybe when we are all together on Mars."

Losses
June 2093

Even with CIPHER and MiXes, some people still went to the local pub, especially lonely people like Gareth. It was that or spend all your free time in Experiences. After the bad time with *Blissful Moments*, he avoided them. The disgust of that memory was still vivid for him.

That left the corner pub as the way to fill the loneliness void. It wasn't bad; it had a decent selection of beer and whiskey. The food was unimaginative, but tolerable. This is a night, Gareth thought, that I could use the company. He threw on a jacket and made the short walk down the street to downtown Takoma Park.

Gareth heard light jazz music as he walked up to the door. He went in and saw a quartet playing off to one side. There were a few couples sitting quietly together at tables.

Gareth noticed Seth waving to him from the bar.

"Hi, Seth. How's it going?" He sat down on the empty stool next to Seth.

"Good, now." He shook his head and sighed. "It was kind of a rough day." He was holding a glass in his hand, likely bourbon, neat. Seth was a snob when it came to his liquor. No mixed drinks for him. He took a sip.

Gareth motioned to the bartender and said, "Same for me, thanks." He often found Seth here, sitting at the bar. Since he didn't have CIPHER, there was no chance, or choice, to lose himself in an Experience. Bourbon was his escape. He held his liquor well, though. He was a quiet, amiable drunk.

"Bad day at *Happy Meadows*?" asked Gareth as the bartender brought his drink. He enjoyed spending time with Seth, a simple sharing between friends without CIPHER in the way. It was like the world was before CIPHER. Someday soon, there will be a generation of people who never knew that world. What would it be like then? Will we forget how to talk? Will babies be injected with CIPHER implants at birth? He took a sip of the bourbon, pushing the thoughts away.

"Terrible day," said Seth. "A new Fugue patient came in today. Just a young girl, it said fifteen on the intake form. She's only had the implants for a month. Just

CIPHER 1; it seems like her parents were being responsible and not getting her CIPHER 2 right away."

Gareth frowned. "I don't understand. She was in Fugue?" Seth nodded. "But that's not possible! No CIPHER 2, no Experiences. No Experiences, no Fugue."

"You're right; that's what I thought, too. There was a researcher there, working on something for the Phillips Foundation. He's pretty much always around. He scanned her CIPHER implant. Turns out that her implants had been altered. They had CIPHER 2 capabilities."

"Altered? How?"

Seth shrugged. "Fuck if I know. I heard the Doc say something about a 'Builder Virus'. I guess it upgrades the implants. You can get it on the black market. Kids always find a way."

Gareth nodded. "Yeah, I heard of that. Something the Ludds cooked up? That's the rumor, anyway. It reprograms the implant's nanobots. It's a scary world out there. Poor kid."

"Uh-huh, somehow it must have let her run Experiences; that's how she fell into Fugue. The doc tried to bring her out of it with this FAR gizmo. No luck." Seth shook his head and threw the rest of the drink back. "You know, it wouldn't surprise me if the Ludds were behind the Fugue."

"Don't get carried away, Seth. The Ludds are bad enough without looking for other conspiracies to hang on them."

"Probably right. So, that was my shit day. How was yours?"

Gareth shrugged. "You know, the same old thing. But I did meet this really intriguing girl. Well, not meet really. I'll get the next round, and I'll tell you all about it."

They continued to order rounds with a beer or two mixed in, as Gareth recounted the encounter and Seth talked more about his job. The conversation moved on to the latest soccer match, and how CIPHER was making refs obsolete.

"Damn CIPHER ruins everything!" said Seth, throwing back the rest of his bourbon. He gestured for another round.

"Um, not for me. I'm good. Really, Seth? I mean, it's done a lot of good, too."

Seth shook his head. "Just look around this place. Those guys playing jazz over there. Great stuff, too. Is anyone listening? Better yet, except for you and me, is anyone talking? Before CIPHER, this joint was hopping! You could barely find a seat! Now people are ciphering each other or killing time with an Experience."

Seth pounded the bar counter. "Everything's ruined!"

"Hey," said the bartender. "Take a breath, buddy."

"It's all right," said Gareth. He placed a hand on Seth's shoulder. "Maybe we should call it a night? I have to get up early tomorrow."

Seth glared at the bartender and threw back the last of his bourbon. "Fine, let's go." Seth stood up, tipping his stool over. Gareth barely caught it before it hit the floor. He steadied Seth, helped him with his jacket as they made their way out of the bar. Outside, the fall chill seemed to have a restorative effect on Seth. His gait became steadier on the short walk back to the apartment building.

"I'll enter the code," said Seth as they reached the entrance to the building. "Damn, fat-fingered it." Gareth waited as he tried again and failed. "Third time's the charm! Fuck!"

"It's OK, Seth."

Cipher, send the entry ID to the door.

The door unlocked. Seth glared at Gareth. "Sure, everything's so easy for people like you. The world is built for you and is leaving *me* behind!"

Gareth didn't know what to say. He's right, he thought. But what can I do about it? No one asked for CIPHER. I didn't want to be left behind either. It's not my fault that CIPHER worked for me and not for Seth.

"Come on, Seth. Let's go in."

Gareth caught Seth as he stumbled on the way in. The sobering effect of the night air had dissipated, and the evening's drinking was catching up with a vengeance. Seth probably won't remember any of this, thought Gareth.

"Let me help you into your apartment." Gareth took his arm and guided him down the stairs to the basement. "Do you have your key?"

"Yeah, sure. Here it is," replied Seth. He handed the key over to Gareth, his hand trembling. "No CIPHER lock for me! Old-school lock."

Gareth smiled. "Don't worry, I remember how they work." He winced. That was a condescending thing to say. He opened the door and searched for the light switch. He found it and flicked it on, revealing the small apartment.

"Not much, I know," said Seth. "Had to move in here after Grace left me."

Gareth closed the door and guided Seth to a large easy chair. Seth fell into it and sighed. "Thank you, Gareth. I guess I had a little too much to drink."

"No worries. You had a bad day at work. It happens."

"It shouldn't. But sometimes, I just get really lonely. You all are running around ciphering each other, whatever the hell that means. People like me, we're left out."

Gareth found a blanket on the sofa and laid it over Seth. "Maybe you should join the Isolators. They don't like the whole idea of CIPHER."

"Hell, no!" said Seth, nearly shouting. He had a brief coughing fit and wiped his mouth with a handkerchief. "Don't you get it? I want CIPHER; I want the world it can bring to me." He paused. "It would bring Grace back to me. Funny that, Grace." He settled back into the chair.

Gareth waited silently, looking around the small apartment. The kitchen was tidy, unlike mine, he thought. The old digital picture frame on one wall cycled through photos of Seth and a woman. Must be Grace. It seemed that they had traveled a lot. There were pictures of the Eiffel Tower, canals in Venice, and the Grand Canyon. Seth looked younger and happier. They looked happy. The world had changed so much.

Soon, he heard snoring. He stood up and left as quietly as he could, closing the apartment door behind him. "I guess we have one thing in common, Seth. CIPHER took away the best things in our lives."

The Procedure

August 2093

Gareth met Alex outside the CRI headquarters for his appointment. He arrived late, having overslept. I'll need to check on that *Serenity* MiXe guarantee, Gareth thought. I feel like I haven't slept at all. "Hi, Gareth. Today's the big day!" Alex is chipper as ever in the morning. But I can't blame him for being excited.

"Hi, Alex. Sorry I'm late."

"No problem, Gar, it's not like they can do the procedure without you, right?"

This will be my third CIPHER implantation, Gareth thought as they entered the reception area. But this time it is different. At least CIPHER 1 and 2 had made it through the FDA approval process before I got them. CIPHER 3 is still in beta testing, not yet approved by the FDA. If it weren't for the contract, I'd wait. It's disconcerting that it integrates with the endocrine system. What did that mean?

The contract was explicit in terms of the requirements for the next two assignments. CIPHER 3 beta was required. The client must have had some pull with CRI to arrange the implants for me. Sure, it was a little risky. But I'll have a tremendous advantage over other Experiencers. I should be able to ask for double the current rate. Then I can retire early and get out of the game.

A large, stocky man intercepted Alex and Gareth just as they entered the building. "Good morning, gentlemen. I apologize for the inconvenience, but all visitors must submit to additional security protocols. Please proceed to the examination room. This will not take long."

"Do you have any idea who I am?" protested Alex.

"Not a clue, and it doesn't matter. You could be Doctor Moloi for all I care."

"I'm Alex Phillips, Isolde Phillips' grandson—you know, the founder of the company you work for?"

Alex rarely mentions that, Gareth thought. Since she 'retired', he hardly mentioned her. Although he's not above invoking her name and their relationship.

"Alex, relax," said Gareth. "He's just doing his job. With all the Ludd attacks lately, it's sensible. Besides, Isolde doesn't work here anymore; dropping her name isn't helpful."

"I know, but it's annoying, all these Ludd attacks." Alex shrugged. "That's what drove her away, you know. The attack on Moloi's lab was too much. Fine," Alex said to the guard. "I'll go. But none of this will stop the Ludds! Physical attacks are not their style, not anymore. CIPHER attacks are what you need to worry about."

The guard ignored Alex's comments and directed them to the examination room. It was a small alcove outfitted with four Experiencer chairs. "Please take a seat." Alex and Gareth sat down, and Gareth's cipher pinged.

Gareth, I have an incoming request from CRI Security. Do you accept?

Yes.

Please remain seated, as we review your CIPHER logs. Done. You may enter the facility. Have a nice day.

Security had finished with Alex as well. "Alex, what was that about? What do they mean logs?"

"CRI has built in a kind of a black box into all CIPHER's. Everything you think, see, or do is recorded and saved in encrypted storage. With your permission, CRI can review it."

"You're kidding me!" Gareth said, his voice was shaking. "I never consented to that!"

"Um, yes. You did. It was all in your employment

agreement. I told you to have a lawyer review it. Besides, if you have nothing to hide, why worry?"

"That's not the point! It's creepy. I don't like people poking around in my brain. How do I know what they've looked at? What they'll do with it?"

"Jesus, Gar, calm down. You're making a scene. No one would mess with your brain!"

"OK," Gareth relented. "I still don't like it. Let's get this over with." He walked up to the reception area.

"Hello, may I help you", asked the young man at the desk.

"Yes, I'm Gareth Williams. I'm here for the CIPHER 3 implantation. If we're late, you can blame your intrusive security."

"And I'm Alex Phillips, CIPHER Tech Specialist with *Multitudes*. I'm here to monitor the implantation and gather baseline data."

"Right, Mr. Williams. I see you are scheduled for ten am." The receptionist seemed perplexed and turned to Alex. "Mr. Phillips, this is most irregular. We rarely permit observers."

"If you check your records," said Alex, "you will find that I have special authority from the financial party and CRI. As Mr. Williams will travel to Ritz Lagrange One, he will be out of CRI monitoring range. I will monitor

CIPHER 3 during that time and will have permission to adjust the implant as needed."

"Very well. Mr. Williams," the receptionist turned back to Gareth, "with your permission, I'll send over a packet for you to sign, authorizing the procedure."

Gareth instructed Cipher to accept the packet from CRI reception. *Connection approved, responded Cipher, packet received and scanned. It's clean.*

Gareth reviewed the packet contents: non-disclosure, informed consent, approval to implant CIPHER 3 nanobots in the hypothalamus, and so on. Gareth had reviewed all the forms earlier. They seemed like the forms he had approved for CIPHER 1 and 2, except for the Informed Consent. The Informed Consent packet included an experience.

Cipher, open Informed Consent experience.

The CIPHER 2 implant shut down his native senses and began feeding the Experience directly to his brain. The perspective for this Experience differed from normal Experiences. Gareth did not feel like he was reliving something that someone else had lived through. In that kind of Experience he became the other person. CIPHER 2 sent his brain's sensory processing centers the same input as the person who had created the Experience. He perceived what that person perceived: nothing more, nothing less.

This was not the same. It was an AI-augmented reality Experience, typically used for education and marketing. For this experience, he is still Gareth Williams interacting as if this were happening in real time. His CIPHER transported him to a virtual world in the Moloi cloud. Gareth could interact with this world as if it were real. Gareth sat in what looked like a standard doctor's office. What would happen if I got up and walked out the door? he wondered. A question for another day.

He recognized the doctor sitting at the desk across from him: Doctor Francis. He was the doctor for his first two implant procedures.

"Hello Mr. Williams."

Gareth understood this was not really Doctor John Francis, but the AI had used CIPHER 2 to mine his memory for a physician he would recognize and would make sense in this context. It had created this avatar based on Gareth's memories of him. He *seemed* real, though—as did the hard chair he sat on. Doctor Francis continued.

"How nice to see you again! I will take you
through the informed consent. This augmented
reality experience allows us to interact, and you can

132

ask questions at any time. The CIPHER 3 Beta implant differs from your current implants as it integrates with your endocrine system via the hypothalamus. The nanobots record the dopamine, serotonin, and epinephrine levels during an Experience, as well as the five senses that CIPHER 2 records. Are you with me so far?" Doctor Francis pauses to allow Gareth to ask a question. He shuffles some virtual papers on his virtual desk to enhance the illusion that he's a real person.

Gareth nodded his head for him to continue. If Cathy were here, he thought, I'm sure she would have a lot of questions. As usual, I haven't any.

"This is an achievement in its own right. You may have heard of the MiXe *EmpHance*? It stimulates the cannabinoid and endocrine systems via sound and scent. Well, we used it to research how nanobots could record and stimulate these systems. We've put that research into practice with CIPHER 3. This is the true leap forward! It regulates these levels in the body when a user runs an Experience."

"Could this lead to more cases of Fugue?" Gareth interrupts, finally thinking of a question.

Avatar Doctor Francis looks mildly

annoyed at the question. "Absolutely not! All this talk about Fugue is overblown and affects less than 0.5 percent of all Experiences. And in those cases, there were often co-morbidities. In fact, CIPHER 3 will eliminate even those. The safeguards built into this system will detect Fugue onset and automatically adjust to exit the Experience before Fugue."

"You must cease use of any Micro Experiences other that those specifically prescribed by your CIPHER tech, Alex Phillips." The avatar pauses to give Gareth a chance to ask more questions. "Mr. Williams, I've given you all the information you need for informed consent. Oh, wait, one other thing," added the flustered avatar. "There is a research rider. CRI is granted access to your CIPHER 3 implants to monitor them and the associated integration. The data gathered will be de-identified when logged to CRI servers. CRI will also be able to disable the CIPHER 3 implant should circumstances warrant it."

No more *Serenity* or *SexyBeast* MiXes? Well, it was fun while it lasted. Not that *Serenity* worked as advertised. Associated integration? wondered Gareth. What does that mean? I've already annoyed the doctor enough, and really, I'm going to say yes, anyway. So why bother asking?

"Do you, Gareth Williams, consent to the
CIPHER 3 Beta implantation and the associated
research rider? Send your response, and you will exit
this Experience."

I've come this far, thought Gareth. Might as well go all in. *Cipher, send acceptance of the informed consent, as well as my consent to the procedure.* The Experience ended, and Gareth found himself sitting next to Alex, facing the receptionist.

"I see you have consented, Mr. Williams," said the receptionist. "Please follow me, and we will get you prepared for the procedure. It should take less than half an hour. Mr. Phillips, please wait here. When I return, I will take you to observation."

Gareth nodded to Alex and followed the receptionist. The procedure room was similar to the rooms for the last two procedures. A reclining chair and a table prepped with a vial and a syringe. The room for the CIPHER 1 procedure had monitoring equipment, which was absent here. Since Gareth already had nanobots, monitoring would be done using them. He sat down in the chair, and the clinician walked in and inspected the vial.

"Please confirm your identity via CIPHER using your public key," the clinician instructed. Gareth confirmed, and the clinician promptly injected him in the neck. "Hey, wait!" Gareth protested. "You could have warned me."

"Sorry," replied the clinician. His expression, however, carried no sign of regret. "The integration will take ten minutes or so," the clinician continued. "There may be some discomfort during this integration as the nanobots calibrate your endocrine responses. This will be transient, as we move the nanobots and you through a set of hormonal adjustments. The injection also included a muscle relaxant so you will not injure yourself during the integration, as some adjustments can be quite intense. Don't worry, I'll be here with you the whole time."

Muscle relaxant? That wasn't in the informed consent, thought Gareth. Frantically, he tried to tell the clinician to stop the procedure. Panic crashed into him like a tsunami, carrying him away. He screamed, but no sound came out. The muscle relaxant stifled it. His panic had no outlet. Wait, I can cipher him, thought Gareth, his brain trying to maintain rationality. Gareth sent to the clinician, *No one told me about this! You've got to let me go!* He ignored Gareth, but soon the panic abated, the wave receding.

Anger chased it, his brain losing the fight to keep perspective—losing the hormonal battle. You have no right to do this to me! he thought at the clinician. You fucking bastard! When I get out of this chair, I'm going to break both of your legs and send you to the hospital! Then when you get out, I'm going to break them again! The anger dissipated as quickly as it had come. He felt calmer now, the hormonal ocean smoothing.

What was I so upset about? Gareth wondered. This really isn't so bad. Gareth felt a blanket of contentment. He didn't know what he had been so angry about. It wasn't like him to lose his temper that way. Sorry, man, lost it there for a minute. I'm good now. I feel so at peace. Then Gareth noticed the clinician as he walked by him. Really noticed him, as if for the first time.

The feeling of contentment transformed into sexual attraction, lust. He was so young, well-muscled, with beautiful green eyes, and such pleasant features. He looks like Sam. Sam? Yes, I remember her now. From the café assignment. Why didn't I remember her before? The clinician's features changed again, looking even more like Sam. Suddenly his perceptions shifted as if in an Experience. He didn't recognize it. It wasn't one he had created or loaded. Where did it come from?

    Gareth saw Sam sitting across from him at a
sidewalk café. It looked like the one in Dupont
Circle where his last assignment took place. "Hello
again, Gareth," she said. He was holding an
Americano in his hand. It was hot, and he gripped it

tightly. He focused on the coffee, and how it felt. Willing himself to be in this moment, struggling against the hormonal fog being produced by the procedure. I need to think, he thought. He took a gulp too quickly, too much at once. It burned as it went down.

"You're Sam, I remember you now. Why do I remember you now? I keep meeting you and forgetting you. Why?"

"I know it's difficult, Gareth." He couldn't tell whether her expression was one of sadness or of a remembered pain. "This moment you are in, the hormonal rush you are experiencing, allows me to come back to you from your CIPHER storage. At the same time, I know it's hard for you to focus. This will be easier after the new implants are fine-tuned. For now, try to stay with me." She reached out and grabbed the hand not holding the coffee. It helped to root him in the moment.

"Your memories of me are buried in your lower-level CIPHER secure memory. I'm riding the wave of the hormone storm to be with you. This implantation procedure produces oxytocin. Oxytocin is a hormone that increases the feelings of love and trust. The sexual arousal you are feeling also comes from it. These feelings help keep me with you."

Even though Gareth knew the feelings he

had for Sam were because of the procedure, he couldn't resist them. He had to have her, had to be with her. He would do anything for her.

"Not long ago, I had an experience with CIPHER 2 which linked me to two other people in a way I had never thought possible. It was like we were more than just three isolated people, struggling to connect. We were really connected for a brief time. But it faded. We lost it, and one of us never came back. Rick and I are trying to reclaim that feeling and maybe bring Ruth back."

She gripped his hand tighter, so tight it hurt. "This feeling, this oxytocin-induced connection is what we were missing. CIPHER 3 can bring that to us." She paused, staring at him. "Gareth, do you understand the difference between sympathy and empathy?"

What is she talking about? Gareth fought to concentrate. "Vaguely," he managed. "It's not something I think about much. I think sympathy is like understanding what somebody is feeling. Like if they're happy, you understand what that's like. I think empathy is somehow more than that?"

"Honestly, I didn't think about it much either. But then I had this moment with my friends. It gave me a glimpse of what the difference was. You create Experiences that others consume, right? Like skiing in the Alps. When I consume the

Experience, I feel like I'm there. As if I'm going down the slopes, the icy wind lashing at me, the sun reflecting off the snow nearly blinding me. I'm feeling this all from my perspective. That's what CIPHER 2 gives us."

"Yes," said Gareth. "I understand that."

"Empathy means that I feel what you feel at a basic level—a shared feeling. Like the adrenaline rush you feel as you go down the slopes, the fear that you might wipe out. It's like I am you. That's what I think when I think of empathy. CIPHER 3 is designed to do that."

She paused, studying Gareth to see if he understood. Then, she sighed and said, "Gareth when this procedure is over, I will again retreat into your CIPHER secure storage, and you will forget me. This whole contract has been for you to imprint on me on a subconscious level. When you see me in person, you will be attracted to me and trust me. I need you to do that; I need you to trust me. We will talk more then. There is much we need to accomplish when you get to Mars."

Mars? Gareth wondered. As his awareness gradually returned to the procedure room, his memories of Sam also receded. Meanwhile, the feelings of lust and desire intensified, focused again on the clinician. He was feeling aroused. Maybe when we're done here, he thought, I can ask her out. Her? What am I thinking? I'll ask him out and get to know him better. With that body, he's got to be fantastic in bed! I bet he meets a lot of people here, lots to choose from.

Yeah, what was I thinking? The arousal faded and withered. No way he'd be interested in me. Even if we got together, he'd just leave me like Cathy did. The sadness welled up, and he wanted to cry. Damn that relaxant! He thought. Let me cry! It was all hopeless. I'll just end up alone, he thought, feeling certain of it now. What's the point of it all? Day in, day out?

"We're almost done, Gareth," the clinician announced. "You're doing great! The endocrine calibration looks good. I know it's been rough, but your CIPHER will erase the calibration from your short-term memory. You won't remember it. There, all done."

Gareth felt sore all over and spent, as if he had just finished running a marathon. At least, that's what I imagine running a marathon would be like, he thought. He struggled to get up from the chair, and the clinician came over to help him up. Gareth waved him off. Just then, Alex arrived with a wheelchair. He fell into the chair. "Thanks, Alex."

"No problem, Gareth. That was some procedure! I

141

can't wait to review the data with CRI. I'll take you to recovery and catch up with you after!"

Gareth was grateful for the wheelchair. That was a lot more intense than they led me to believe, he thought. "Hey, Alex. When you're done, can you give me a lift home?"

"Sure thing! See you soon."

What could go wrong?
August 2093

Cathy lay in her bunk, killing time before meeting up with Rick and Jagan. Cathy perused the *Bradbury's* daily activity feed for something to do tomorrow. What hadn't she tried yet? Zero-G laser tag? Done that. Wallyball? Check. Indoor Soccer. Of course, on a spaceship like the *Bradbury*, playing outdoors was not a good idea. But yep, done that. It was day 83 of the 90-day trip to Mars, and Cathy had tried everything—even Mahjong.

There we other possibilities, of course. Without Sam, they were out of the question. Coupling and decoupling occurred frequently on the ship. There were a lot of fights among family members and friends. It was impossible to keep the 800 passengers busy enough to avoid such conflicts. The *Bradbury* was a pressure cooker for many.

She reminded herself that in the 18th and 19th centuries, three months sailing from Europe to America was not unheard of. The conditions were much worse, of course. Beyond boredom, there was disease and often death. There was still disease on this trip, rare and mostly treatable. The 21st century brought something new: CIPHER Fugue. The boredom and claustrophobic conditions on the ship drove many to use Experiences as an escape. Some never returned from that escape and became lost in Fugue.

So stop feeling sorry for yourself, she thought. It is a good thing you never got CIPHER 2. You have a private cabin with a bathroom. The journey is nearly over. Soon you will be at New Nottingham and soon after that (another 3 months!). Sam will be there.

In the meantime, Cathy had Rick. Sam had been right about him. She had said that Rick would be good company, and he was. He was the sort of person who made friends easily. Still, she sometimes sensed an undercurrent of melancholy that he tried to cover with his outgoing nature. It wasn't obvious at first. Yet, three months on a spaceship is a lot of time to get to know someone.

Mostly, Rick jumped from new friend to new friend, pulling Cathy along with him. It kept things from getting boring. One time there was a couple who were going to be part of the terraforming project on Mars. They were passionate to the point of exhaustion. Rick tired of them and pivoted to a man who had sold everything and booked passage based on a dream. He had left his wife and family behind. Now, he talked only about his regret and planned somehow to raise money for a return passage. Cathy was glad that Rick moved on quickly from him. The theme of abandonment hit too close to home for her.

There was one person whom Rick kept going back to. Drinks, dinners, and card games with Dr. Jagan Bhatnagar quickly became regular occasions. He was a small, slightly pudgy, calm man, well-read and polite. Jagan was a Cloud researcher on his way to the CRI Advanced Projects Center on Mars. It seemed odd to Cathy that two Isolators would spend so much time with a lead CIPHER researcher. Jagan projected a serene presence, a sense that he was satisfied with his life. She felt at peace in his company. Cathy liked him.

Cathy gave up on figuring out what to do tomorrow. She got out of her bunk and headed out to meet Rick and Jagan.

###

Seated at their usual table in a corner of one of the *Bradbury's* bars, they finished a game of three-handed pinochle. Rick had won. "Well played, Richard," said Jagan. He saluted Rick with his drink glass.

"I can't let Cathy win all the time," said Rick. "Winner buys the next round?"

"Nonsense! I will take care of it. It is such a pleasure having you two for company."

"If you're sure, Jagan," said Cathy. "It seems that we owe you. Or at least, Rick does with him making you talk about your work all the time."

"I don't mind. If I talk about work, then maybe I can deduct it. After all, what's an expense account for if one does not use it?" Jagan must have had a sizable expense account, as he always treated Rick and Cathy. For a small man, he held his liquor and was well into his third Martini—gin, of course.

"By the way, Jagan, about your research," said Rick— Dr. Bhatnagar had insisted they should be on a first-name basis. "I'm still not sure I understand it. What is there really to know about the Moloi Cloud? Isn't it just a repository of Experiences? A way to connect with other cipher users?"

Here we go again, Cathy thought. Well, Jagan did open the door, and Rick is in one of his earnest moods.

"Rick, stop pestering Jagan! I'm sure he's tired of explaining his work to people like us." After Sam's experience at *Happy Meadows,* the subject made Cathy uncomfortable. "Besides, there's only a week before we reach Mars. Let's enjoy this time together!"

"That's perfectly fine, Cathy. Really, I don't mind. Allow me to cipher the barkeep for another round. The cards have not been kind to me tonight; you and Rick keep winning! So, I am quite happy to speak on my favorite subject." Jagan raised an eyebrow. "For an Isolator, Rick, you seem unusually interested in CIPHER technology."

Rick smiled and said, "I can't help it. While the tech has definitely had a negative impact on society, it is fascinating. I keep hoping there might be a way, finally, for it to do some good."

"I disagree with you concerning the negative impact, Rick. In many ways, CIPHER has been a boon. And yes, I can still see more good coming." He sighed and took a sip of his newly arrived martini. "I know we must agree to disagree on this. Now, regarding your question, Rick. The Cloud is much more than just a repository of Experiences and a communications network. So much more! True, when Nomusa Moloi performed her famous experiment, it was simply a server. It connected, as you say, the

147

CIPHERs implanted into the mice, creating a shared experience for them navigating the maze. Over time, the cloud evolved as CIPHER technology evolved. It not only connects all our CIPHERs, but it also learns from them using artificial intelligence programming. The Experiences seem more real, and we can now create virtual environments and virtual entities, avatars of people, if you will."

Cathy accepted the Scotch refill from the server. She recognized the introspective look on Rick's face, no longer the outgoing Rick. He was now a person seeking to understand something. This was not merely idle curiosity.

"How real *is* this virtual environment, Jagan? How do I go about creating one?" asked Rick.

"Creating one? It's quite simple, really. If you have CIPHER 2, everything you've seen, everywhere you have been, has been recorded by your implant." He gestured to his head. "Stored in your nanobots, up here."

"Isn't that just memory?" asked Cathy.

Jagan shook his head. "Cathy, it is much more than just memory. Memory is fallible. CIPHER is not. Cloud AI works with CIPHER to build a virtual environment based on what had been stored in its nanites. This," Jagan waved at the bar, "can be recreated by the AI capabilities of the cloud. You can then enter it with your CIPHER, similar to an Experience. How real is that environment? Very. But some things it cannot recreate."

"What do you mean?" Rick said.

"Cathy, indulge me. Take a drink of your Scotch."

Cathy gave Jagan a questioning look. She shrugged her shoulders and took a drink.

"How was it?" Jagan said.

"Well, good, I guess. It tastes like a good-quality single malt. Peaty and smoky, with a hint of citrus."

"That's what it *tastes* like. CIPHER can recreate that, as it interfaces with your senses, in this case smell and taste. How does it make you *feel?*"

"Relaxed, I guess. Calmer."

"Good! A pleasant feeling, yes? I quite enjoy it. CIPHER cannot recreate that feeling," said Jagan. "That requires an interface to the human systems which control mood."

Cathy smiled and said, "That's one advantage of memory over CIPHER, then."

"How do you mean, Cathy?" said Jagan.

"Human memories come with feelings. When I remember the first time I met Sam, I *feel* happy. I smile."

Jagan laughed. "You are quite right! I hadn't thought of it that way." He frowned. "This vast vault of CIPHER recordings, to the finest detail of our senses, and it is ultimately sterile, void of emotion."

"Yes!" said Rick. "I see. CIPHER is incomplete."

"For now, indeed. However, there has been work on a CIPHER version that could provide the missing piece—our emotional responses. Progress, however, has been problematic."

"Problematic, how?" said Rick.

Jagan sighed. "You have heard of Isolde Phillips?"

"Of course," Rick said. "She used to run CRI."

"'Used to' is correct. This has to do with the cloud virtual environment I was speaking of earlier. You see, it is theoretically possible to upload all of one's memories to the cloud and create a virtual copy of yourself there. In many ways, it would be indistinguishable from the original. For a dying person, this could mean a new life. Except for one thing."

"No feelings," said Cathy. "That's what's missing."

"Correct. This is something Phillips desperately wants to fix. She ran several special projects at CRI with this end in mind. I was involved in some of them. These included new CIPHER implants to interface with the endorphine system. They could record and stimulate endorphine levels to provide that missing piece. However, there remains a major problem. The cloud AI alone cannot simulate emotions as it can the environment. A human host is required to simulate emotions."

"You are saying that for Phillips to accomplish this upload, for it to be 'real', to have feelings and emotions, that she needs people. How could that even work?" said Cathy.

"Good question. Phillips had an answer: use Fugue victims. They are still connected to the cloud."

Jagan paused and peered into his martini glass. "I fear I am saying too much." He shrugged. "I must tell you this. I overheard an exchange some time ago, when both Moloi and Phillips were still at CRI. You see, Phillips expressed this very idea to Moloi. She responded in shock. 'Why not?' said Phillips. 'They have no meaningful existence, anyway!'" Jagan shuddered and shook his head. "Truly, a terrible person!"

Cathy recalled Sam's description of what had happened to her at *Happy Meadows*. How she had seen and talked to her father. Still conscious, still aware, but living in a virtual environment. She felt her hands tighten around the whiskey glass; pain started between her temples. She took her hand away from the glass and began massaging her head.

"Cathy," said Rick. "Are you all right?"

"It's just that, my God, that's horrible! Jagan, this is personal for me. My father is in Fugue. I can't explain it, but I think he is conscious. You are saying that, in some way, he could be existing in the cloud? Thinking, aware, and feeling abandoned?"

Jagan gave Cathy a sympathetic smile and placed his hand on her hand. "I hope that is not the case, but I think so, Cathy, yes. I'm sorry, it is one of the things I want to study. It is possible." He removed his hand and sat back. "This last incident with Phillips was too much for CRI, a step too far. They have forced her out and have denied her access to all test versions of CIPHER 3."

"Why was she so obsessed?" said Rick.

"There are rumors. Perhaps she has a degenerative brain condition, or maybe just paranoia that the Ludds might finally succeed in killing her." He lowered his voice and said, "She seemed desperate."

"Did you say that there were problems with it? CIPHER 3, I mean," said Rick.

Cathy half-listened to the conversation. *So academic for them, so personal for me.* She took another drink, trying to calm herself. *There's nothing I can do for dad, now. Sam was probably right, after all. I had needed to say goodbye.* She took another sip and forced herself to pay attention to the conversation.

"Yes," said Jagan, "the fine-tuning of the responses has proven difficult. In particular, when replaying an

Experience. It can be too real. The user often loses their sense of identity, confusing themselves with the person who created the Experience. As of now, no one has been harmed. We must be very careful. Personally, I think we will need to abandon it. I believe there may be one last trial? We shall see."

"I hope," said Rick, "that it doesn't work. This is why people join groups like the Isolators. There are some things that shouldn't be done! The impact on society could be even worse that CIPHER 2."

Jagan smiled. "Ah, Rick, we have finally returned to our usual disagreement. True, CIPHER 2 has been disruptive, but you cannot argue with the benefits. We are traveling to Mars! The possibility of such a journey had lain decades in the future. But CIPHER 2 and the enhanced collaboration made it possible. However, I too am concerned that CIPHER 3 may be more than society can handle. It may be too much for any human to handle," said Jagan. "I weary of this subject now. Too many terrible memories. Shall we play another hand? I do so enjoy three-handed pinochle. There are so few games that three people can truly play. And they must be the right three people!"

Rick smiled and said, "You are right about that, Jagan!"

Just then, Cathy heard a ship wide announcement:

Attention! The satellite launch will occur in two hours and can be viewed from any observation lounge. For those of you with CIPHER 2 implants, check your ship messages for the live Experience link. Remember, we are running a limited-time offer of discounts, special financing, and other opportunities to get CIPHER 2 implants. There is still time to get your implants before the next launch! See the ship infirmary for details!

"Anyone interested in the launch?" asked Cathy. "I've yet to see one."

"I understand there are one or two more before we arrive at Phobos station," said Jagan. "I have seen them already, so I am not terribly interested. By all means, go. It is worth witnessing once. Maybe Richard can join you after this hand?"

"Sure, I need to run to my cabin after this hand," said Rick. "I'll meet you in the lounge, Cathy."

Jagan seemed tired, or, more likely, the martinis had caught up with him. He overbid each hand; Cathy reached 1500 and won with an hour to spare before the launch. "I think I am well past due for a lie-down," said Jagan, yawning. "Enjoy the launch. Another game tomorrow night? Same time? Yes? Very good." He rose unsteadily from the table and made his way out of the bar.

It was a quick trip to the mostly empty observation lounge. Entering, Cathy noticed that many of the Experience chairs had been taken. The transport ship had ten such lounges. They were usually empty, as most information and visual feeds could be consumed via CIPHER. There was an array of tables and chairs, with a bar at one end.

She looked at the passengers in Experiencer chairs. Their eyes were open, focus constantly shifting, pupils dilating and contracting in the absence of external stimuli. She hated that look, the way her father had looked at *Happy Meadows.*

Cathy wandered over to the bar and ordered a glass of the ship's red. There wasn't much variety of wine on the ship, but what they had was tolerable. She could see the view screen and watched as the communication satellite deployed from the transport ship. Taking a sip, she envisioned all these satellites orbiting Mars. Then the Mars habitats would be connected to a Moloi Cloud, all except New Nottingham. The satellites, along with servers at the Earth and Mars Lagrange point—the location where the gravitational pull of Mars and Earth are in balance. The satellites will connect Earth, Moon, and Mars Moloi

Clouds. New Nottingham would be isolated from that.

Cathy felt a different kind of isolation on the trip. Rick and Jagan had been good company, but she missed Sam. She remembered the farewell at the airport as Cathy waited to board the plane to the space elevator. She was still angry with her then. *I never should have visited Dad,* she had thought. *Sam had meant well, talking me into visiting him at Happy Meadows. It just hadn't brought the expected closure.*

It was easier to think of Dad being lost in Fugue. The story Sam had related to her was hard to bear. *There's no way of knowing for sure. It could have been Sam's subconscious creating the dream world she saw. Either way, there was nothing she could do about it.* Ultimately, Cathy had forgiven her.

They had kissed and hugged. "I'll see you soon," Sam had said. "I'll be on the next transport. And no shenanigans with Rick on the trip, OK? You're my girl!"

"No worries on that account," Cathy had said. "He's not my type. I don't know what you saw in him."

"He has some good qualities," Sam had protested. "Yes, he can be arrogant; ultimately, though, he's a good guy."

The sound of some coughing shook her out of the memory. She turned and saw Rick, sipping what looked like a whiskey. He must not have stopped at his cabin for very long.

"Did you notice the zombies?" he asked. "I hear that the special shipboard offer for CIPHER 2 is a contract to test the satellite relay. I'd never bite on that. What if something went wrong, and you succumbed to the Moloi Fugue and never came out? Stuck somewhere between Earth and Mars? No way, not me!" He grimaced, as if in response to a memory. "Wherever we go, we can never escape the Moloi Cloud. Except for New Nottingham, of course."

They watched as the satellite deployment was just finishing. The satellite's solar panels were unfolding. Rick resumed their conversation. "Cathy, I would like to find some time after this to sit down and talk about what's really..." He never finished the thought, as there was a bright flash from the viewscreen. Cathy heard some commotion from across the room where the Experiencers sat. They were spasming, and some were moaning. She heard one of them exclaim, "My God, it exploded! So bright, like the sun. I can't see!"

The view screen abruptly switched off as calls for medical help rang through the ship. A shipboard announcement came through Cathy's CIPHER, as well as the ship's speakers:

Attention! All cabin doors are now locked! There has been an incident. Please remain calm as the crew investigates. There is no danger. We will provide more details as we get them. Your safety is our primary concern.

"Rick, what the hell is going on?" asked Cathy.

"I don't know, but something happened to that satellite, or the video feed. Judging from the people viewing on CIPHER, it sure seems like it blew up. The poor bastards, they don't look so good."

Cathy saw a man and a woman checking on them, probably medical personnel. How well trained are they in CIPHER issues? she wondered. Will they end up like Dad? It seems the incident is affecting them badly.

"Do you think this is a Ludd attack?" asked Cathy.

"Who knows? It's most likely an accident."

"But there will be an investigation, right? Half of the passengers are Isolators. I'm sure some of them could be more radical. Ludd sympathizers?"

"No," Rick said, but then stopped. He frowned and seemed to get lost in thought, as if he was weighing Cathy's question more deeply. "No", he repeated. "I'm sure it's an accident. There'll be no investigation. Excuse me, Cathy, there's something I need to do."

Cathy watched as Rick walked over to a crew member standing by the locked lounge door. He began talking to him, and the conversation became more animated. Finally, the crew member called another person over. The door to the lounge opened, and they escorted Rick out of the lounge, the door closing behind them. What the hell? Cathy wondered.

What Goes Up

August 2093

Even a week after the procedure, Gareth still felt stiff and sore. Alex told him that the nanobots were likely still integrating and sending some false signals to his brain. This did not reassure him.

I'm glad, he thought, that the flight from Washington DC to the *Arthur C. Clarke* space elevator terminus had been smooth. The business class seat had been comfortable, and the food and drink were quite good. He had convinced Alex that he needed sleep to deal with the effects of the nanobot adjustment, which kept Alex from annoying him too much during the trip.

As the plane approached the terminus, Gareth could see the elevator platform from his window. It was a combination airport and embarkation station, floating in

160

the Pacific Ocean south of the Hawaiian Islands. Alex nudged him. "I can see the elevator just coming down, almost to the platform! How fast do you think it's going? It's a lot bigger than I imagined." Gareth looked down at it. It must be quite a way up still; it appeared large even from this distance. Large enough to accommodate two hundred passengers and several bars and restaurants. "Five days to get to the end station! And I don't even need to pay for an Experience to enjoy it! I get to see it for real!" Gareth began to think that this was going to be a long five days.

"Don't worry, Gar," Alex continued. Gareth recognized the signs of Alex trying to rein in his own excitement, casting his eyes downward, staring at his hands—trying to keep them still. He's like a twelve-year-old sometimes. He was like that even as a precocious teenager attending college four years early. We all teased him mercilessly. I knew it was cruel, but I went along anyway. Why is it so easy to be cruel? I should be nicer to him. He is the best tech at *Multitudes* and he's been a good friend.

"From now on, you won't see me," Alex promised. "We wouldn't want to take away from the Experience you're creating. I'll keep to myself. Besides, it's been long enough since Cathy left. Maybe you'll meet someone on the trip. There's no need for a long-term commitment; just have some fun. Maybe you'll get lucky and meet up with someone nice."

"I don't know, Alex," said Gareth. The plane had landed, and he gathered his carry-on. *Maybe he's right. I'm not fully booked with assignments for this trip. I should be open to opportunities.* "OK, Alex. I'll keep my options open. You try to have some fun too, OK? There's not much for you to do until we get out of CRI monitoring range."

"Sure! Let me know if you need a wingman!"

Gareth made his way off the plane to the first-class outdoor passenger lounge. He confirmed with CIPHER that his bags would be delivered to his suite on the elevator. CIPHER also advised him that he had two hours until boarding. *Plenty of time for a drink,* he thought, *and it's a beautiful day.* He and Alex accepted the offered Mai Tai to start. *All part of the Experience,* he thought. He sipped the cocktail and observed his fellow passengers in the lounge.

He recognized a few people from the plane. The well-to-do family and their obnoxious kid who cried the entire flight. *Good thing he and Cathy never got around to having children,* he thought. *We'd never even discussed it. God, I hope they aren't in the cabin next door. A five-hour flight was bad enough, but five days on the elevator?*

"Don't look now, Gar," said Alex. "But I see a possibility heading our way. I'll make myself scarce." Alex took his drink and headed over to the hors d'ouvres table.

"Excuse me? Is this seat taken?" A blond woman had come up behind him and nodded at the bar stool next to him.

"Well, no. My friend is off in search of snacks. Please help yourself. My name's Gareth. Friends call me Gar."

"Mine's Sam—short for Samantha, of course. I thought you might be traveling with someone."

"Oh no, that's Alex. An old college friend. We work together, but we are not traveling together. He has his own cabin." She seems pleasant, Gareth thought, and certainly not bad looking. Alex was right. He should be open to the possibility. "Can I get you a Mai Tai? They're great."

"Sure, sounds like the perfect drink for today. Where are you headed?"

"The Ritz. How about you? Where are you off to?" Gareth replied as he ciphered for the drink.

"Mars, but I'll be stopping off at the Ritz on the way. Business or pleasure?"

"A little of both," he replied as her drink arrived. "I'm an Experiencer. Someone's paying me a lot of money to have a good time." She's really easy to talk to, he thought. Maybe this trip will be more fun than I thought. He finished his drink and ciphered an order of a beer and some appetizers to share. "You look familiar. Ever been to DC?"

"Of course, everyone should visit the museums there. I know I could just run an Experience, but it's so much better in person—don't you think?"

Just small talk, Gareth thought. But what do you expect? It's early days. There's something about her that reminded him of Cathy a bit. They talked some more and exchanged CIPHER addresses, not something he usually does, but she seemed trustworthy and very much a 'what you see is what you get' sort of person. Apparently, her cabin was just two doors down from his.

The boarding announcement came over the loudspeaker, as well as CIPHER.

Arthur C Clarke elevator is now cleared for boarding. First-class passengers may board at any time prior to our five PM departure. Other passengers, please wait until your group is called. CIPHER-capable passengers should allow the station access for identity confirmation. All other passengers, please have your passports and boarding passes ready for examination.

Gareth instructed his CIPHER to allow identity access

to the station. He noticed Sam was finishing up her drink. He polished off his beer. "Are you planning to board now?" he asked.

"Sure. Hey once we get settled, how about dinner? Say around seven?"

"That'd be great. I'll make reservations", Gareth said as they made their way to the boarding area.

###

Gareth walked into the *A View Above* restaurant and glanced at the other diners. They were all well-dressed in suits and cocktail dress finery, jewelry, and expensive watches. Who needs a watch these days? he pondered. They've been obsolete for over fifty years. Only the rich can afford obsolescence. The rest of us have no choice but to move forward.

Alex, sent Gareth.

Yes, Gareth.

Just wanted to let you know that I'm going off the clock for a bit. I'm meeting Sam for dinner.

Sure Gareth, I got it, Alex sent. I hear the view is great! You get to dine with Earth at your feet! Enjoy yourself for a change!

Thanks, Alex! I'll catch up with you tomorrow.

165

Gareth had to admit that Alex was right; the view was spectacular. The dining room was at the bottom of the elevator. A single large window wrapped around the full circumference of the elevator and curved under, creating a panoramic, if somewhat unsettling, view of the ocean around the base of the elevator. Gareth felt that of all the people he saw in the room—the beautiful, the thin, and the tan—only he had earned his place here. He had worked and sacrificed for it. If only Cathy could be with him, he thought. He missed her at times like this. He would have loved to share this with her. Where was she now? Had she made it to Mars?

"Good evening, sir," greeted the Matre'd, bringing Gareth out of his reverie. He gave him the once-over, clearly thinking Gareth didn't belong in his fine restaurant. But Gareth had satisfied the minimum requirements: suit jacket, ill-fitting, even so, slacks and loafers, somewhat worn. "Welcome to *A View Above,* where the cuisine is out of this world. Do you have a reservation?"

"Yes, Gareth William. A table for two, Earth side."

"Ah yes, I see your companion, a very fine-looking young lady, may I say, has already arrived. Francois," he summoned a short young man, "please show Mr. Williams to table 17."

Francois, or Frank as Gareth surmised, guided him to

the table. The view of Earth he could see through the large panoramic window took his breath away. As the elevator rose above the Earth, the atmosphere growing thinner by the minute, Gareth reflected on how unique Earth was. It's such a fragile-looking thing, he thought. There is no place else. Sure, there's the Moon and Mars, but the Moon will never really be a home to humans, and it will be generations before Mars is terraformed so that people can live there comfortably. Not just survive in habitats with little between them and death but live and thrive.

"Hey, Gareth!" Sam said as he made it to the table. The Maitre'd was right, Gareth thought, as Francois pulled the chair out for him. She was quite fine-looking. She had a nice black dress offset by a small, tasteful white gold necklace.

"Can I get you a drink, sir?" asked Francois.

"Thanks, sure. What are you drinking, Sam?

"An Old-Fashioned."

"Sounds good, same for me."

"It's quite the view, isn't it?" asked Sam.

"Yes, I was just thinking the same thing. I'm kind of lucky in my line of work. I could never afford to travel this way on my own."

"Yes," said Sam. "I remember you said that you're an Experiencer. I'd really like to know more about what that's like. It must make for an interesting life. Have you created any that I may have seen?"

"Maybe some, but I'm kind of new at the job. I was lucky to snag this contract. Although honestly, most of the Experiences are pretty mundane."

"No offense intended to your profession, but I think you are right," Sam said. "It's like when the old Internet first became available to the public, not just for researchers to share information and collaborate. It was supposed to democratize access to knowledge, change the way we learn and create a 'global village' where we could all learn to respect and understand each other. I studied early 21st Century history in college, and I can tell you it did not turn out that way. Instead, it turned into a platform for pornography and crackpot theories. It tore us apart."

"I know. My ex-wife talked about this a lot. But somehow, we survived it. I work for a respectable company and would never take part in any of those Experiences you can find in the dark cloud."

"No, of course not! I'm sure you wouldn't. In fact, I think we can still turn CIPHER into a kind of connective tissue that brings people closer together. I heard Moloi became disillusioned and has become a virtual hermit. And who was it that co-founded CRI, Phillips? She kind of disappeared, too. Something about an illness?"

"I don't know about Moloi. Phillip's grandson, Alex, is an old friend of mine. He mentioned there was some kind of a Ludd attack. It changed her. Other people say she became paranoid and was disruptive at CRI. She wanted to start all these odd special projects. She was working on uploading consciousness to the cloud. Crazy shit like that." Gareth paused and frowned. "Maybe the Ludd attack made her feel like she needed some way to protect herself. Like a backup copy. As I said, crazy. They finally had enough and frog-marched her out, banning her." It's a good thing I put CIPHER in private mode. Alex would not be happy with my talking about his grandmother this way.

"What she was working on," said Sam, "it's what people used to call 'Digital Ascension'. I guess I remember my history classes, after all. Anyway, that never happened as far as I know. Crucial elements were missing. Beyond intelligence and memory, you need, not the soul exactly, but the way we are driven by our emotions: happiness, fear, attraction, and all that. Somehow, you need to record and reproduce all of that."

Gareth thought of the way CIPHER 3 could do some of that. It's odd having this conversation when he has the nanobots that could make this possible. He felt he should tell her about it. She seemed like she was trustworthy, but he had signed the nondisclosure agreement. He turned the conversation to something more social.

"Look, this is all a little over my head. I'm just a simple Experiencer trying to make it through the day. Besides, I'm getting hungry. Do you know what you'd like? I can call Frank, I mean Francois, over."

"Sure, I didn't mean to go on like that. But you are easy to talk to. I hope we get some time to talk about other things. I'd like to get to know you better."

"Absolutely! We have four more days left on the elevator." Maybe, Gareth thought, she'd like to join in on some Experiences on the trip, before she heads on to Mars. Too bad I can't use *SexyBeast* now. Oh well. "Look, would you mind joining me on some of the contract experiences? It would make them more authentic, and we'd compensate you. There'd be zero-g sports, and a spacewalk if you're up for it."

"That'd be great! There's no need to compensate me. I'd love to spend more time with you."

Gareth grinned at her enthusiasm. Fantastic! This trip just keeps getting better, he thought. I'm sure I can talk Alex into it. I'm going to spend time with her, whatever he says. Nothing could be better than that.

Cathy's Arrival
August 2093

The *Bradbury* reached Phobos Station and docked with the transit station, which was the terminus for the elevator down to Mars. The lower gravity and thinner air of Mars meant a much shorter trip, just one day, than the Earth elevator. Phobos Station had no gravity to speak of, simplifying landings and take-offs. The ship that had been her home for the last three months was refueling and preparing to take on other passengers for the return flight to Earth. It would be someone else's home now.

Cathy grabbed her duffel bag and met her assigned group to make her way to the elevator. Since the *Bradbury* had stopped spinning to dock with Phobos station, there was no longer artificial gravity on the ship. Cathy had practiced during the journey in the weightless section of the transport ship, but it was still an unnerving experience as she made her way.

Some people she encountered along the way were chatting nervously, but most were quiet. She had heard that some had regretted the decision and had frantically tried to book a return on the *Bradbury*. The long voyage to Mars in a rotating steel cylinder had convinced them that migrating to Mars was a terrible idea. Mars would not be much different. For those who could not immediately afford a ticket, they would need to remain on Mars until they earned enough for the return voyage.

Maybe they would decide to stay. Eventually, the Martian habitats would look more earth-like with artificial gravity, trees and fields, even flowing water. New Nottingham had already made significant progress with most of that. Many of her fellow travelers were headed to Mars to do the same for other habitats. It would take time and a lot of hard work. Even then, in reality there would not be much between them and the harsh Mars environment except another rotating cylinder; this time made of glass.

Cathy recognized Rick just ahead of her. He was being escorted through the crowd towards the elevator shuttle. She had met his escorts briefly: Mary and Mitch. They had some kind of security role among the Isolators. They reported directly to the chief of New Nottingham.

Rick's confession didn't ring true, thought Cathy. Sam had told her Rick had left the Ludds. It was a brief flirtation. He would never jeopardize the people Experiencing the launch. They might have gone into Fugue. Fortunately, they seemed OK. Still, he did stop at his cabin before joining me in the lounge. Why? He never said. Is he protecting someone? Maybe someone on the ship is a Ludd?

As Cathy caught up to him, Rick caught her eye and gave her a sad smile. "Hi Cathy," he said as he noticed her contemplating his escort. "At least I have some help to make sure I don't bounce off the floor and bang my head on the ceiling."

"Aren't you lucky? It seems all you need to do to get some attention around here is to blow up a satellite."

"Well, I wouldn't recommend it. Hey, when you get settled, come by and see me. I'm sure they'll set up someplace nice for me to serve my sentence after the 'trial', which I don't expect to take very long. There are some things I'd like to explain to you. I know it's a lot to ask, considering I lied to you. But I had my reasons. And the lie is not what you think it is."

Cathy wondered what he might have to say to her. She also wasn't clear why he would drop these hints in the presence of Mitch and Mary. Fanatics always have reasons, or they think they do. But there would not be much to do for the first few weeks, so why not? "Sure, Rick. I'll clear my calendar."

"Very funny. Thanks, Cathy. OK guys, let's catch our shuttle to the elevator."

Cathy watched as they escorted Rick to the transit car. They entered the car, took their seats and buckled up. Cathy followed and settled in as the car filled up. The ventilation system wasn't coping very well with the group of anxious, sweaty travelers. The door closed, and the car proceeded to the Phobos elevator. Yep, there is still a long way to go, she thought.

###

The shuttle left the elevator terminus at Pavonis Station and made its way to New Nottingham at Deuteronilus Mensae. The location was chosen because of the presence of ice, guaranteeing a good supply of water. New Nottingham was one of three habitats, either built or in the process of being built there. The Isolators' wealthy benefactors had paid for its construction. It was the smallest of the three, even so, it was significant as being the only privately funded habitat; governments and large corporations funded the others.

Cathy could see the cylindrical habitat on the viewscreen as the shuttle approached. It looked like a large glass ice cream cone, nestled in a shiny metallic-looking cradle. There were glints of bright reflection as the weak sun struck the rotating cone. The cone was spinning to create artificial gravity. The cradle did not spin; it provided stability and the power and machinery to spin the cone. It was still at Martian gravity, about half of Earth's gravity. The shuttle docked at a port in the cradle, close to the Martian surface.

They made their way along the gangway that connected the shuttle to the lower section of the habitat. Passing through the security checkpoint, facial recognition and retinal scans confirmed Cathy's identity. As if anyone could have stowed away on the *Bradbury*. Anyplace else, CIPHER communication would confirm identity. There was no Moloi cloud to connect to; so, there was no way to confirm identity with CIPHER.

The lower section was used only for entering and exiting the habitat, so it was sparsely furnished and merely functional. Cathy glimpsed several sealed-off sections. Perhaps for further expansion, she speculated. She saw Mitch and Mary escort Rick into one of the side corridors after security. Cathy followed everyone else to a tram station with a set of waiting cars.

She entered an open car and waited as her fellow immigrants entered. It would be devastating to get all the way here and then be denied entry. But, as far as she could tell, it had all gone smoothly, and the tram began its ascent up and around the cylinder, gaining speed as it wrapped around the cone. Cathy could feel the pull of gravity increasing gradually to Earth's standard gravity as the tram sped up to match the speed of the cone's rotation.

Eventually, the tram matched the speed of the spinning cone, and she heard a loud thump. It was the sound of the tram connection to the habitat station. The door opened. Cathy caught the first glimpse of her new home. She had seen videos of the interior of the habitat, but was still surprised at how vast it seemed. It took her eyes some time to adjust to the change of perspective. The diameter of the cylinder wasn't that large. They were standing on the interior wall, and the circumference surface area was usable living space. She understood it was about one kilometer high and half a kilometer wide, but the curvature took some getting used to. Since it curved in and not out, there was no visible horizon.

As she and her fellow travelers stepped out of the tram, she could make out green areas and pathways with clusters of buildings. There was a forest of what looked like banyan trees. Cathy noticed what appeared to be another tram station, which Cathy assumed was used for transit within the habitat.

She saw a young man standing among several people. He greeted them as they exited the car. He was slim, with curly dark hair and bright, energetic eyes. The man waved at them as if they were all long-lost friends. "Welcome to New Nottingham!" he said. "My name is Tim. You all have that 'My God, this looks so strange' look on your faces. Don't worry, you will adjust. We are here to help you find your quarters and get settled in. After being cooped up in a spaceship cabin for four months, you will appreciate your new living space."

"We have two ways of getting around here: by foot and by tram. The habitat has a lot of water to shield us from radiation, so taking a boat will someday be another possibility." If Cathy wasn't so overwhelmed taking it all in, she might have found his enthusiasm infectious. He's a lot like Gareth in that way, she thought. Like a puppy happily running around, trying to please everyone.

"The trams," Tim continued, "run in a loop inside the habitat: up-cone and down-cone. You'll see kilometer markers along the path and starting with zero at the base of the cone. You are at the .5 kilometer marker up-cone, so about halfway up. With the way the cone spins, it won't feel like you're going up or down, just moving along a level path."

"Is the tram we took the only access from the cradle to the habitat?" someone asked.

"Good question," Tim replied. "There are a multitude of access points connecting to the cradle for maintenance, waste disposal and material intake, as well as an emergency access corridor should the tram break down. New Nottingham has all the required safety features, as well as many others. It is a well-built habitat. In fact, I work on a team that frequently uses those other corridors to perform routine maintenance."

"If we had to evacuate," the man persisted. "How long would it take to reach the base of the cradle?"

"There are many points where the rotation needs to synchronize, from the peak, two days—from here a day to the base. You will get briefings on this and other matters over the next few days. But really, you have nothing to worry about. OK then! It's time to get you settled. We have welcome ambassadors to take you to your lodgings. Let's pair up!"

As it turned out, Tim would help her find her quarters. After everyone else was matched with an ambassador, Tim guided Cathy down one of the paths. He walked quickly, and Cathy was having trouble keeping up. Tim probably hasn't done this very much, and he's forgotten how long it took him to adjust to one gravity again. He pointed to a cluster of cabins. "You are in cabin C26. It's a one-bedroom with a small kitchen with some starter supplies. I think you'll like it. At the center of each cluster is a small automated café where you can get something to eat at any time of day. Speaking of day, we have artificial morning, day, and night—basically the same as on Earth. This is also my cluster. I'm in C5. Everyone here is friendly. If you need any help, just ask. You can usually find me at the café in the morning before I head off to my day job."

Tim walked her up to the cabin. "The door is already set with your handprint. Go ahead, try it."

Cathy pressed her hand on the door, and it opened. She walked in, Tim following behind. Well, it's a lot smaller than the place I had shared with Gareth. It was a single room, dining area, kitchen, living room and bedroom, all combined in one space. "I didn't see a partner joining you here. I assume you are on your own?" Tim asked.

"Just for now, my partner is on the next transport," Cathy replied.

"You're very brave to do this on your own," he said.

"It was the same for me. Jared and I split up. It was complicated, but **CIPHER** was a problem in our relationship. I had a hard time until I found the Isolators." He looked around the cabin as if to make sure everything was in place. His earlier cheerful mood had dissipated. "Sorry, that was more than you needed to know. This place can be good for finding new beginnings without the complications **CIPHER** can bring. I wish I could just kill these damned nanobots in my head!" Tim paused. "OK, that was a little over the top. Anyway, I know that it's been a long trip. There will be an orientation tomorrow at the café at 10 AM. Unless you have questions, I'll be on my way."

He's a little moody, Cathy thought. I guess I'm not the only one having to make adjustments. We seem to have something in common. Maybe we're all running away from more than just **CIPHER**. But **CIPHER** is the common denominator. It broke the things we treasured: me and Gareth, Tim and Jared. Or is that just an excuse? Were those things already broken? Maybe my father would have finally succumbed to something if not **CIPHER**, then depression, MiXes, gambling.

Now I'm becoming moody. It's all so overwhelming, and I'm tired. "No, I think I'm fine for now. You're right, I am tired. You've been very helpful." I don't know, she thought. I think I need to hang on to what and who I can until Sam gets here. Tim is nice, and it would be good to have a friend here after what happened with Rick. "I'm good for now. I will see you tomorrow at the orientation. You will be there, right?"

Tim smiled and headed back out of the cabin. "Yes, I will be there, and I look forward to seeing you again."

Lagrange One Day 1
August 2093

Gareth climbed down the steps from the zipline tower. What a rush, he thought. I've sweated right through my shirt. He smiled up at Cathy as she followed him down the tower's switchback staircase. It's fantastic that we're together again. Laughter spilled out of him like floodwater over a dam, his feelings no longer restrained. How long had it been since he had felt so free? "Hey Cat, that was incredible! What a fantastic view of the forest canopy! Did you see that big red bird fly by? Was that a macaw?"

He began taking the steps two at a time, lost his footing, and stumbled. Cathy called down to him, "Gareth, be careful! You're such a little boy. Watch where you're going!"

"I'm fine! But did you see it? The bird? The sounds,

and my God, the feeling of the wind as we zipped along! How many was that? Ten platforms? The fog too—that was intense! One minute you're gliding along, the fog hiding everything, and then suddenly you see the next platform! Boom, you land! What a blast!" Gareth reached the bottom where the Land Rover was supposed to meet them.

"Let's go again," he called up to Cathy. Wait, where is she? he wondered. Oh, no! Did she fall? His earlier ecstasy was now exchanged for panic. He couldn't see anyone on the stairs. He looked frantically around the base of the platform. There was no sign of her. All he saw was red earth and dust.

Red earth? There were no trees, and there were no plants, only an arid red plain. It was getting darker, and the stars were becoming visible. Gareth was having trouble breathing. It's just panic, he told himself. Get a grip! But where's Cathy? Where is everything? What is this place? I still can't breathe right. Where is everybody?

Finally, he saw a man sitting at a desk, alone on the red plain. It was Dr. Francis, the avatar from the CIPHER 3 implantation. What's he doing here? Where *is* here?

"Good morning, Mr. Williams. I'm just reviewing the data we have gathered so far."

"Data?" asked Gareth, struggling to breathe. "What do

you mean? What is this? I'm dreaming. That's it. This isn't real."

"Yes, you are dreaming, but yes, this is real. We go through this every time," Francis sighs, "naturally you keep forgetting. Not your fault, really. You will forget again. I see that *EmpHance* and your CIPHER 3 have integrated well with each other. The feedback loop is coming along nicely. Although a little tweak here and there will help move things along."

"Feedback loop? What do you mean?" Gareth asked.

"CIPHER 3 improves continuously. *EmpHance* helps with that improvement. It's unfortunate that you must encounter me in your dreams as *EmpHance* does its work. However, this helps with further calibration. At some point, it will no longer need adjustment. For now, it is a necessary annoyance. It doesn't matter; in any case, you'll forget this part of the dream."

"But," Gareth protested, gasping for air. He collapsed to the ground on his hands and knees. He looked up at Dr. Francis. "This was never explained to me when I agreed to this. This needs to stop! You can't do this to me!"

Dr. Francis ignored the outburst. "Over the next few days, your *EmpHance* level will increase to the optimal point. Your connection to other people will grow stronger.

Likewise, your sense of identity may become blurred. Don't worry, as your brain adapts to the implants, this will be less of an issue."

Gareth harnessed the little breath he had left and yelled, "I told you I didn't agree to this!"

"Gareth! Wake up!" He felt someone shove him. He rolled over. It was Sam. The bedroom came into focus as his breathing gradually returned to normal. OK, I'm still in my suite at the Lagrange One resort, he thought.

"Sorry," he said, "a bad dream." His mouth felt dry, and he reached for the glass of water on the stand next to the bed. He took a long drink. "It's these new implants. I wish Alex would get them calibrated. Ever since we got here, I've been having the strangest dreams. I hope I didn't wake you."

"No. You didn't—don't worry. Yes, you should get Alex to adjust them. That's his job, after all," Sam said. She rolled over towards Gareth and rested on her elbow. The sheets fell away from her, revealing the gentle curve of her breasts, the fine strands of blond hair partially obscuring her green eyes. She is beautiful, Gareth thought; she reminds me of Cathy, somehow. I guess that's part of the attraction.

He stroked her hair and kissed her. The last few days with Sam had been exhilarating. He felt a connection with her from the moment they met at the space elevator; the connection grew stronger all the time. The dinners and late-night talks at the bar continued as they traveled on the transport ship to the Ritz at Lagrange One.

Alex complained that Sam was a distraction. He seemed almost jealous. So what? What did it matter as long as the contracted Experiences got done? Gareth was enjoying himself for the first time in ages. There had been no one since Cathy left. He hadn't been able to let go of the memory of her, keeping the apartment like some kind of museum of their time together. The change of scenery was liberating! He had freed himself from the mausoleum of memories that was his apartment. At least for now.

Surprisingly, he trusted Sam from the start. She wouldn't hurt him. He felt sure of it. She canceled her room at the Ritz and moved into Gareth's suite. Partly he trusted Sam because it felt like he had known her for a long time. There was something familiar about her. He must have met her before, but where? It was more than that, almost like she knew him better than he knew her. That created a kind of power differential. Where she led, he would happily follow. He was fine with that. Why, he wondered?

Then there were the sex games. They were fun, definitely. He was happy to give control to her there as well. Let her lead. More and more, he trusted her. He felt safe with her. I've always felt like I need someone to lead me, he realized, to give me direction. But why Sam? I've only just met her. Sometimes, I feel like I should be more assertive. But I can't resist her. Ha! Why should I?

Sam was a relief from the dreams, sometimes nightmares. Maybe it was the new implants, but they were much more vivid than he was used to. They were no longer memories, like before. They were almost premonitions. Lately, they have been very confusing. Almost always the same situation, but sometimes it's Cathy with him, and sometimes it's Sam. They start great, always an adrenaline rush and the sense of a happy relationship. But then everything comes crashing down, and he is abandoned on a dusty red plain. Gareth took another drink of water and lay back in bed. If they are premonitions, what are they trying to tell me?

What else could CIPHER 3 be doing to me? Is it more than just vivid dreams? How much can I believe in how I feel? The nanobots both record his hormonal levels and affect them, which creates more intense Experiences. All of this—the dreams and Sam—it was all happening at the same time. Why?

He looked over at Sam again. She was still on her side facing him and grinning, with a mischievous look in her eyes. She leaned into him, placing a hand behind his ear, and kissed him. Sam caressed his chest with her other hand, moving down to his stomach and lower. She put her mouth next to his ear and whispered, "If you're in the mood?"

"Maybe I could be convinced," he whispered back.

He moaned as she bit his ear gently. "I don't think you'll need much convincing." She pulled the covers back and looked down at him, already hard. "I've heard of guys and their morning stiffies, but *that* is a bit much."

"Too much?" he teased.

"We'll see... Let's crank up *EmpHance* and have some fun."

Cipher, sent Gareth, set EmpHance to level 3.

Gareth kissed her and moved down her neck, kissing as he went until he reached a breast. He caressed the nipple with his tongue and kissed it. Sam sighed as he bit it gently.

"Not so fast, Gar." Sam grabbed his shoulder and pushed him over onto his back, throwing her leg over his thigh. She kissed him, their tongues playfully darting around each other. Cathy climbed on top of him and placed a hand around his neck. She squeezed gently, then placed the other hand over his mouth and nose.

Gareth struggled to breathe. He felt excited by the

play. She would let him get his breath for a moment, then squeeze again. He was safe with Sam, and the feeling was intoxicating. She released him and rolled onto her back and pushed him down between her legs. "Now, let's see how good your tongue is," she said.

He began licking her slowly, making her more wet, tasting her. She grabbed his head, bringing him into her even closer. She was moaning now; the sounds punctuated with small cries. He moved his tongue around more quickly, losing himself in the joy of it, sensing her pleasure. Sam cried out as she came.

Gareth moved up, wanting to enter her. Sam pushed him back. "No," she said. "Roll over. Let me watch you. Play with yourself. I'll hold you."

"But, Sam," Gareth started.

"No, I am in charge here. I'll see how you do and then, maybe." She was teasing him, Gareth knew. But he sensed also that there was more to it than that. "Don't wait too long. You might lose that beautiful hard-on, and you'll need to start over. You wouldn't want that, would you?"

Gareth did as he was told and rolled over onto his back. He began stroking himself, conscious of Sam watching him. He was excited though, not self-conscious. Gareth could still sense her excitement as she began touching herself between her legs. He quickly reached the point of no return as Sam's moans got louder. He came, cum spurting up and then down his stomach.

She nestled her head on his chest. He felt so many things now. Her gentle breathing, which he followed, led him to her sense of happiness. He had agreed against his better judgment to grant her a direct connection to his CIPHER, as she had to hers. The *EmpHance* MiXe connecting the two as they played—not making love, really. It was both less and more than that, a different and more intense sharing. When he came, he felt his sense of self melting away, merging with Sam and everything she felt. When Sam came, he became lost in her pleasure. The separation between them faded, becoming blurred.

"Well done, Gareth! I promise you will enjoy it even more next time."

Whose Cloud Is It Anyway?
August 2093

It goes by various names, including *You shape it, you own it* and *My world, love it or leave it*. Gareth had played it a few times but quickly lost interest. Since Cathy had left, there was no one he trusted enough to team up with. Cathy could never have played, anyway. She needed CIPHER 2 implants to play. She refused to get them. That left co-workers and casual friends that he could team up with. But defending a shared virtual reality against attacks from the game's cloud AI might expose too many personal vulnerabilities, things he wanted to keep hidden.

Sam insisted on playing. She said it would bring them closer, working together to control the mini-Moloi game cloud. That was the goal, after all. A battle waged to determine which team would repel the attacks the longest and gain ultimate control of the cloud and win.

Sometimes, it was more than a game. Marriage therapists would use it to gain insights into issues in relationships, businesses for team-building exercises; military and security forces to find the most compatible team members. Gareth wasn't sure it was a good idea at this point in their nascent relationship.

"Nonsense!" protested Sam. "We have a great bond already. This will just strengthen it. It will bring us even closer together." She had already finished the omelet she had ordered at the café. Most everyone else had left, leaving a few stragglers eating at other tables. She sipped her coffee, waiting for Gareth to say something. *God, she loves coffee*, thought Gareth.

"But things are great now. Can't we just keep going on like this?" He grew despondent, playing with the eggs he had ordered for breakfast. *Where do you get fresh eggs on a space station? Is there a chicken coop in space?* He stared at the yellow yolks, still unbroken. They stared back.

After the nightmare last night, he was so happy waking up and finding Sam lying next to him in bed. The nightmare seemed like a premonition. It had left him feeling alone and worried that something bad was going to happen. Sam's quiet presence helped to erase it from his memory, reinforcing their strong connection. He feared that the game could endanger that. What if they weren't so compatible, after all? Why risk it?

"Sure," Sam continued, "things *are* great. They will continue to be great. Stop being so gloomy; you have such a tendency to overthink. I promise this will be fun! With your background as an Experiencer, we'll win easily."

"You realize how this goes, don't you?" Gareth asked. "It's not so simple. Each team creates a virtual environment in the cloud, and the Game Center AI works to take it apart, making subtle changes. It's a kind of gaslighting, fooling us into thinking something is real. We need to recognize the changes it makes and reverse them by remembering what was there before. The team that holds it together the longest wins." He frowned. "We haven't known each other long enough to have much common ground. How would that even work?"

"Yes, of course. I know how the game works; I've played it before. That's part of the fun! We pick a 'reality'—something we can both identify with; someplace we've spent time together."

He grinned despite his mood. "Like the bedroom? That *would* be fun."

"No, silly! I don't think that's allowed. Not this version of the game, anyway." She finished the last of her coffee.

"Stop playing with your food, Gareth," she teased. "We've shared so much already. We can do this!"

Gareth pushed his food around the plate. *It's too cold now. I can never say no to her. Why is that?* "OK, you win."

"Great! It's almost time for the game. I already know what reality to set up!" She pushed back from the table. "Finished?"

"Yeah, I guess so." He stood up and followed her as she walked out of the café.

Hey Alex, he ciphered. *Guess what I'm doing this morning?*

Oh, hey Gareth. What, again?

No! Not that, although I wish... Sam and I are going to play 'You shape it, you own it'.

I see. You know, that's interesting. I've always wanted to try that, could never find a partner.

Gareth winced at the statement. Despite their college friendship, they had never been close. *I need to be a better friend to him.*

Maybe when we get back to Earth, we can try it out? Gareth sent.

After a slight hesitation, atypical in CIPHER communication, Alex sent back, *Sure, I'd like that. You know there's a cloud researcher, Bhatnagar, I think is his name. Anyway, he thinks that the basis of the game, which is, you know, taking control of a cloud by imposing a reality, could be a kind of Trojan Horse flaw.*

How do you mean?

The flaw is triggered as part of the game. The imposer of the winning reality would then get complete control of the cloud. Not just the game cloud. The main CRI cloud.

That's crazy!

Hey, most things with CIPHER are a little crazy, Alex sent back. Remember that CIPHER tech is still new and has been pushed out quickly. I wouldn't be surprised if there were flaws. Maybe taking advantage of the way all clouds are networked to the main CRI cloud. It's how CRI keeps control. In fact, someone at CRI was working on a Trojan Horse attack—as a proof of concept. He used a firewall-protected cloud, of course.

And how did that go?

Not well. He went into Fugue just as he finished the research and was about to test it. He's at Happy Meadows now. The odd thing is, he was not big in running Experiences.

So, Gareth ciphered back, I don't understand. Only Experiences cause Fugue.

Yep, it's a mystery, all right. There's a rumor that the Ludds hacked his research. Maybe they had something to do with it? Somehow infecting his lab's cloud with a Fugue-like virus?

Sam slowed down and looked at him, nodding at the door to the Games center. *Looks like we're here. Talk to you later, Alex.*

"How's your friend?" asked Sam.

"Good," said Gareth, smiling. "You really do know me well. I have no secrets from you! How could you tell I was ciphering Alex?"

"Easy! You get a kind of melancholy expression. I can't describe it, but I feel there's a history between you two. Not all of it is good."

"Yeah, some bad. It's complicated, and it wasn't his fault. Not really. Anyway, we're here. Let's create us some reality!"

A young woman greeted them as they entered. "Welcome! You must be Samantha and Gareth! My name is Kimmy."

"Call me Sam, and yes, we must be."

She waved at a couple reclining in Experiencer chairs.

"Here is your competition. They just settled in. I see that you have signed the waivers via cipher. You are going to have so much fun! Have you picked a reality, yet?"

"Gareth, I hope it's OK that I picked out a reality. Luckily, they had someplace we've been together."

"Really? But we've only been together for a few days."

Sam turned to Gareth and grinned. "They have the restaurant on the space elevator."

He grinned and said, "Ah, good choice! I enjoyed that dinner so much. I remember it well."

"Wonderful," said Kimmy. "You two have played before, so I will just review briefly with you how the game works. The restaurant setting is a place you have been together. The Game AI will reconstruct that environment in the cloud. Your ciphers have stored the memories of your time there. The Game AI will integrate them into the created reality. With me so far?"

They nodded, and Kimmy continued. "It will make subtle changes, which you must correct. If you fail to do so within the time allotted, you will be forced out of the cloud and lose. You have five minutes to detect and correct the changes. The time will become progressively shorter. The team that stays in the longest wins the cloud. After one hour, if both teams are still in, a tie is declared."

"Yes, that sounds right," said Gareth as he settled into the Experiencer chair. He felt the chair conform to his body. As usual, Gareth had the sensation of floating. His cipher bypassed his physical senses, feeding him the sensations of the virtual world.

The Game Center AI announced the start of the

game.

Gareth found himself seated at the table in the restaurant. He looked around and saw again the panoramic view of Earth, slowly receding as the elevator ascended. The restaurant, the aptly named *A View Above*, was as he remembered. Sam was across from him, silhouetted by the Earth. She wore a black evening gown with a pearl necklace around her neck. "You look great, Sam! But I don't remember the elegant gown."

She felt the necklace around her neck and looked over at Gareth. "I like the tuxedo you're wearing, but that's not right, either," she replied.

"Right, I've never owned a tux. This is part of the game," said Gareth. "These clothes are the default setting. We need to remember what we wore that night. That's how we make this our reality. I remember you wore a black dress with a white-gold necklace." As he spoke, Sam's outfit changed to match his memory.

"And you wore that ugly sports jacket and slacks," Sam noted.

"Hey, I hadn't planned on fine dining during this trip!" He reached for the whiskey glass in front of him. "I hope the Old-Fashioned tastes as good as I remember." He took a sip and appreciated the fine, peaty flavor. "Damn, this is scotch! That's not right! Not bad, but it needs to be an Old-Fashioned. Sam, take a drink—focus on the flavor, smell, and taste as you remember it."

Sam closed her eyes and took a drink. She smiled. "Now that's what I remember: a perfect Old-Fashioned!"

"Nice, we fixed it in time. Now let's enjoy our dinner. We both had prime rib, as I recall."

Gareth and Sam settled into the meal and began talking as if the restaurant and the meal were all real.

It seems real to me, Gareth thought. He felt relaxed and happy again in Sam's company. He almost forgot that they were playing a game. Maybe CIPHER 3 has something to do with that?

"Sam, this feels different from a typical Experience."

"What do you mean?" Cathy asked, sipping on the Old Fashioned.

"I'm not only remembering the evening as it looked

and felt, sounded and smelled, but also my emotional reaction to it. Not remember so much, but feel it."

Sam shrugged. "I enjoyed it, too. So, I'm probably feeling the same as I did then."

Gareth shook his head. "No, no. It's different. I'm not sure how to explain it." He took a bite of the prime rib, chewing it. "It tastes like it did then. The feeling in my mouth is the same. I should enjoy it and your company. But I feel nervous, apprehensive, shy. I shouldn't feel that now. But I do." He closed his eyes. "It's exactly the way I felt back then."

"I don't get it. Why?"

He opened his eyes, looking around the restaurant. "It must be the CIPHER 3 implant! I had them when we dined here. It recorded my endocrine levels and is reproducing them now. This is not something CIPHER 2 can do. You are feeling this moment spontaneously."

"I think I understand."

"Yes! Right now, I feel excited about getting to know you for the first time. I feel the anticipation that if this goes well, we'll head back to my suite. I am hoping we'll make love, and you will spend the night. But we did all that. It should really be a happy memory. Which it is, but my body, my feelings tell me that this is something I'm hoping for and not wanting to mess up."

"I see what you're saying. You are feeling all this the same as you did the first time."

"Yes, my mind and memory are telling me one thing; my body, my endocrine system are telling me something else. This is something I experienced, not something that a company like *Multitudes* could make."

"That's great!" said Sam, her eyes lighting up and smiling. "Think of what this means. You could really feel what another person feels, understand them better."

"Maybe, but it's dangerous; I could stay in here forever. My **CIPHER** could just keep playing this moment or any other moment that made me feel happy. I would never need to line through an awful moment: none of those times I kept my feelings hidden to protect myself. Only the times like this, where I feel free and connected to someone else. I would never want to leave."

"Well, the game will end eventually, and we'll pop back out into reality. We can talk more about this later. Don't let the prime rib get cold. It's delicious. And the waiter was right about the wine. Enjoy!"

Gareth grinned. "OK. Sure, and I can't wait for dessert. Then maybe we can linger and enjoy some coffee."

Yes, I could live any kind of life I want in the cloud, he thought. Sam is right. This moment will end, but there are others. They would all be real to me. I could even create whatever reality I wanted and live it. As long as my physical body is taken care of, then why not? That's the problem. Someday my body would wear out, and that would be the end. Or would it? If I uploaded myself, I could still live in the cloud. But that wouldn't be the same—not without a physical body for CIPHER 3 to interface with to create the hormonal responses that I feel now. He noticed Sam trying to get his attention. Damn, I let my attention wander!

"Gareth!" said Sam. "You're losing focus! It's all fading away!"

"Wait! I can hold it; I can bring it back. I just need something to remind me." He tried to remember something. Something he could visualize, some object. Yes! He remembered drinking an Americano; Sam was sitting across from him. She was wearing a dress with an intricate design of flying birds.

There was a look of panic on her face. "Gareth, no," she said. It's not right, he thought. Why is Sam so upset? This is a café, not the restaurant. But I don't remember this. It faded, too. Abruptly, he found himself back at the Game Center. The dining room had vanished.

"Damn! Sorry, Sam, I got lost in thought. I remembered something, somewhere else, at the last minute. It was so odd."

She smiled at him. "You? Get lost in thought? You just can't help it, I know. Hey, it was just a game. You must have confused some memories. It happens."

"Wow, that's one of the shortest games ever!" said Kimmy. She frowned. "I'm sorry; there are no refunds. But I can give you a discount, say twenty percent, if you want to try again."

"No, that's all right," said Sam. She nodded to the other couple. "I see the other team is still playing?"

"Yes, they own the cloud now. They can stay in for the maximum time."

"I hope they picked something good," said Gareth. He was determined to shake off the last confusing part of the game. The dress, the scene at the café. It seemed so familiar. Sam's right, just some jumbled-up memories, nothing that really happened. "You know, after that meal we just kind of ate, I'm starving. I think I'll take another run at breakfast. Care to join me, Sam? I think I'll get an Americano, haven't had one in a long time."

Lagrange One Day 2
August 2093

"I'm really not looking forward to this, Sam," said Gareth. He continued loading his backpack with a change of clothes. "Alex and his stupid ideas! Zero-G Laser tag! *Multitudes* already has a good inventory of those. The last thing they need is an Experience created by a klutz like me. *You shape it, you own it* was bad enough. That was just between us, and I'm still a little unsettled by that." Try as he might, Gareth still thought of the bird-adorned dress he saw Sam wearing in the game. I don't recall seeing that before, he thought. It's distinctive; I'd remember it. Yes, it had been an AI-generated game, yet the dress seemed familiar, and at the same time, not.

"Relax," said Sam. "Just have fun. The game isn't that hard, not really. I promise no clouds, no virtual reality. A good, clean, physical game. You like physical games, don't you?"

Great, she played that card. He grinned. "One-on-one, I'm your guy. But I've never been good at this kind of team sport." That's not what she meant, he realized. More than one partner? Or did she? "I'm afraid I'll let you down. Who are we playing again?"

"Do you remember Rafe and Peter? We met them at the bar last night. Just how much did you have to drink?"

"Hey, look who's talking," Gareth replied, smiling. "I was just trying to keep up. Of course, I remember. I thought we were joking."

"Sorry, big guy. We committed to it. Don't worry, you'll do fine. Besides, Rafe and Peter are on their honeymoon. They're probably hungover too, and all worn out. You'll never see them again after this, so who cares? This will be good practice for the spacewalk tomorrow," Sam said. "I'm really looking forward to it."

Gareth zipped up his bag. "OK, I'll try to relax and have fun. Are you packed?"

Sam smiled. "Yep, let's go, space-cowboy!"

Gareth and Sam met the competition while suiting up. They were both young and athletic looking. They don't look tired at all, Gareth observed. Where do they get their stamina? We're going to lose and lose badly.

Sam did well, of course. But Gareth kept getting shot. At one point, Rafe and Peter both zapped him—and kept zapping him, laughing the whole time. Sam used the distraction to capture the flag, so it wasn't a total loss. She scored their lone point. They all shared a drink later, after showering and changing. They even bought Gareth a Lagrange Old-Fashioned, which the bartender smoked using a laser torch.

Sam tried to console him back in the suite. "Really, you did well! And it looked like you had fun. I even saw you smile once." She grabbed a couple of beers from the suite's mini-bar and offered one to Gareth.

He cracked it open and took a long drink. "No, that was a grimace." He smiled and added, "Yes, I had fun. I really don't mind losing. I just hope I didn't let you down. You are very good. Where did you learn to handle yourself in zero G like that?"

"Experiences. There are a lot of training Experiences. You spend so much time creating Experiences, do you ever use them?"

"Not much lately." Gareth frowned. "I sometimes get too involved in them. I have a hard time pulling myself away. Not like a Fugue or anything, but just ..."

"I think I understand."

He took another drink of his beer and shook his head.

"After Cathy left, it was just too tempting. Being alone, it's too easy to get lost in an Experience."

"Hmm, yes. But you're not alone now, are you? I can certainly think of other ways to spend time. Together. Are you interested? Take your mind off the game. I have an idea that could be fun. We could crank *EmpHance* up to level 9, too."

"Sure," Gareth said, grinning. He finished his beer. "OK, I'm game. Let's push it. What do you have in mind?"

"First strip and get on the bed."

Gareth began taking off his clothes. "Yes, ma'am! What about you?"

"Oh, I'll stay dressed for a bit. And drop your CIPHER firewalls. I have a packet I want to send."

"Really, Sam? I shouldn't..."

"Hey, you trust me, right? Don't worry, it's harmless."

I shouldn't do that, Gareth thought. I do trust her, though. Why is it I'm so accepting of her? It's only been a few days, but it feels like we already have such a deep relationship. He gave in. *Cipher, drop firewalls and accept packet from Sam Brown.*

"OK, send it." He finished stripping and lay down on the bed. *Packet accepted, executing.* "I've got it, Sam. What does it do?" Now I'm naked and no CIPHER firewalls, he thought. I can't believe I'm letting her do this!

"I'll explain later." She grabbed a blindfold from the nightstand. "Put this on." Gareth complied. It was a blackout sleep mask. He put it on and the room went dark. He couldn't see anything.

"Good, now raise your hands!" He felt her tying his wrists. She must be using the belts from their bathrobes; very resourceful. He had a sensation of his CIPHER reaching out, trying to find visual inputs it no longer had. Gareth had opened his CIPHER totally, and Sam had done the same. A Near Field connection occurred between them.

His senses shifted, as if he were running an Experience. Not completely; he still had an awareness of himself, but with Sam's senses overlaying his. Gareth still felt the bed underneath, the belts tied around his wrists, his erection growing. He also saw a belt tying his wrist to the bedpost. Then he saw his blindfolded face. His CIPHER must have connected to Sam's, he realized. He still had all his senses, but now Sam's as well.

As she got up to admire her work, he saw himself spread out on the bed. She looked down at his now fully erect penis. Gareth felt his own excitement, and somehow Sam's as well. He longed for her pussy, as he felt her longing for his cock.

The *EmpHance* and NF connected them. The combination was overwhelming for Gareth. It was compounded by his happy helplessness. But there was more. He felt Sam's reassuring presence, too. Was it the packet Sam had sent? There was nothing to fear, said the presence. He let go of the fear and concern and let the pleasure take him.

Sam ran a fingernail along the underside of his penis up to its head, then grabbed it firmly with one hand as she moved down to his balls. He sensed how he tasted to her as she licked and gently bit them. His own arousal increased with hers.

More of Sam's senses opened to him. All the boundaries separating them crumbled like mud walls. The gale force of her sensations swept away the dusty remnants of those walls. He felt her pleasure and excitement as she looked at his body; how slender he looked to her. How she enjoyed watching him quiver and shake with excitement, struggling against the belts.

It was strange and exhilarating to be seen and sensed by another person. Is this how other people saw him? How Cathy had seen him? No, she and Sam are not the same. How would it have been with her? He was Gareth, with his own senses and excitement. At the same time, Sam's senses and excitement flowed into him and merged with his. The two perceptions and feelings created a kind of harmonic wave convergence—more intense than each on its own.

How he saw himself: naked and vulnerable. But also, he saw how Sam saw him, Gareth, in that same body. She looked at his body with intense excitement, strongly attracted to him. Gareth didn't need to guess how she felt; he did not need to hope that was how she looked at him. He *knew* it; he *felt* it. She wasn't faking anything. That was impossible with this connection.

His CIPHER 3 added her excitement and arousal to his own. Its ability to modulate hormonal levels supplemented his own response with Sam's. The separation between them lifted like an early morning fog. Does it feel this way for her as well? he wondered.

Gareth sensed Sam taking her clothes off. He felt the cool air touching her naked skin as she disrobed. She sat on the bed over him. *I feel you are with me, Gar. You are connected to my CIPHER. That's good. I've felt this only once before. Are you enjoying it?*

God yes, Gareth sent back. *It's scary though; I am losing track of who I am.*

Don't worry, Gareth. You won't get lost. Open up more of yourself to me.

He watched through Sam's eyes as she tied his legs to

the bed. She climbed onto the bed, kneeling between his now-spread legs. Sam licked his right nipple, then bit hard. The pain and the pleasure generated more activity in his CIPHER, interfacing with his sex hormones: vasopressin and oxytocin.

She saw himself as she moved down to his penis. She licked it from the base of the shaft to the tip. It was exciting for him to see himself through her eyes, for him to feel her touch and experience how he felt to her. She teased him with her fingernails, sending a shock of pleasure through him. All at once, it seemed as though he was both the giver and receiver of pleasure.

Sam took him into her mouth and began sucking him—nearly to the point of no return. She stopped, causing him to cry out. He was breaking down, losing himself. She started in on him again with renewed vigor.

Have you had enough, Gareth? Do you want to come? I can feel your excitement. I'm ready to come with you.

God, yes, please!

She went back to sucking him. Again, he was reaching the point of no return.

Please let me come! he pleaded.

Yes, I know you are ready. I can feel it. Come now!

She released him, and he came.

She took off the blindfold. He felt a momentary vertigo as his CIPHER switched off the sensory and hormonal feeds from Sam. He lay motionless as she untied him, and the sense of her presence faded. The NF connection to Sam finally ceased, leaving him isolated again—only himself. The loss immobilized him. "Sam," he said. "I..." He couldn't think of what to say next.

"Gareth, are you all right?" He felt her wiping the tears from his eyes.

"I don't know. I think so."

Sam curled up next to him, resting her hand on his chest. The touch revived him, and Gareth wrapped his arms around her, holding her. He searched for the feeling he had before, the connection, desperate to regain it. There, he thought, I can sense it. Somewhere in his CIPHER, in his consciousness, as well. He felt better now, reassured. What is it, though? Some kind of imprint? It's as if another awareness had moved in; mute, but the feeling of it was so strong.

Gareth knew about avatars, programs that ran using the CIPHER bots as networked computers. Is that what this awareness is? He had dropped all the defenses earlier, opened the CIPHER firewalls. Did Sam send an avatar of herself over? Not such a big program that CIPHER would alert him, but something. Why?

"I wish you didn't have to go back to Earth," she said. "Can't you stay with me?"

"Maybe. This is the last assignment on the contract." I have to stay with her, he thought. After being so close, I can't bear being separated from her. "I'll apply for a vacation. I haven't taken one in a long time."

He sensed her happiness at his answer. The connection is still there. I can't lose it, he realized. I can't be without her. What would I be then?

Gareth toweled off after his shower. He dressed and walked into the living room portion of the suite. Sam was sitting on the couch, looking out the window at the field of stars.

We had been so close, he thought, so connected. But now, we seemed closed off to each other. What is she feeling now? He searched for her presence left behind in his CIPHER. It was there, but ephemeral: a ghost.

"Sam," Gareth began. She turned to him and smiled.

Hi Gareth, I hope I'm not interrupting anything...

"Sorry, I just got a ping from Alex."

Alex, you better not be eavesdropping....

Sorry, but I can tell when you are not otherwise

occupied. You know I need to monitor the new nanobots. I set the equipment to tell me when your endorphin levels are more normal, which is not that often lately, I tell you. It was really crazy, man! I'm glad you and Sam hit it off. Maybe we've got a new marketing approach for CIPHER 3, 'You're always ready'.

Hilarious Alex. Although I admit that it's a nice side benefit. What do you want?

You have a Space Walk Experience set for 2 PM today. You might want to think about having a good lunch beforehand, as it seems that you've skipped breakfast.

What makes you think I missed breakfast? Oh, right. Sam and I will be there.

As much as I think Sam is good for you, I wish you wouldn't mix business and pleasure. It means more editing for me as it screws with your endorphin levels.

I don't care; she's coming along. He thought back to his dreams, how Sam had often been in them, and how calming that was, and now this. It would be his first spacewalk, and he wanted her there. *I'm sure you can correlate how she makes me feel versus the excitement of the spacewalk and edit out what you need. Or do you need more data?*

No, no. I think I have quite enough of that, thank you. On second thought, the marketing campaign should have a warning 'Repeated and overuse could lead to ...'

Enough, Alex! We'll be there! Now disconnect.

"Sam, it looks like we have someplace to be at two this afternoon. So, do you want to grab some lunch before we take a stroll outside?"

"Sure. Was there something else you wanted to say just now?"

"Not really. It can wait."

"OK. How should I dress? Do you think it will be cold today?"

"It's always cold in space."

A Good Walk Spoiled

August 2093

After a light lunch, Gareth and Sam made their way to the excursion deck. They went to bay three to meet the shuttle, which would take them a safe distance from the hotel before they went for the spacewalk. They had already had several briefings and had practiced in the simulator.

Gareth had got the hang of it after a few lessons. He learned how to tether and untether, maneuver with jets, and operate the suit radios. Sam did nearly as well. But it seemed that she was faking it somehow; in truth, she was catching on faster than Gareth. He teased her, "You're just pretending you don't know what you're doing." She gave as good as she got. "Well, I need to protect your fragile male ego." The instructor, Hector, had grudgingly passed them. It was, after all, only a resort class.

He greeted them today at the shuttle. "Hi you two! We're going to have a great day outside!"

Gareth pinged Alex to begin recording the experience. "Absolutely! What's the forecast?" Gareth asked.

"Mostly dark, but no showers," Hector replied. Gareth and Sam boarded the small four-person craft; the pilot and Hector made up the crew. The pilot was more taciturn than Hector and barely acknowledged them. As the ship left the resort, Sam and Gareth got into their spacesuits— each double-checking the other. By the time they had finished, the shuttle had taken up position a few kilometers from the station.

Alex, sent Gareth, are we still within the Ritz Moloi Field?

Yes, Alex sent back. You are well within limits and I'm getting clear data from your CIPHER 3 implant. Remember, the shuttle also communicates with the resort using the field, but on a narrow band. It has only an emergency beacon, which they've never had to use. The field will not extend to you outside the shuttle, but I'll download the Experience from your CIPHER when you get back. You are good to go. Have fun!

They headed to the airlock at the back of the shuttle. The door closed behind them, and the exterior door opened after the pressure equalized. Gareth went first, after attaching his tether line to the shuttle exterior. Sam did the same. They exited, and the airlock door closed behind them. Gareth could tell his adrenaline was increasing based on his CIPHER 3 implants.

He looked back at the Ritz Lagrange One resort. He remembered his first view of the resort as the transit ship arrived from the elevator terminus. How small it had seemed then. This close in, as he hung in space, the resort looked immense; yet, at the same time, it seemed small and vulnerable as he surveyed the surrounding emptiness—so black. It was like a delicate, beautiful piece of jewelry laid out on a black velvet cloth surrounded by tiny motes of diamond dust, which were stars.

"Sam", Gareth called on the suit radio. He did not use CIPHER so as not to cloud the data Alex was getting. "Can you hear me?"

"Loud and clear, Gar. This is amazing! What a view! Let's go to the other side of the shuttle. We can get a view without the resort."

Gareth followed as she used the maneuvering jets to go to the other side. Show off, he thought, as he clumsily followed. She is far better at this. They used the jets to stabilize their position and waited for their eyes to adjust to the darkness.

He felt once again that presence of her, the imprint inside his mind, within the implant's nanobot structure. It had faded after they had had their CIPHER enhanced sex. Now, away from the station's Moloi Field, it was stronger. Perhaps the lack of a field allowed the NF connection between their implants to be stronger.

"Sam, earlier, back in the suite, you know, after we, you know, I was going to ask you about something. You sent that packet to me. I really shouldn't have let you do that. What was it?"

"It was harmless, really, just a memento of me. Nothing to worry about."

"A memento? I don't understand. It seems like it left an imprint of you in my mind. Is that what you mean?"

"In way. I'm sure that you have interacted with AI Augmented Experiences in the past, right?"

"Yes, at my CIPHER 3 implantation. There was an AI avatar of a doctor I had met previously." Gareth had a sensation that he had met Dr. Francis after that, as well. But that can't be, he told himself. I've only met him once in real life, though the sense of the meeting was quite strong. "He seemed real to me, like a person. Is that what you mean? Once the Experience was over, he was gone. Yet your avatar is still there; I am sensing it more. Almost a part of me. I see you there in the spacesuit, but I feel you in my head as well. Am I making sense?"

"Yes, I feel it, too. I think the MiXe and our NF connection and the intensity of physical and emotional sharing—I think that created something—a kind of bond. It's making the avatar I sent you stronger. I should have thought about how you have CIPHER 3, how the avatar might take advantage of that."

Gradually the stars appeared, followed by the river of suns that made up the Milky Way's arm. Looking out at it, Gareth was nearly overwhelmed. "Yes, I feel it—very intense, very strong. It feels like a real person. It doesn't talk to me. I think someday it might. Right now, I sense when it's happy, sad, or anxious. It's a reflection of what you might feel. I'm not sure Alex and CRI will be happy about this."

"Really," Gareth continued, "I should be angry with you. This can cause me some problems with CRI. I guess I can always delete it, but I'll keep it for now. It came from you, so I'll call it Sammie. That's a good nickname, right? And looking at all this, all the stars, I feel that I'm sharing it with you in so many ways," he said. He added softly, "Beautiful, isn't it?"

"Yes, it is, and you don't need to give the avatar a name..." she replied. Her voice was hesitant.

"Is everything OK, Sam?"

"Um, yes. Just let me check on something with Hector. Hector, this is Sam. Can you hear me?"

"Yes, Sam. What's up?"

"Do you see that we have company? I see what look like running lights. Is that another shuttle on the starboard side?"

Gareth looked in the direction Sam was facing. She has good eyes, he thought. He could barely differentiate the lights from the stars. It's probably no big deal, but the resort should not allow two ships so close to each other. Sam sounded worried about the other ship. I'm sure Hector will clear this up soon, he thought.

"Let me check," replied Hector.

Gareth noticed the lights were growing brighter, and he could now make out the outline of the ship they illuminated. There were a lot of running lights, many more than their shuttle. He felt another CIPHER connection, this time not the NF connection with Sam.

Incoming connection from Alex Phillips, accepting per protocol, Gareth's cipher announced. Alex? What's he doing? Where is he?

"Hector," Gareth said. "The ship! It's getting closer. Do they know we're here?" There was no reply. "Sam, I'm not getting a response from Hector. Can you hear me? Alex must be on the ship; he's trying to connect to me!"

"Gareth, you need to stop him! Abort the connection! I'll try to raise Hector."

The ship continued to close in; it seemed larger than a shuttle to Gareth. *Alex, what are you doing? Abort the connection now!* He felt the ephemeral presence Sam had left in his mind stirring, growing stronger. It was worried.

Gareth, I'm here to help, Alex sent back. Gareth felt his mood changing, relaxing. His earlier panic about the new ship subsided. *Gareth, I'm here with my grandmother, Isolde Phillips, on the Mangala. We've come to rescue you. You can't trust Sam! She's using you. Come to our ship; we can help.*

Yes, that seems right, Gareth thought. Alex is an old friend. He wouldn't hurt me. I trust him. At the same time, Sammie's presence flooded him with worry, unhappy with Alex. He began to doubt what Alex was saying.

"Sam, is he telling the truth? I don't know who to trust. Sam?"

"No! He's lying! Remember Alex can control your CIPHER 3. He can manipulate your hormones; he can try to control you. Come back with me to the shuttle. We'll be safe there. I can help. Remember how you opened yourself up to me earlier? Let me in again, please. You don't want to go with them! Gareth, please!"

Gareth, come to our ship. Trust me, we'll take you back to Earth. You'll be safe there, Alex sent.

A voice in Gareth's head said, think rationally. What Alex is saying makes no sense. It wasn't really a voice, Gareth thought; it was more like a stray thought. Where did it come from? Did it come from the imprint Sam had left? It *felt* like her. That connection had been so strong, he was certain it came from there, from Sam in a way. Wherever it may have originated, it was right. It didn't make sense for Alex to come all the way out here. Why not meet me back at the resort?

Suddenly, he felt ripped away from that feeling. It had been shoved aside, and Gareth now felt a sense of affection for Alex. He remembered the years of friendship with him and Cathy. He's always had my back, he thought. He just wants to help me. That's what good friends do.

"Please, Gareth, let me in!" Sam called. Dammit, Sam! Can't you see Alex just wants to help? He's a good guy. The inner voice, Sammie, urged him to take control of CIPHER 3 back from Alex. It seemed to counterbalance Alex's attempts to manipulate his CIPHER. How can it do that?

"Gareth, if you really trust Alex, he wouldn't need his connection to CIPHER 3. Shut it down. Then if you still trust him, you'll know it's real."

Of course you would say that, he thought. Can I do that? Just shut it down? Yes, the inner voice nudged him. Try it. Put it to the test. If it still feels right after, then it is right.

Alex, I'm shutting down CIPHER 3. Don't worry, I just need to prove something to Sam.

Gareth, no! Don't listen to that bitch!

Sorry, Alex. Cipher shut down CIPHER 3, verification code phrase For the Snark was a Boojum.

Acknowledged, shutting down CIPHER 3.

FUCK, thought Gareth, as his hormones abruptly returned to normal. Alex, what did you do to me? Go to Sam, the inner voice said.

"Sam, help!"

"It's OK, Gareth. I'm here." Suddenly, she was there beside him, and she spun them around back towards the shuttle. "Hector!" he heard Sam call to the shuttle. "We're coming in fast! Be ready to head back to the station as soon as we get in."

"Acknowledged. I've already alerted the station concerning the *Mangala's* unauthorized presence."

The *Mangala* moved away as they entered the shuttle. Why were they here? Alex came out here to kidnap me, he realized. But why? That was his grandmother's ship.

What did she want with him? If it hadn't been for Sam and that inner presence.

All Roads Lead To New Nottingham
August 2093

"Sam, I don't understand what's happening," said Gareth. "How can the station let Phillips get away with it?" They had returned to his suite after a discouraging meeting with the station authorities. "Hector backed us up. Phillips' yacht was there. But she's getting away with just a fine! For not obeying station control orders? That's not right!"

"I know, Gareth. I'm frustrated too. But Phillips claimed it was a misunderstanding. They thought we were in trouble, and they simply tried to render aid. She denied attempting to kidnap anyone. As far as the station controllers could tell, you headed first for the *Mangala*, then changed direction to head back to our shuttle. They figured you were disoriented. We have no proof that

Phillips was doing anything other than trying to help. They won't even look at our CIPHER logs! Alex and Phillips are heading back to Earth, so that's it, end of story."

Gareth collapsed on the small sofa while Sam retrieved beers from the mini-bar and sat next to him. He managed a 'thank you' as she handed one over to him, and he took a swallow. "Why me? Why try to kidnap me? And Alex using my implants to control me! I don't get it. We're friends! Damn him! What are they after?"

Sam shrugged her shoulders and slouched back into the sofa. "Good question. My guess—it looks like Phillips, Isolde, I mean, needs you for something. You told me Alex is her grandson, right? Blood is thicker than water, or something like that. He must feel that helping her is more important than your friendship."

Sam took another drink of her beer. "We need to think about this. It's all got to be connected somehow: Phillips, you, Alex. Is it your CIPHER 3? Could that be it? You are the only one with the beta, right? That makes you unique. She wants them and sees you as the way to get them."

"But she is CRI, right? She founded the company, for god's sake!" Gareth protested. "Can't she just get them? Get the CIPHER 3 Beta implants? Or just wait until it becomes available to everyone. Why can't she wait?"

"Maybe she can't get the beta from CRI. Remember, you told me they kicked her out. The special projects, right? They are afraid of what she might do with CIPHER 3, and they do not want to lose control of the technology. It's a good question, though." Sam looked out the window and tapped on the bottle with her ring. Gareth noticed the ring—a man's ring. Whose? he wondered. He had never thought to ask. "I mean, why can't she wait?" Sam continued. "The final version—the one the public gets—will it differ from what you have now?"

"They should be pretty much the same. The final version will be totally locked down, of course." He pointed to his head. "What I have now is more open; it can be adjusted, modified, fine-tuned. That's why Alex could control how I felt. He can make changes based on the feedback he sees when monitoring them. That won't be possible when the final one comes out."

"Yes! That's it! What you are telling me is that the beta is hackable; it can be altered. She can change it to make it more suitable for her 'Special Projects'. That's why she wants it! She can copy it and then change it the way she wants. That's why she wants you. But if Alex has access to them and can modify them, then why can't he just copy them?"

Gareth leaned forward on the sofa. "The cloud. CRI

owns the cloud here and on Earth. As long as my CIPHER is connected to it, CRI won't allow him to copy it. Sure, adjust it within parameters. But not copy. That's why he tried to grab me during the space walk." He took a sip of his beer. "What do you think these 'Special Projects' could be?" asked Gareth.

Sam paused, and Gareth felt she was thinking back to something. "I don't know. Not for sure, anyway. That Ludd attack you mentioned. I heard about it, too. It must have had some effect on her. People say that she became super-paranoid and doesn't trust anyone to meddle with her implants now."

He could feel the avatar presence trying to tell him something. But it wasn't at a conscious level, just a kind of unformed thought. What was it trying to tell me? That Sam sitting next to him, the real Sam, wasn't telling him everything? How do I deal with the avatar of Sam in my head and the Sam in front of me? I need to give it a name, maybe 'Sammie'? The presence, the program running on his CIPHER seemed uncomfortable.

I need to listen to it. There is something there. I can sense that Sam isn't being totally honest. There's just too much going on. Phillips is after me, but is she the only one? Could there be others? Sam was able to reason out so quickly what Phillips was up to. Who is Sam really?

Her knowledge of NF, MiXes, the way she talked me back to the shuttle. It's more than a layperson would know or be able to do. It's too much of a coincidence that we met. Could she have planned it? But how? Only CRI and the client would know that I was traveling to LaGrange One.

Who is the client? The one that required me to get CIPHER 3 for these assignments. Assignments that have brought me here. Assignments that have led me to Sam. I *am* being led! I need to stop letting people decide what I should do. It's too easy. I need to take back some control.

"Tell me," he said, his voice trembling. "How do you know I'm the only one with CIPHER 3? When we met at the elevator, we hit it off so quickly. It was, I don't know, so easy. Like we were old friends. As if, somehow, I already knew you. Right from the beginning, I was comfortable with you."

Sam looked away, avoiding eye contact at first, regrouped, and then smiled at him. "Gareth, you've been through a lot. We both have. Look at it from my point of view. I'm here on holiday. We were going the same way, up here to Lagrange One, and we have a connection; I felt it. We hooked up and had a lot of fun. What's wrong with that? That's all it was then. After all of this, what's happened, I've come to care for you. But now, I'm in the middle of something I don't understand. I admit it; I'm afraid. Phillips is a powerful person, and we've pissed her off."

"I get that. This is more than you bargained for," said Gareth, taking another drink of the beer. He looked into her green eyes, searching for something, something that said he should trust her. She turned away again. She's avoiding the subject. It's uncomfortable for her. He put his hand on her knee, forcing her attention to him. "There's more, though. I can tell you are not telling me everything. That part of you in me now—that avatar—I don't know if you meant it to happen, but the MiXe and the NF connection created a very strong and distinct presence in my CIPHER. It's as if you, as if you're in my head. I don't understand how CIPHER 3 and the *EmpHance* MiXe interact with the avatar you sent me. It feels like maybe they could have created something like this: a virtual presence of you running on my implant."

Gareth paused, waiting for Sam to say something. He continued, "Whatever this presence is, I can sense it's uncomfortable. It is trying to tell me something. I believe you care for me, but I also think that our meeting was not a chance encounter. Somehow, it was planned, maybe by you. You are like Phillips. You need something from me. Tell me what that is. I deserve to know."

Sam removed Gareth's hand from her knee and stood

up. She walked over to the suite's window, looking out into space for a few minutes.

"I'm waiting," said Gareth.

She took a drink, turned and said, "There's nothing to say, really. Yes, I know a lot about CIPHER. Many people do. A friend of mine was an Experience hacker. Not a legit thing, I know. Her name was Ruth. But she was good and kept under the radar. She was always talking about it. Talking about Moloi and her mice, about the latest research. Ruth was so excited about its potential to bring people together. I learned a lot just by listening to her."

Sam dropped her head and sighed. She said, "Something went wrong with one of her hacked Experiences. Ruth was always trying to push CIPHER's limits. She must have pushed it too far. She went into Fugue. After a while of visiting her, I just had to get away. That's why I'm here. Perhaps that's also why I fell in with you so easily. Kind of a rebound, you know?"

"Maybe," said Gareth, seeing her framed by the window. The special window glass enhanced the star field behind her. In the dim illumination of the suite, it seemed as if fireflies surrounded her. "I still think there is more to you than that."

"You know what I think?" she said. "You are on the rebound, too. How long has it been since Cathy left you?

A year, I think you said."

Sammie twitched at the mention of Cathy, and he felt a sense of familiarity with Cathy. He wondered, did I ever mention Cathy's name to Sam? I remember saying I had split up with someone, but did I mention Cathy's name? I'm certain I haven't.

"How do you know Cathy's name?"

"Oh Gareth, I'm sure you mentioned her at some point." Sam came back to the sofa, leaving the fireflies behind, and sat next to him. She put her head on his shoulder and moved her hand below his waist. He felt himself stirring. I'm so easy to control, he thought. No! I've had enough of being manipulated! He grabbed her hand and pushed it away.

"Sam, not now! You're trying to distract me. Trying to keep me from asking questions about you, about us, about how easily we fell in with each other. It doesn't seem right."

She raised her head, looked at him, and smiled. The smile weakened his resolve. "Just one more time, Gareth. Let me in. I'll let you in. I want to try again, to see if I feel what you feel. It's important to me. I can't explain it now. But please, I need this." She undid his zipper and felt his now stiffening penis in his shorts, squeezing it. "Then we can talk, OK?" She released it and kissed him.

Gareth felt an urgency, more than just the sexual arousal, prodding him on. His hormones and Sammie's presence conspired, making it inevitable. You know you want her, he thought. The confusion and suspicion he felt just now crumbled in the force of his desire for Sam. She sat on his lap and kissed him softly on the cheek and then, more forcefully, his lips. He kissed her, their tongues playing.

Gar, open yourself to me, Sam sent. I want to see what you see, feel what you feel. Like I did with you last time.

Gareth instructed his CIPHER to accept the NF connection from Sam. She closed her eyes, as if willing herself to see with his eyes. She gasped. "Is that what I look like?"

"If you mean beautiful, then yes. Sexy, too," he said, smiling.

"It was that way for you, wasn't it?" Sam asked. "The other senses too, like touch."

Cipher, sent Gareth. Accept connection from Sam, flow her senses to me.

Like an Experience, Sam's perceptions merged with his own.

"Yes." He led her to bed and laid her down. He began taking her clothes off, and she saw her body as it was revealed to him. "Follow what I see towards what I feel when I touch you," he said.

He ran his hand through her hair; she felt a tingly electric sensation. She also felt how it felt to Gareth, the softness of it. Through him, she smelled what she smelled—a delicate, sweet fragrance. He moved his hand between her legs, and she felt how wet she was, how excited she was becoming. Then she felt buttons and fabric as Gareth stripped. Then the sensations on his cock as her vagina received his penis, the sense of friction on it as he began moving in and out of her. She knew he must be close to coming, but she only felt her nearness. She felt the cum escaping from him, and she came as it flowed into her. He withdrew and rolled over, lying next to her.

Gareth's CIPHER told him that Sam had broken the NF-Connection. He no longer received her perceptions. She lay silent, not moving. He felt her drifting away; the presence becoming melancholy. "Sam, what's wrong?" he asked.

She seemed to focus on a spot on the ceiling, vacantly. "I didn't, I didn't feel what you felt. I mean emotionally. Yes, I saw what you saw. I even perceived your sense of touch. That was exhilarating. But it's not what you experienced before when I let you in. You were connected to me emotionally. You felt my ecstasy as if it were your own. That's right, isn't it?"

"Yes, that's the best way I can describe it. Is that what you are looking for?"

"I can't explain it, but yes."

Gareth was silent for a bit; he listened to Sam's breathing. He breathed in rhythm with her. It was a kind of synchronizing; he knew he could follow that, NF-Connect to her and lose himself in her. "It scares me, Sam. What can this connection do? Is it a good thing? I didn't know who was feeling what. I felt all of it. It's like I merged myself into you, losing my sense of self." He smiled ruefully. "That's not very strong to begin with."

Gareth could feel her tremble. "I would give anything to feel what you felt, to be that close to another person," she said.

"It is an amazing feeling, yes. I guess I am afraid of losing myself in that and never coming back."

Sam untangled herself from him and climbed out of bed. Searching for her robe, she tossed their discarded clothing around until she found it. "Sam? Are you OK? What's wrong?"

"You don't understand. What you felt—that connectedness—I want it! You have it, and it scares you! I could feel a bit of that connection. It doesn't scare me! I want more of it! Maybe if I had your implants, I'd have it. But this version you have, maybe it will become available someday, maybe not. It might be different. But this version, it works!"

"You talk about this feeling as if it were a kind of an illegal MiXe, the kind that people get addicted to," said Gareth. "Is that really what you want? Or is it something you need? I'm not sure that's a good thing. It may not matter anyway; CRI may decide it's a dead end. Right now, I think it might be a step too far. The feelings are too intense, too dangerous, too addictive. Sam, what is it you are really looking for here?"

"I don't care about the danger. The result is worth it. I'd love to be that close to another person; to achieve that level of empathy," said Sam.

'Empathy', thought Gareth. He rolled over onto one side, looking at her. We've talked about that before. When? Someone had said, 'means that I feel what you feel'... Was that Sam? "Sam," Gareth started.

"You need to come with me to Mars," said Sam.

"Mars, I don't understand. Why Mars?"

"New Nottingham. Phillips is too powerful, too strong. She'll follow you back to Earth. She'll try again to get you. Next time, she'll probably succeed."

"Yes," he said with a sigh, "you're right. It's hard for me to think right now. This is too much! All she really needs to do is copy them—the nanobots—and their programming. Alex could do that. Do I care? I should let her take them. But then, CRI wouldn't be happy. My career would be over." He got out of bed and began pacing the room. Finally, he collapsed into the chair next to the bed. I'm falling back into old habits again, he thought. Let someone else decide, make the choices. Still, he trusted Sam, despite everything that had happened.

"I know someone who can help. She's at New Nottingham," Sam said.

"OK, New Nottingham?" Gareth asked, stunned. "Who is this person?" And Cathy's there, he realized. She went there with the Isolators. What if she sees me? How could she not?

"Doctor Moloi. She can help us. I'm sure of it."

"How do you know that she's there? How do you know any of this?" None of this was accidental, he realized. Sam being at the elevator, moving in with him, the sex, all of it. Sammie began to stir and intrude more on his awareness. The avatar brought up memories he didn't know he had. Like someone pulling keepsakes from an old-time steamer trunk and throwing them around an attic. The attic was his consciousness. The cabin and Sam faded. Is this a Fugue? Gareth wondered. Is this how it starts?

An Experience came up. Where was this? He

recognized the procedure room where he got CIPHER 3. Sam was there. That can't be right. I'd only just met her at the elevator. Where was this? What is she saying?

"Your memories of me are buried in your
lower-level CIPHER nanobot memory."

And another experience, a café in DC:

"…because we've met before."

And Sam in the CIPHER 3 procedure room, again:

"Empathy means that I feel what you feel,
the adrenaline rush you feel as you go down the
slopes, the fear that you might wipe out. It's like I
am you, that's what I think when I think of
empathy. I think CIPHER 3 can do that."

He emerged from the Experiences. Sam was looking down at him. No, watching. Concern mingled with fear on her face. She knows that the memories have come back to me. Did she plan for this to happen? All of this buried in my **CIPHER** memory. Now they are rising to my conscious level, like bubbles of air from a drowning man rising to the surface of a lake.

"Gareth," Sam began as she reached over to him.

He pushed her away and rose from the chair. "You planned this!" he cried. "I remember now all the times we met. How did you make me forget? You must have been working with Alex. The headaches, *EmpHance*, somehow you got me the CIPHER 3 Beta. Shit, you're the client!"

What do I do with this? Cathy was right all along. CIPHER was a mistake. I'm taking the easy way again, letting Sam control me. And now, I'm going to New Nottingham to join the Isolators?!

"Why, Sam? Why did you do this to me? The time we spent together, the games we played, the sex! Were you laughing at me the whole time?" Suddenly, he felt his nakedness, how exposed he was. "Watch what I can get Gareth to do, so pathetic, so sad!"

She found his robe and offered it to him. He ignored it, and she laid it on the bed. What was the point of covering up now? She already knows every bit, every little detail about me. Putting on the robe would just be pretending, denying the truth. I have no privacy from her; she knows everything about me. She is still a mystery to me.

"No, I wasn't laughing at you," she said. "It's who you are; there's nothing wrong with that. But you're right. You are easy to guide, to nudge. I'm really sorry; we didn't mean to hurt you. It's just that we need you, what you carry with you. We wanted to get you to Moloi, you and your **CIPHER** 3. We can copy it there. We're trying to save someone; someone close to me. We need you for that."

"You're no better than Phillips! You're just more subtle, but you both want the same thing. Not for the same reason, I get that. But you still used me!" Gareth felt defeated now, the earlier rage evaporating, leaving resignation behind. He put the robe on, trying to compose himself. Get a grip, he told himself. This is no time to indulge in self-pity. "What do you know, Sam?"

"I'm not sure, but I had a near-fugue experience not long before leaving for Mars. I was in a Fugue sanatorium, a nice one, private. My **CIPHER** accidentally NF-connected to a victim, like you and I did earlier. Well, not quite like that. I'd been using *EmpHance* for a long time, and I think it made me susceptible. It was as if I had entered his mind. It wasn't like he was trapped in an Experience, not the way people think. And this guy kept talking about Phillips. She needed something he was working on."

"Wait," Gareth interrupted. "I remember when I first met you. We talked about how Phillips was working on Digital Ascension? Uploading herself to the cloud. Am I the missing piece, my CIPHER 3?"

"Yes, I think it is. That's why we need to get you as far away from her as possible. Please, Gareth. Come with me to New Nottingham."

What choice do I have? I need to find a way through this. Maybe if I get to Moloi, with her help, I can get out of this mess. Sam gets what she wants, and Phillips will leave me alone. I have to go along for now.

On the Lowell
September 2093

Gareth rolled over in bed. He could hear Sam's quiet breathing. Even knowing that she'd been using him all along, he felt comfort in her nearness. Was that feeling genuine? Or was it a result of the conditioning? All the times they had met left an impression, an imprint of her. Then there's the program, the avatar she had sent him. He could still feel it there, a warm feeling like the memory of an old, trusted friend; the presence he called Sammie. He knew it was an AI avatar. That's how it started, anyway. But it's been growing, changing. Somehow, it was using his nanobots, the CIPHER 3 version, to do this. It already seemed different from Sam. It cautioned him with hesitant feelings that Sam was not telling him everything, that she's holding something back.

Even though Sam had only just convinced him they had to go to Mars, she had already added him to her suite on the *Lowell.* She had always intended to have him join her, confident that he would go along. One month's journey to get to New Nottingham. It's ironic. Cathy went to New Nottingham to get away from CIPHER. Now I'm going there, bringing all this CIPHER nonsense with me. He did not know what they would do when they got there, or what Sam had planned.

She stirred, waking up. Gareth got out of bed and put the coffee on. She always needed a cup before she could converse coherently. He felt the beginnings of a headache; the coffee might help with that. Gareth found a robe in the closet and put it on. He took the other one from the closet and took it over to her.

"Thanks," she managed.

By the time he had brushed his teeth, the coffee was ready. He poured a cup for himself with some milk, and black for Sam. He sat the mugs on the table in the small kitchenette, waiting anxiously for Sam to emerge from the bedroom. His hands were absently gripping and then releasing the arms of the chair.

Sam arrived with the robe wrapped around her and sat down across from Gareth. They sat quietly, sipping the coffee, with nothing but the ambient sounds of the *Lowell* for company: the distant low thrumming noise of the engines matching the throbbing of Gareth's headache. The coffee wasn't helping the headache. He massaged his temples, trying to relieve the pain. How do I reconcile the conflicting feelings I have for her? he wondered. She used me and is still using me. But I feel connected to her. I feel the need to please her, to make her happy. Yes, she did that. All this time she had been creating that need, subliminally, with Alex's help. Even though I know it isn't real, I still can't deny the power of what we shared and the impression all of that left on me.

Finally, the caffeine kicked in, and Sam could utter, "Good morning."

"Really? Good morning, that's it?" The headache, the silent mornings and nights, the accumulation of suspicions and the trapped feeling of being used burst from him.

She glared at him. "What do you want from me, Gareth?"

"I want, I want something from you. Something that tells me you're sorry about all this. About dragging me into this crazy plan. About fucking with my mind and my memories!"

"Fine," said Sam. She took a sip of the coffee. "If that will make you happy. We should have left you alone in your quiet, meaningless life. Happy now?"

He threw the mug at the kitchenette wall. "Fuck you! That's what you say? After all that you've done to me? I have no life now. You own me! You people and your plans. Do you have any idea what you're doing? The harm you've done?"

Sam barely acknowledged the outburst, a slight hand tremble. She sipped her coffee. "No, I didn't think it would go this way. You weren't supposed to get hurt. I was hoping to have more time with you, to get you to understand what it could be like. You could see how much of a change it would be for people. CRI shouldn't have a monopoly on CIPHER. With your help, we could bring this technology to many more people and free people from the Fugue. That would be great, wouldn't it? I'm sure you would have wanted to help. Then, you could have gone back to Earth, back to your job if you wanted to."

"You sound like you are trying to convince yourself," Gareth replied. "I think you know this was wrong. You've always known that."

"No! It wasn't wrong! Sometimes you need to use people to make things happen. I don't apologize for that. It's not like you've been hurt, really. You've made a lot of money on this contract and had mind-altering sex! Literally. As far as I can tell, making money is the only thing you really care about. You have no one in your life, right?"

"Really!" Gareth shouted. "That's what you come back with? Pathetic Gareth, an easy mark? Screw him and he'll follow you anywhere? Do you think that excuses all that you've done to me?"

Sam looks away, avoiding eye contact. "I'm sorry, Gareth. That was cruel—and I didn't mean it. I guess that, I'm just desperate. We didn't count on Alex betraying us. I'm angry at myself. We thought we could just get everybody where we needed them, positioning people as if they were pieces on a chessboard. If we could do that, nobody would be hurt, and we could get what we needed." She gripped her mug, as if willing the heat to burn her hands. "We didn't realize that there was another player, someone countering my moves."

"I am not a chess piece! Do you hear yourself?"

"Of course! I've liked you from the first time we met at the café. And I've grown to care for you, to love you. I am human! All the time we spent together, that was real for me. I wouldn't hurt you. Isolde Phillips will. She doesn't care about anyone other than herself. Gareth, please, can we move on from what's happened? I'll bet you she's probably going to Mars, that she has no intention of going back to Earth. We must go there, and she knows that."

"If Phillips is going to Mars, then why are we going there?"

"Moloi. I told you she can help."

"Fine. It seems like you will get what you want. Me on Mars, but what happens when we get there? What's your plan then?"

"Just give me a chance to explain. Please?"

Gareth shrugged. Why not? There's nothing else for me to do. He refilled their coffees and said, "Sure, I'm not going anywhere. Or I guess I am. I just have no say in it."

"What you experienced when we made love that time on Lagrange One, what we shared, you felt it more intensely than I did. That's because of the CIPHER 3 enhancements. *You* can have empathy with other people. Your hormone levels match the levels of the person you are sharing with. So, if I'm afraid, you feel that fear. If I'm in love, so are you. If two people can share like that, it's ..." Sam paused, searching for a way to explain things.

"Like right now," Sam continued. "I can't figure out how to tell you in words. They are insufficient. But if I had CIPHER 3, we could connect and you would know. You had that then, right? When we made love."

"It was, it is still, something I am trying to sort out," Gareth said. He took a sip of the coffee and closed his eyes. "I sensed your physical, I guess, reactions while we were together. When I kissed you, I felt my lips. When I touched you, I felt the coarseness of my fingertips. You don't have CIPHER 3, so my nanobots could not create the hormonal responses you had. So I think they tried to interpret them."

Gareth stared down at his coffee. "After you put the blindfold on me, my CIPHER latched on to yours for sensory input. That was an NF connection between them. It was ... disorienting. Then, I realized I was looking at myself through your eyes. It was exhilarating and confusing. I felt it was me, and it wasn't me. I can't explain it. What it was like to *really* see myself through someone else's eyes. Like I said before, it scared me."

He took a sip of his coffee and shook his head. "Despite everything I've said to you about being used, that you don't care for me, I know it's not true. At that moment, I felt the love and caring you had for me. I'm still overwhelmed when I recall it."

"That's it, Gareth! Exactly what I want. What I want for everyone, that feeling of being known and loved."

"Sam, maybe it's too much; it's like a drug. I keep wanting to go back to that moment and stay there. That's what happens to people with Experiences, right? They never want to leave and end up in Fugue. I worry, can I recapture that feeling? How awful it would be if I can't. I think that's part of why I'm angry with you. You've shown me something beautiful, and I'm afraid it will be gone forever. What then?"

"No, I don't believe it," Sam said, talking faster—with certainty. "Once you have it, it won't go away. You'll always have it! I know. I almost had that feeling with two friends, that kind of sharing and knowing. I still feel it! I want what you have! You're so lucky to have it, can't you see that? CIPHER 2 and *EmpHance* are not enough. We need the interface to the endocrine system that CIPHER 3 provides. If we can get it to Moloi, she can perfect that."

"But how are you going to convince her?" Gareth challenged. "I thought she gave up on CIPHER. How do you even know where she is?"

Sam looked back at her coffee, seemingly lost in contemplation of its darkness. She's stalling, Gareth thought. Like she was trying to decide how much to tell me. Is that my intuition? Or is Sammie trying to tell me something? "There's something else. I know you want to tell me."

"No, nothing," Sam said, returning to her contemplation of the coffee.

A Murmuration
September 2093

Cathy had read the news about Rick's trial on her tablet. It was the topic of nearly all conversations in her cluster's café. Some were sympathetic to Rick's case. Everyone at New Nottingham was an Isolator. It's not surprising that a portion of the population supported action to oppose the expansion of the Moloi Cloud to Mars. Most, though, were unhappy with the attention such an act brought to their cause and to New Nottingham. They didn't like being associated with crazy.

The trial had begun shortly after Cathy and Rick arrived in New Nottingham. As Rick had predicted, justice was swift. He hadn't bothered with a defense. He admitted to once being a member of a Ludd group. That was almost enough to convict him. It was all circumstantial, but on a closed ship there were only so many suspects. If there were any co-conspirators, he didn't give them up. The prosecution increased the charges to terrorism because the satellite could have exploded before launch, potentially killing many people on the transport ship.

Rick was found guilty and sentenced to fifteen years. The Isolators negotiated an agreement for him to serve the time in New Nottingham. He's our problem, they said. We'll take care of him.

Living quarters were transformed to create a makeshift prison. No one had planned on a prison, in this case, for one convict. The scandal faded after the trial ended. Conversations returned to more mundane matters as everyone adapted to life in the habitat.

Cathy was surprised when she got a message from Rick. Could she come to visit? He had something he wanted to tell her. She had promised Rick she would visit, and this was as good a time as any.

Cathy worked her way around the habitat to the "prison". She was still getting used to the fact that New Nottingham was an enormous cylinder. Inside, as she looked at it now, it seemed like a bucolic English countryside. Or how she imagined it would look, as she had never been to England. There were grassy fields interrupted by streams, lakes, trees and clusters of cottages, like her own. You would never guess that you were on an alien planet.

The spinning cylinder generated a centrifugal force. It essentially pushed everything and everyone to the outer wall on which the landscape rested. The spin created Earth's normal gravity and made the habitat more livable for humans. So now I'm walking on the walls, she thought. I hope the thing doesn't stop spinning anytime soon.

She made it into the prison with little fuss. Security was lax, but then where could he go? Rick greeted her as she came in. "Cathy, hi! Thanks a lot for coming. I don't get many visitors." He was still handsome, and the beard looked good on him. But he had lost a lot of weight. Rick sat on his bed, and he motioned her to take the hard metal chair across from him. It was a sparse room, with just the bed, an end table, and a sink. There was a door to another room, probably a toilet.

"Oh, Rick," Cathy sighed. "We all got along well—you, me, and Sam. It still surprised me you would do something like this, not fight the charges, I mean. I never figured you for a Ludd. I still don't believe it. Sam would never have been with you if you held such extreme views. Also, you seemed genuinely surprised by the explosion."

"Yeah, you're right. I was surprised. Of course I'm not a Ludd! Far from it. But I had to stop the investigation."

Cathy frowned. "Are you telling me you didn't do it after all? If you're innocent, why was it so important to stop the investigation?"

"Space law."

Cathy sighed again. "Rick, that is not an answer."

"Right. Well, the captain of the *Bradbury* has a great investigative tool at his disposal." Rick points at his head. "CIPHER 2. It records everything. On Earth, you would need a warrant to access it. The captain doesn't need a warrant. He would dump all our CIPHER logs either to find the culprit or clues to their identity." He shook his head. "I couldn't let that happen. There are things I need to keep hidden."

Cathy arched her eyebrows. "What? I don't understand. What could be so important that you had to keep it secret?"

"Sam and I are working on something. Something we need to keep quiet. We can't risk people finding out."

"Working on what? Why am I just finding out about this now?"

"We didn't want to involve you. But now I have no choice. We would have to tell you, eventually. I guess now is the time. You know we have something in common. Both of us have lost someone we love to the Moloi Fugue. You lost your father. Truly, I understand the pain you must have felt, and I'm sure still feel. We also lost a loved one to the Fugue, and that's when things changed for me."

He paused for a moment, pushing himself to remember a pain he had long hoped had healed. "I wasn't always an Isolator. If anything, I thought CIPHER and the Moloi Field were great. An awesome new playground where you could be as adventurous as you wanted, and you would never get hurt. When CIPHER 2 came out, Ruth and I were early adopters. Ruth was my wife, you see. I know Sam has mentioned her before. We had high-paying jobs; we could afford all the latest toys."

"Ruth," interrupted Cathy. "Yes, Sam mentioned her. She was your wife? I don't understand. I thought that Sam and Ruth were lovers?"

"Yes, well," Rick smiled, "I will get to that. Ruth and I, we had the CIPHER 2 implantation procedure and spent months exploring Experiences people like Gareth created. All kinds of adventures. But that wasn't enough for us; it got boring after a while. I apologize if this offends you, but we knew there was a lot of porn out there, and we began Experiencing it together. Like I said, it was a vast playground. We were kids trying out all the swings and slides and building castles in the sandbox. With the occasional *SexyBeast* MiXe thrown in."

"OK, but what does this have to do with blowing up

satellites?" said Cathy.

"Trust me, I'm getting to that. This is going to make sense, although it's going to get weird first. Ruth was a techie and had found some open-source CIPHER software that allowed us to create our own Experiences. So, we did. Ruth would then upload them to our private server; some, we even uploaded to the dark cloud for others to experience. It was kind of a high for us, as we saw people play the Experiences we created. Think of it! Other people wanting to experience what we did. To be us!"

"We were hooked, and we wanted to push it even further. Ruth had gone to college with Sam, and they had had a relationship back then. That's how I met Sam. They were both much more adventurous than I was. Sam would sometimes join in when Ruth and I made love. Mostly, I think I was just allowed to join them occasionally. Honestly, I think Sam leans more toward women than men."

"Good thing for me," noted Cathy.

Rick smiled. "Yes, I admit to a little jealousy there. Anyway, Sam joined in with us as we created the Experiences, each of us recording. Let's push the envelope more, we thought. Honestly, it was wonderful. But then we had a great and terrible idea. We wanted to create a different and more intense experience with Sam. We couldn't just do what everyone else did; we had to take it further."

He paused and looked at Cathy for a bit. He seemed embarrassed by this revelation, Cathy thought. Maybe he was looking to see if I disapproved. Honestly, I don't care. We all did crazy things when we were young.

He continued. "Have you heard of a MiXe called *EmpHance*? It was originally designed for socially awkward people to enhance empathy and a feeling of connectedness with others. That's what *EmpHance* stands for—Empathy Enhancement. It does this through sounds and scents acting on the endocrine system." Cathy nodded but had a bad feeling about where this might be headed. "Well, it's more than that; it can connect to other CIPHER's running *EmpHance*. They connect to each other using NF. Do you understand what that means?"

"Yes, I know what NF means: Near Field connection. I was with Sam when she had that experience at *Happy Meadows*," replied Cathy.

"That's right. Sam had entered a kind of virtual world. Somewhere that existed in the Moloi cloud. Her awareness interacted with your father, as if that world existed. Even then, it was still a CIPHER 2 Experience. What I am talking about is more immersive, more real.

You see, CIPHER has always been about reliving someone else's Experience. Nonetheless, there's a separation. You know you didn't skydive or spacewalk or cook and eat some wonderful meal. That always belonged to someone else. Now with *EmpHance* and NF, your CIPHER's really connect. What I see and feel, you see and feel, even at the emotional level: happy, sad, aroused. You share all of that as a gestalt, a single person. No one owns it."

"Wait," said Cathy, "that's dangerous, right? These things are in our brains, CIPHER, nanobots whatever. You'll just let anyone connect?"

"No, not just anyone. We're not stupid!" Rick sat back, embarrassed. "Or maybe we were. We knew and trusted each other. We wanted to build on that. Take down all the walls, all the barriers, and let each of us in to the other. We were young and foolish, so, fuck it! We wanted it."

"Sam had a friend who could get *EmpHance* for us, as CRI hadn't approved it yet. We agreed we would each record our experience of having sex while using it. We all ran the MiXe and connected, all firewalls, all barriers down. It was incredible! *EmpHance* really brought everything to a new level. We had cranked it up to 10. We shared everything: everything we felt, being touched and aroused. It was overwhelming, but so joyful. At some point, it felt like we were truly one. Later we had another crazy idea, or maybe Sam did. I don't remember. The lines were becoming a bit blurred thanks to *EmpHance*. Who was who? Who wanted what? I don't know."

"As I said, Ruth was a techie. She used software to blend our three Experiences. It's like having multiple audio and video tracks all playing at once, somehow in harmony. I can't really explain what she did. It took her a few days. When she was done, she uploaded it to our private server. We got into bed together, connected our CIPHER's with *EmpHance* and NF. We started the Experience."

He got a faraway look in his eyes and shivered. "It wasn't at all what I had expected. All of us shared the same feelings and the same sensations. There was a heightened awareness of each other and how we connected. We were three joyous birds flying around each other in ecstasy. We were in sync. Each of us knew and accepted everything about each other: the good and the bad, all our shortcomings. Even the things that are so ugly, we hide them from ourselves. There was no judgment."

"I keep trying to describe it." Rick paused and closed his eyes. "You know what a murmuration is, right? The way starlings fly in a complex formation of twisting and turning. Each bird somehow flies in this complex pattern, each individually, but together making a larger entity. The gestalt I mentioned earlier. Yes, I know three people do not make up a flock, but that's what I think of when I remember it."

Rick smiled. With his eyes still shut, Cathy no longer existed for him. He was reliving the memory for himself, not for an audience.

"We were all moving together. Twisting and turning emotionally and physically in and around each other—in perfect point, counterpoint, and harmony. It wasn't sex anymore. I had lost my sense of self, and I felt like I was part of a greater whole. You know, like the whole being greater than the sum of the parts? We were the parts, and we created something greater, better."

"I lost track of time and could have stayed there forever. I didn't want to leave. That's how some people think of oneness: the loss of the self. It was such an all-encompassing feeling. Suddenly, I felt anxious. It was more than I could handle. What if I truly lost myself? Who would I be? I'm ashamed to say that it scared me. I had to stop. I fell away from the experience and have regretted that ever since."

"It had been hours; I was starving. Sam had come out of it as well. She was sobbing. I realized then that I was crying too. I felt a great sense of loss. Would I ever get that feeling of oneness again?"

"We noticed Ruth hadn't come out of the Experience. We argued: should we try to rouse her? What right did we have? Sam said we should leave her be. Why take that joy away from her? I panicked, or maybe I was jealous. Why should she get to stay in that moment? I shook her and shouted her name, but I couldn't bring her out of it. She was in Fugue."

"We never get her back. She's now housed with other Fugue victims, being fed, bathed, and cared for. This may seem odd to you, but in a way, I'm jealous of Ruth. She gets to stay in that moment of happiness for the rest of her life. The rest of us are stuck with reality. It's like I'm on the outside looking in. Why does she get to be so happy and to be taken care of by the rest of us? So yes, I was jealous. I'm also glad I couldn't rouse her. I'm happy for her."

"I don't understand," said Cathy. "Why didn't you and Sam go into Fugue?"

"It's a good question. Sam and I tried to figure out what had happened. We talked about it and realized that we both felt that fear at the end. Maybe there was a spike of adrenaline? Was that enough to shock us out of it? We came up with a theory. If CIPHER had some control of the endocrine system, then it could modulate the adrenal response. We could stay in the experience for as long as we wanted. When it's time to come out, then shock it with adrenaline at the right time. They've tried it with some Fugue victims, but they died. Somehow, it needs to coordinate with the Experience. That requires CIPHER."

"So," Cathy said, both curious and cautious. "Is this the special project? The one you are trying to keep secret?"

"Exactly! We heard that CIPHER 3 would include an endocrine system interface. The Experience would also influence the hormones, adrenaline, as well as the normal five senses. We believed that a system like that with better control could be the answer. Sam and I are trying to get it."

"In New Nottingham? How? It's not likely it's going to show up at a hotbed community of Isolators!"

Rick nodded. "That's why this is the perfect place. It's on its way now. But there are complications. Based on what Sam learned from your father at *Happy Meadows,* I think that the Phillips Foundation is doing more than just researching the Fugue. I think they are behind it; I think they created it. People could live in that virtual world as uploads. CIPHER 2 would work as a gateway to upload a person's consciousness. They would have their memories and brain patterns, how a person thinks. That's most of what we are. CIPHER 3 would provide that missing piece, the endocrine system supporting our emotions."

"That's incredible!" said Cathy. "Do you really believe that? Phillips created the Fugue? That's not possible! Is it? Are you saying that they are part of some experiment? Why?"

"It's more than an experiment. From what Sam told me, they've become a kind of virtual workforce. I think there's even more to it than that. There must be some kind of connection between them and CIPHER 3. Phillips created the Fugue victims, and she wants CIPHER 3. This has become more complicated and more dangerous than I originally thought."

"Do you think they're behind the destruction of the comms satellite?"

Rick paused for a moment and shook his head. "No, I don't see that it would help them. I didn't blow it up, either. I had to stop any investigation that might expose us, so I confessed. Maybe it was the Ludds, someone on the *Bradbury.* Or just an accident. It happens. I couldn't take the chance that an investigation might also uncover our plans."

I don't know what to make of all this, thought Cathy. Has Rick lost it? This crazy story and now a conspiracy. I keep thinking of what Sam saw at *Happy Meadows*: her father. "Rick, why are you telling me this now? What do you want from me?"

"Sam is on her way here. She is bringing CIPHER 3 with her. Also, we know Phillips wants it too, so she is likely on her way here too. I can't help Sam from this cell. You need to help her. I hate to do this, but there is no choice. Sorry about this, Cathy."

Cathy, alerted Cipher, firewall breach, incoming packet.

"What the hell, Rick! What are you doing?"

Virus detected, cannot quarantine. Storage compromised.

"You should hurry now and get back to your cottage. You will need to get some rest." Rick's eyes lost their focus on Cathy, pupils dilating as if in Fugue. He collapsed onto the bed.

"Rick, don't do this! Guard! Help! We need medical help!"

Cathy felt a little dizzy and weak. After the guard came and called for help, she made her way back to her apartment, assaulted by a rising sense of vertigo. She retraced her way back. Everything about the habitat was still so unfamiliar. She found the path from Rick's cell to the tram station. So, which direction was her cabin? Up-cone or down-cone? Down, that was it.

Focus, Cathy said to herself. Just two stations to C Cluster. The car was almost empty. Thank God for that. One more station. What's happening to me? I feel so tired. There's someone in the car behind me—tall, dark hair. Mary?

Good, my station, she thought. I can get out now. I just need to follow the path to my cottage. Focus, Cathy! Just the next block over. I'm still not used to navigating here, she thought.

Finally, she saw her cottage and pressed her hand on the lock to open the door. She entered, closed the door, and collapsed onto the floor. Cathy wondered what Rick and Sam were trying to do. How is Sam bringing CIPHER 3 with her? Cathy's head was pounding with the worst headache she had ever had. Is this what a Fugue is like? she wondered. But she hadn't connected to an experience. What did Rick do to her? Feeling feverish, she passed out.

Recovery
September 2093

Cathy heard voices. Swirling voices, thoughts and memories surfacing and sinking again, like debris from a shipwreck.

... don't leave, we can work something out...

... should have kept an eye on them...

...doesn't matter, what's done...

.. Burning up ...

... a doctor...

... will join you soon ...

The voices faded. In a moment of awareness, she glimpsed a woman with a washcloth in her hand; she had curly dark hair. She said, "Awake again, I see." The woman rose from the chair and walked over to the sink. She rinsed and wrung out the washcloth and wet it again.

How did she get into the house? Cathy wondered. Where's Sam?

Cathy looked around and saw simple furnishings in a small room: a dining table, a small kitchen where the woman had rinsed the washcloth, and a sofa. Slowly, they took on familiarity, and she recognized her cottage at New Nottingham. She knew then that she was lying in her bed.

Sam's not here yet, she realized. Who is this tall woman? "Who are you? What happened? What do you mean, again?" Cathy asked as the woman applied the cool washcloth to her forehead. How did she get in? Did I invite her in? She looks familiar. Didn't I see her walking Rick off the *Bradbury*?

"My name is Mary. I work in security. We've met a few times on the trip here."

Oh, that's right, Cathy realized—security. She can probably get into anyone's cottage.

"You had a mild fever when we found you passed out here, and you have been drifting in and out of consciousness. You'd wake up long enough for us to feed you; you wouldn't say much, just ask for food and water and go to the bathroom. Then you would drift off again." Mary paused and stared at her, her eyes signifying a question. "Your fever seems to be gone now, so maybe you'll stay with me this time."

"How long?" Cathy managed to ask. Her mouth felt dry; it was hard to talk.

Mary poured a glass of water at the sink and brought it over to Cathy. "Here, can you sit up a bit?" Cathy struggled but could prop herself up with Mary's help. "Drink this." She managed a few sips, her mouth feeling a little less dry.

"Five days," Mary replied. "Five long days, Mitch and I took shifts staying with you. Waiting for this moment; for you to be fully awake. You are awake? Do you know what happened?"

"I, uh," Cathy started, still groggy. *I'm remembering now, but it's hazy. How much should I tell her? I'm not even sure myself what happened, what Rick did. It was all so weird. First, his going on about fucking birds flying around. Second, that thing about Sam—something about a new CIPHER?* "I can't remember," she continued. *That seemed safe.* "Maybe I have a touch of vertigo? I am feeling better."

Mary frowned and challenged her, saying, "You must remember something!"

"I don't know! Last thing I remember ...," Cathy started. *I can't tell her the truth,* she realized. *I need to know more. But how? I need to know who to trust, and Mary is not a good place to start.* "The last thing I remember is saying goodbye to Rick and leaving the cell. That's it! Sorry, I don't even know how I got here."

"I can help with that," Mary said. "I was checking on Rick after I saw you leave his cell. You did not look well, so I followed you. You barely made it to your cabin. But I figured you would be OK. I went back to check on Rick. That's when I discovered he was in Fugue."

"Fugue?" She remembered her father at *Happy Valley*, how he looked. What happened to Rick didn't seem like that.

"Yes, Fugue! Now he's hooked up to IVs and monitors. He can't tell us anything. When I told the chief what happened and that you were the last person to see Rick, she sent me to check on you. You didn't answer when I rang at the door, so I overrode the lock and found you collapsed on the floor. I called Medical. They couldn't find anything wrong with you, just a mild fever. How do you know Rick? Why were you visiting him?"

"We have a mutual friend," Cathy replied.

"Would that be Samantha Brown?"

"How do you know that?" asked Cathy.

"We know that she originally booked passage with you on the *Bradbury*. Just a guess on my part, but it made sense," she said. "Since you visited Rick, we looked for any connections between you. Her name came up. It's our job to know these things. It doesn't matter, though. She's another Isolator like the rest of us; she's not a Ludd. As for Rick, I'm not so sure about him. He has history with them. His behavior after the satellite exploded is suspicious." Mary shrugged. "I can't figure it out."

Cathy tried to follow all of this. I can barely keep my eyes open. Why is she badgering me? "Rick didn't blow up anything, or so he told me. That much I remember." Wait, should I have told Mary that?

"He confessed," Mary countered. "That should be the end of it!" She paused and collected herself. "I'm sorry I pushed, but we had to know. We know the explosion was an accident. There was a defect in the propulsion system—that's the current thinking. Rick is innocent. But why confess? It doesn't add up. There's something going on."

Mary stared at Cathy, looking for some kind of reaction, some kind of response. Finding none, she sighed. "You seem well enough now, but Medical says you should take a few days to recover." She stood up and headed for the cottage door to leave. "Get some rest, and please take a shower. There are algae protein drinks in the fridge. If you need anything else, call security." She left, and Cathy was on her own. Still so tired, she thought and drifted off to sleep.

It was a restless sleep, populated with images of herself and Sam and some other woman she didn't recognize. But it felt like she knew her. It was more than just recognition; there were powerful feelings of love and loss. The name Ruth came to her. Yes, Sam had a picture of her back at the house on Earth. That's who it is.

So odd, she thought on waking up. I've never seen myself in a dream before. It's not like the image I see in a mirror. It's like I'm turned around. But that's what a mirror image is. I'm seeing myself as someone else might see me—my true image. Like in a photograph. And how is it I dreamed of that woman?

She climbed out of bed and went to the kitchen. The images—they're probably left over from Rick's attack. Whatever he had sent to my **CIPHER**. I need to think. She set the coffeemaker to brew a cup. Happily, there was coffee on Mars, of a sort. It wasn't real coffee, just like the milk she added to the cup wasn't real milk. Close enough. Then again, I don't even like milk. She stared at the brown color of the coffee, confused. Why did I add milk? Reflex? As if I were preparing a cup for Sam? For the last three months, I've always only made coffee for myself. Never with milk. She tasted it and remembered why she hated milk. She tossed it and brewed another cup.

Satisfied with the taste, she drank some of the algae

protein drink Mary had left behind. It was not the best flavor combination, but she felt better after she finished it. The coffee isn't helping much, she thought. I still feel so sleepy. She went back to bed and lay down. What did Rick do to me? She fell asleep again.

This time, instead of a dream, she heard a voice. "I'm sorry about this, but I had no choice. You will feel better. By the way, what do you have against milk? Coffee tastes so much better with it." It sounded like Rick.

"Rick, is that you?" Still groggy, Cathy looked around the room. "Where are you? How did you get in?"

"I'm not in the room," came the voice. "I am in your head. Remember, I sent something to your CIPHER just before you left my cell."

"Right, I remember. Then the vertigo and fever started, and I barely made it home. Thanks for that."

"Sorry, I had no choice. It was a small program that cracked the door to your nanobots open just enough to get started. But you'll need to command your CIPHER to allow me more access."

"I don't understand. More access? To what?"

"I'm active on a subconscious level in your thoughts. You're sensing me there, confusing you a bit. I'm why you added milk to your coffee, why you see yourself in your dreams—and the other woman you never met. You were right; she's Ruth."

"I still don't understand how," thought Cathy. "Wait, am I thinking or am I talking? There's no one here with me, is there? I'm sleeping. But I feel like I'm having a conversation."

"You kind of are," said Rick. "I'm a program that's running on your CIPHER, an AI image of the original Rick. Your brain conceives of me as a separate entity. It's easy for you to think that you are talking to me. This works now because you're sleeping."

"You're what?! A program? What are you talking about? What's this about you being in my head?"

"Cathy, please try to focus here. We don't have much time. Simply put, the program I sent to you is an AI simulation of me. You've heard of AI avatars, or maybe not... you only have CIPHER 1, until now, anyway. Trust me, this AI simulation is a kind of avatar, a representation of me. Right now, it can access your subconscious, which allows us to talk while you're asleep. When you are fully awake, that won't be possible. We need to fix that. You need to grant me, the program, full access."

"Access! Why the hell would I want to do that? This is bad enough. Whatever you did to me put me out for five days! Five days! You did all this so that you could run a program, a fucking avatar, on my CIPHER! Now you want to be constantly in my head, all the time? Not just when I'm sleeping. No way would I do that."

"I'm sorry, Cathy, but you need to do it. Gareth's in trouble. That's the last message I got. Look, once you grant me access, you can still control that access. You can shut it down when you want to. Really, we need to do this."

Can't I just have dreams like normal people? thought Cathy. What's this about Gareth? He's in danger somehow? What did he get himself into? He was always acting without thinking. What kind of danger? How did Rick know? A message from whom?

"Cathy, you are becoming more awake. We need to do this now!"

"OK."

OK, grant access to Rick.

Acknowledged.

Cathy's room faded away, replaced by the apartment she and Gareth had shared. She saw the bed he had never made up and the clutter of knick-knacks he had always thought important to save. She thought they were tacky. But they had meant so much to him, so why not let him keep them?

Rick was sitting in the easy chair Gareth had always liked to sit in. Cathy wondered, is this a memory? No, she met Rick long after she and Gareth had split up. Rick must have somehow dredged this up from her memory. Why did she give him access?

"You bastard! Why show me this?"

Rick grimaced and said, "Sorry, I thought this would make you feel more at ease. Sam can tell you I have no sense of such things." The apartment faded away, replaced by the observation lounge on the *Bradbury*. "This is probably still not great, but at least it's neutral ground."

"This is before the explosion," said Cathy. She wandered around the lounge. It seems so real, she thought. She touched a chair at the bar. It seemed substantial, cool to the touch. "Am I still dreaming?" she asked.

"No, you are fully awake. This may be hard for you to understand, but this is what an Experience is like for people who have CIPHER 2. Your brain thinks this is real because CIPHER controls your perceptions; what you see, hear, touch, smell. You talk to me because I seem real to you."

He pointed to the chair. "Sit down and see what it feels like."

She sat on the chair, having to lift herself up onto it. Cathy shifted her weight as she settled in and felt the momentary panic of almost falling off before she was fully seated.

"Well done," Rick said as he offered her a glass of wine. Where did that come from? she wondered. "Here, have a sip. I promise it will taste better than the ship Zinfandel."

She took a sip and realized Rick was right. She tasted the full flavors of raspberry, cherry, and juicy blackberry. Yummy, she thought.

She shook her head. "But this isn't real."

"Doesn't matter." He pointed to his head. "In here, it seems real. The program I sent to you—this avatar—makes this possible. It makes it possible for us to talk and interact here."

"I still don't understand. I'll go along with it anyway. More to the point, why did you do this? What do you want from me?"

"OK, this is the thing." He took a drink of a beer that he had conjured for himself. Do avatars drink? Can they get drunk? "I'm in jail, right? For all intents and purposes, I'm in Fugue. Except I am and I am not. Remember when you were getting up to leave my cell? Your CIPHER reported a firewall breach? Well, that was me. There are small cracks in the CIPHER firewall, which, under certain circumstances, allow for Near Field connections to be made. I inserted a program into your CIPHER nanobot structure."

"You mean a virus, right?" Cathy asked, anger creeping into her voice. We are having a conversation in my head, Cathy thought. I don't really have a voice. How do I convey to Rick how angry I am? "You sent a virus to my CIPHER, which also made me sick. How the fuck did that happen?"

"I had to load a copy of myself into your CIPHER. But I couldn't do that with the CIPHER version you had. You needed an upgrade. You fell sick because the program required a lot of your body's resources to manufacture a new set of nanobots to support this avatar of me. A stripped-down version, but hopefully enough for what's coming. I know you're angry, but I had no choice. You need me, and I need you."

"I don't get it. Upgrade? How is that possible?" Cathy asked as she finished the wine. How do I get another one? She wondered. There's no bartender. I absolutely need something stronger. She looked down at the bar and saw a cocktail sitting there. Excellent service.

"Our nanobots have always had the ability to create more bots in order to replace ones that break down. All they need are the proper instructions. The virus included these instructions. These new bots differ from the ones you had before. They can run avatars like me; they allow us to communicate like this. When there were enough of them, my program unfolded onto your implant. That's where I'm running, where all of this," he gestured around the lounge, "is."

"Yes," Cathy said. "It's like Jagan was talking about. Being able to create a virtual reality from places we've been."

"Yes!" said Rick. "And that's where that drink came from—you're welcome, by the way, I know that's what you like."

"That's creepy, Rick! Just how much do you know about me now?"

Rick frowned. "I'm sorry, Cathy. I know that what I did pushed the limits, was wrong even. But it worked! It's amazing what Doctor Moloi could create. Not just the nanobots, but a whole extensible framework. There is so much potential."

"But why?" Cathy asked. "I hear a lot of how's; you are very short on the whys. You must have planned this for a long time. Even before I met you and Sam at the protest?"

"Please listen, Cathy. Let me explain," Rick pleaded. "Sam and I, we told Moloi about what had happened with us and Ruth; what I told you about back at the cell. She had been bitter about what had happened with CIPHER.

She felt new versions were being rolled out without enough testing. With CIPHER 2 people started going into Fugue. It had been too much for her. She wanted to have nothing more to do with it."

"OK, I'll bite. How did you convince her?" Cathy asked.

"We showed her a new way. A way that could also bring back those lost in Fugue. The key was empathy. Right now, CIPHER keeps us separate, each of us wrapped up in an Experience we're viewing."

"Yes, that's what trapped my father. How is empathy a key?"

"For us, empathy is the key to getting what we, Sam and I, want. The path to that state is the endocrine system. It influences how we feel. It can let us stay in a happy moment or release us back to awareness. That can help the people who are in Fugue."

Cathy finished her virtual drink, confused. She said, "I don't get it. Why do you need me? Can't you just leave me out of this? I want you gone! Out of my head! I should never have given you access. What do I need to do to get rid of you? Do you understand? I want you out! Cipher revoke acc ..."

"Wait!" Rick held up his hand. "I told you Gareth is in danger ..."

"Stop right there," Cathy interrupted. "How do you know Gareth is in danger? You've never even met him."

"Did you hear about the kidnap attempt at Lagrange One?" said Rick. "It happened two weeks before you visited me. The guards talked about it, but you may not have heard. The account left out some details. This was not a Ludd operation; not like when they threatened to kidnap Moloi or Phillips. This time, Gareth was the target, and Isolde Phillips was the perpetrator."

Cathy pressed him, "If that detail wasn't in the news, how do you know this?"

"About that. You will not like this. Sam was with him, and she told me."

"Sam? Gareth and Sam together? I don't understand. How does Sam know Gareth?"

"This plan that Sam and I have—we need the new CIPHER 3 nanobots. They have an endocrine connection. We have to get them to Moloi. When you told Sam about Gareth, we came up with an idea. We engaged his company to create a series of Experiences. One of these would require that he get the CIPHER 3 Beta and travel to Lagrange One. Sam would meet him there and then convince him to come to Mars. We figured that by then he would want to come. They are now on their way."

Sam and Gareth? How could she? Cathy felt so many levels of betrayal coming together in a flush of anger and jealousy. "Just how would she convince him? You mean sex, right? He's such an easygoing guy. He wouldn't need much convincing." She stood up from the chair, pacing around the virtual lounge. She walked back up to Rick. "Of course, that's why you picked him! When I spoke to Alex before I left, he mentioned Gareth had a big new contract. That was you! You waved a lot of money at him! How could he refuse?"

"I know. It took every bit of money we had," Rick admitted. "But we didn't realize what we had started. We also bought off the CIPHER tech, Alex Phillips, to help us prepare Gareth for what we wanted him to do."

Alex too? He's involved in this? I had thought we were all friends. Even after college, we had stuck together. OK, I was angry with him when he got Gareth the job at Multitudes. Even still, I thought that he and Gareth were still good friends. Would he use Gareth like this? Is there anyone I can trust? "You're lying! My Alex, Gareth's friend? He can't be working with you! I don't believe it!"

"Believe it." Rick shifted in his chair, somehow uncomfortable. "Although it turns out that buying Alex's cooperation was a mistake. He must have told his grandmother, Isolde Phillips, about it. We didn't realize they were related. It's such a common name, and why would the grandson of one of the world's richest women be working as a lowly CIPHER tech?"

Cathy glared at Rick. "Really. I don't care," she said. "You and Sam think you can just use people, concocting these elaborate schemes. Sam used me to get to Gareth, and now she's luring him to Mars; you two get what you want. Well, what about me? You've used me, implanted a virus in my head, a version of you wandering around in there. You've endangered Gareth. A kidnapping attempt, really? He could have died! What does Phillips want with him? Why should I help you? Why should we help you?"

She remembered then the times when she and Sam were together, how Sam never really talked about herself. Always listening to Cathy talk about Gareth. Sam somehow got her to talk about him. How they met, how they fell apart. What he liked and what he didn't. Then about his work at *Multitudes*. It occurred to her and hit hard. *I'm not really that different from Gareth. I was so easily manipulated, so quick to trust her. The coffees, dinners, and moving in together. It was all planned. All so that Sam could get to Gareth.*

I can't pin any of this on Gareth. I led Sam right to him; he was what she wanted. Not me. I was just a means to an end.

Now she's with him! Her mind flooded with images of Sam, with her beautiful green eyes flirting with Gareth. Flattering him! The way she did me. God, the lovemaking! I even told her about his fantasies, what he liked. The quiet moments after, too. They belonged to Sam now; she had stolen them. No, I tossed them aside, and she picked them up. They are no longer just mine.

She felt pain in the palms of her hands. Her fingernails had been pressing into them as her rage had been building. The fucking bitch, she thought. I came to Mars to be with her, to build a life free of CIPHER. Of course, she didn't love me! Now she's fucking my ex, all the way from Earth to Mars. Gareth is probably having the time of his life. Why shouldn't he? I left him after all. Cathy stood up and turned away from Rick.

"Cathy, just let me explain..."

"No, I've had enough!" Shut up, you bastard, you pimp! *Cipher, end simulation.*

Rick disappeared, followed by the *Bradbury* lounge. She was once again in her cottage, alone with her rage. Cathy knew she would need to bring Rick back. She and Gareth were trapped, and the only people who could help were the ones who had made the trap: Rick and Sam. But not now. No, not now.

A Choice

September 2093

Cathy tried to sleep. It was fitful at best. She was worried Rick would intrude on her again if she drifted off. I need to rest, she told herself. Sleep had never come easily for her. Her brain was always trying to work something out or just thinking weird shit. Being on a different planet screwed with the usual circadian rhythms, too. It was hours of lying on one side, then the other, staring up at the ceiling. The pillow wasn't right; flip it over—that's better—no, it's not. Get up and go to the bathroom, and then you'll fall asleep.

Then, finally exhausted, the time came when she was most vulnerable. The time when the demons of the early morning would appear. She knew she would be defenseless against them and they would descend on her, attacking her with the countless worries and regrets of her life. She drifted off.

Her father came to her, the first of the demons to descend. He was propped up in his bed at *Happy Meadows*. Eyes staring straight at her now, not dancing around as before. He accused her of abandoning him, judging him. Who was she to judge him? He challenged her. What have you done with your life? She shrank back from him, knowing he was right.

Then she saw a woman hovering over him, attaching probes and monitors. Don't worry about your father, Cathy. I have plans for him and all the others. Soon, they'll all be together, working for me. She suddenly recognized her: Isolde Phillips. 'Izzy won't leave me,' her father said. 'Not the way you did'. He turned away from Cathy, looking at Phillips, with a contented smile on his face.

'You've left us all', a new demon said. It was Gareth. His soft voice rang in her head. No, she wanted to say. I didn't want to, she thought. I wanted to warn you, but I didn't know how. She saw him then, lying naked in bed in their apartment. Sam was lying next to him, her head on his shoulder, hand caressing his chest. 'Even now', he said, 'you abandon me. You could help me, but you won't.' He began stroking Sam's hair, as Cathy used to touch Sam after making love. The memory was still vivid. 'Gareth, don't!' Cathy tried to tell him, she tried to warn him not to trust her.

Sam looked at Cathy. 'This is what you lost,' she said. 'You had him, but now he's mine.' She rolled over and kissed Gareth. Demon Rick appeared next to the bed, wearing a surgical gown and gloves. 'Don't worry, Cathy,' he said. His voice was soothing in her dream. 'We won't hurt him. We just need something he has.' She saw the scalpel in his hand. Sam sat on Gareth's chest and held his arms down. 'Is this a new game?' he asked, grinning. 'I like games.'

Rick made an incision across Gareth's forehead. 'No! Stop!' Cathy yelled.

'It's OK, this won't hurt him,' said Rick. He used a spreader tool to widen the cut, making a large opening. He reached his hand into it and searched around Gareth's head. 'Ah, that's what I'm looking for,' he announced. He pulled his hand out. Cathy saw what he was holding: an infinite number of blank pieces of paper. He fed some to Sam and swallowed the rest himself. An infinity shared between them, leaving Gareth empty.

Sam and Rick merged, no longer individuals. They faded away, abandoning Gareth. His forehead had healed, with no sign of the cut. He looked at Cathy. 'Everything has been taken away from me,' he said. 'I have nothing now. Please, you need to help me.'

"Gareth!" she cried out, the sound waking her up. Fuck me, she thought, as she saw the crimes she had committed against the bedsheets and the pillows, innocent bystanders to the nightmares. She struggled out of bed, gathering the sheets from the floor. She found the pillows and threw them back on the bed. How do I get laundry done around here?

Shaking, she sat back down on the bed. No use trying to sleep now, she thought. She stood up again and went to the bathroom sink. Cathy splashed warm water on her face. Looking in the mirror, she saw that her hair was a mess, pointing in many directions. Cathy ran water over it and dried herself with a towel. I really need a haircut, she thought. Cathy made her way to the kitchen and set up the coffeemaker, and waited for it to brew while debating what to do next.

Cathy could just ignore the whole thing. After all, no one can make her do anything. She could keep Rick's avatar forever quiet. Just go on with life. But then, that dream. Was that from her subconscious? Or was it a fever dream produced by Rick's avatar, its awareness and memories bleeding into mine? Can I live with that, with Rick's presence—forever?

What the hell is he, anyway? An avatar? I've heard of AI-generated avatars used for educational purposes, but this is different. Avatars run as programs on the Moloi Cloud. This is running using the nanobots of my CIPHER. He said the program has a subset of his memories. It certainly has his personality. If the avatar is just a program running on my CIPHER, can I just delete it? Get rid of the Rick in my head?

But I can't abandon Gareth. He needs help. It's not like I can alert the authorities. There's no actual crime. Gareth is coming to Mars of his own free will. No one has kidnapped him. Could I send him a message? Alert him to the danger? Yes, that could work.

What ship would he be on? She was about to ping her CIPHER for a list of incoming transport ships until she remembered New Nottingham does not have a Moloi Field. I'll need to check with Tim, she thought. He'll know or can help me find out. Then I'll send a message. Just what should I say? 'Hey Gareth, it's me, Cathy. Don't trust that lying bitch, Sam Brown. She doesn't want you for your body or your charming wit. She wants you only for your nanobots.' Yeah, that'll work ... or not. I guess I need to give it some more thought.

The coffee maker chirped, letting her know the brew was ready. She poured a cup and continued to ponder the situation. Why does Rick need my help, anyway? Gareth's coming to Mars; that's what he wanted. He said that there had been a kidnapping attempt. Isolde Phillips. Rick's worried about her, afraid of what she might do to Gareth.

She remembered Sam telling her about what had happened at *Happy Meadows* when she had connected with her father in that dream workshop. Was it a dream, though? Is Phillips somehow responsible for putting him into Fugue? She must be involved, and now she wants Gareth. How could such an ordinary person like Gareth be so important?

A reluctant resolve emerged from her deliberations. She had to help Gareth. That meant letting Rick back in. *Cipher, reactivate the Rick avatar, and take us to the Bradbury Observation Lounge.*

She was once again in the *Bradbury* observation lounge. She heard the fusion powered engines, smelled the stale shipboard air. She saw Rick standing at the observation window, looking out at the elevator connecting Deimos to Mars.

"You know," Rick said, still looking out, "I never got to see this view. I was locked up in my cabin before we made it to Phobos. I'm glad that you have this memory and that I can see it now. There's something odd about this simulation of me running on your nanobot structure.

The longer I am separated from my physical self, the more I change—small, subtle differences—but meaningful, perhaps. Your memories and thoughts bleed through to my avatar, changing it. I wonder does that happen to every avatar like mine? I am beginning to dislike that person, the original me."

He turned to Cathy and said, "I understand you have had some bad dreams. I am sorry about that."

"Yes, some bad dreams," she admitted. How much does Rick know? she wondered. I guess I shouldn't be surprised. He has taken up residence, an unwelcome guest wandering through the house that is my mind, opening all the cupboards and drawers and closets. What might Rick find there? The things I've tried to lock up and keep hidden from myself. He can find them and inspect them. Like so much bric-à-brac, he can take them out, examine them, pass judgment, and put them back again. I would never know.

"It doesn't matter," she said, brushing the image aside. "I've realized that I have no other choice. I need your help. Even though you and Sam have interfered with my life and messed with my brain. Despite that, I see no way of getting back on track without helping you. You told me Phillips tried to kidnap Gareth. Why would she do that?"

"She wanted to take him back to Earth."

"Right," said Cathy. "Why back to Earth?"

"I don't know. Maybe the Rick back in the cell knows. If he does, he didn't load that into this avatar of himself. Given that Phillips tried to take Gareth by force, it can't be good. We can't let her get him."

Cathy thought back to the image of Phillips in the nightmare and what Sam had seen at *Happy Meadows*: the virtual Phillips Industries her father was working at while in Fugue. He was working on something for Phillips. Did the nightmare somehow connect her to Gareth? Was Cathy's subconscious trying to tell her that? "OK, I'll accept that for now. But back to you. Why bring Gareth to Mars, to New Nottingham? Couldn't you do what you wanted on Earth?"

"That would be easier, yes. This has to do with the basic architecture of CIPHER, and CRI. They really control CIPHER and the Moloi Cloud on Earth. You see, each CIPHER nanobot is a small computer. They talk to each other in three different ways. You know two of them. The first is Very Near Field, or VNF, which allows all the nanobots in your head to talk to each other. This allows for Experiences; your networked nanobots comprising a computer running programs we call Experiences and Micro Experiences, aka MiXes. The second is Near Field, or NF. It's rare, but CIPHERs can connect to each other.

That's what happened with Sam and your father at *Happy Meadows*. The last one is the Moloi Cloud connection, which allows your nanobots to communicate with a server. On Earth, there is only one server. It's owned by CRI. They have a monopoly, which they protect with extreme prejudice. If anyone tries to create a private Moloi server, it is shut down quickly. The one Ruth and I had didn't last long after the Murmuration."

"OK, I get all of that," said Cathy. "Now why Mars, why New Nottingham of all places?"

Rick looked away from the view, facing Cathy.

"There is someone here who can help us. Nomusa Moloi."

"Fuck, you're shitting me! She's here? Why would she help you?"

"Guilt. She came here with her assistant after the Ludd attacks. Moloi has her own private cloud server for her own research. CRI doesn't suspect anyone would set up one here in the Isolator's habitat. She thinks CIPHER is flawed but can be fixed. We have an arrangement with her assistant. If we get Gareth here, he thinks he can convince her to help."

"Convince her? Is this your plan? She doesn't even know?"

"Of course she'll help! She must! Moloi can enhance

the nanobots, the CIPHER 3 beta Gareth has, by copying them and the nanobot programming. She will create a new nanobot blueprint, a new CIPHER. It will create the connection between people that allows for the Murmuration. Only it will be safer; no one will be left in Fugue. She'll see that it's the right thing to do. I'm sure of it!"

"Yeah, sure. Sounds like you have it figured out. Why do you need me?" said Cathy.

"We need you to find Moloi."

"Wait, you don't even know where she is?"

Rick shrugged. "I was supposed to meet up with her assistant. Of course, that didn't happen since I went right to jail. Sam knows who he is, but I never met him. She was trying to keep things on a need-to-know basis. Sam's read too many spy novels for her own good. All I know is that the lab is somewhere at the base of the cradle."

"OK, we'll take the next tram."

"Sadly, the tram doesn't go there. We will need to find another way. Or, more to the point—you need to find a way."

Cathy sighed. "What choice do I have? I'll see what I can figure out. Once this is done, once you have what you want, Gareth and I are leaving. I never want to see you or Sam again. Got it?"

Rick turned to look out the observation window once more before saying, "Agreed."

The Search

October 2093

Cathy reviewed the public information about New Nottingham on her tablet. There wasn't much: tram locations and schedules, daily events and so on. It wasn't the kind of information she needed. Surprisingly, there was nothing about secret laboratories or corridors.

I need to know more about the habitat and how to move around in it, Cathy thought. There must be passageways not marked on the public map—used for maintenance, and the like. I also need to know whom I can trust. I can't just rely on Rick. Anyway, he only knows what he knew at the time he transferred the avatar over to me. Tim seems as good a place to start as any. He's been here a while and is qualified to guide people around.

Maybe I can convince him that I can help with

something simple. Something that will let me learn more about the habitat and its ins and outs. He's likely still at the café this morning. If I head over now, I can catch up with him. Cathy set down her tablet and headed out of her cottage.

I still need to get a message to Gareth. I've got to warn him about Sam. He needs to know what she's planning. Cathy saw Tim arrive at the café just as she got there.

"Hey Tim," she called.

"Oh, hi Cathy," he replied. "Sorry, I didn't see you there. How are you adjusting? I heard you weren't feeling well. That maybe you had a touch of habitat vertigo?"

"Yes, just a slight attack for me. Mary helped me through it," said Cathy.

"One of my crew is down with that now. He still hasn't adjusted to life here. Some never do."

"What happens to people like that? If they never adjust? Do you send them back to Earth?"

"No," Tim replied, frowning. "We can't afford that. It's too expensive. Sometimes, their family will pay. But most times they're stuck here. There's a program to sensitize people who have this problem. If that doesn't work, we'll find something for them. Essentially, they'll become wards of the habitat. We'll take care of them. I'm still hopeful he'll adjust, though, given some time. After a few weeks, we'll see..."

"I hope it works. By the way, I have a friend who is arriving on the next transport ship. I'd like to send a message to him if I could."

"Sure, I can help with that. What's his name?"

"Gareth Williams."

"Sure, let me check," Tim said, looking at his tablet again. "Yes, he is on the *Percival Lowell*. I'll send you the details, and you can message him."

"Thanks. Maybe I can do you a favor in return. How long did you say your crew member would be out?"

"I don't know. It could be two weeks if the treatment works. For now, I'm shorthanded."

"Well, I'm still waiting for my lab to be set up. Is there anything I can help with? His work, I mean, not the sensitization."

Tim smiled. "Let me get us some coffee, and we can talk about it. You know my team and I work in sanitation. Dirty work, but someone's got to do it. How acute is your sense of smell?"

"So, how was your day?" asked Rick. He had invited Cathy again into the virtual representation of the

Bradbury's observation lounge. The environment was running on her **CIPHER**. She had gotten used to meeting Rick's avatar this way. It made it easier to communicate with him, as opposed to a disembodied voice in the head. It was kind of neutral territory.

They were seated on a bench in the lounge. After several days of working with Tim, Cathy decided it was time to talk with Rick. She had to trust him. If Rick was going to insist on meeting at the Lounge, she thought, he could at least have a virtual bartender on hand. After a day like today, I could use a drink, virtual or not.

"My day? Wonderful, thanks for asking. I'm essentially working in sanitation, thank you very much! I've now learned more about shit than I ever wanted to know. Where does the shit come from? Huge pipes from above. All running around the habitat cradle. Where does the shit go? Processing vats five floors down. What happens to the shit then? Separated into manure for our finely manicured gardens and vital farms. What's left over gets trucked out to a Martian dump." She shook her head. "Why couldn't Tim work at a different job? Like making sausage?"

"You know, I actually don't give a shit," Rick replied, grinning. "I'm glad you've found a job you're passionate about. I've been busy too. The work's not as glamorous as yours, but I've been able to augment the public maps of the cradle with what I've seen from your work trips. There are still gaps, but I think we can figure out from those gaps, and the doorways you've seen, how we can make our way down the cradle and find Moloi."

Cathy wondered again about how much of her brain Rick was taking up. He had seen what she had seen; she didn't understand how that was possible. Were they essentially sharing her CIPHER nanobots? Of course, that's where his program is running. But how much more of her could Rick access? The more she thought about it, the more violated she felt. She had never consented to this. He had forced his way in when he infected her with the damned virus. She sensed her physical body trembling with anger, competing with the sensations of her virtual self in the augmented reality. Here, she seemed calm despite what she felt. It was a strange disconnect between the two. All she could do here was express her anger to Rick in words.

"Will I ever be able to get rid of you? When this is all done, will you leave? Will I know that you've left? You're like a squatter in my home, in my consciousness, which is where I live. You've made room for yourself there. How much of me did you throw out? Have I lost memories? Am I no longer able to speak German? Maybe I could once, and now I can't, and I forgot I knew, because you disposed of all that, like so much rubbish."

"Cathy," Rick said, a gentleness in his voice now, "I'm sorry. Honestly, I don't know. I don't think that anything that makes you who are was disturbed. A friend of ours got the program, the virus, that created this copy of me. It's called the builder virus. He got it from the Ludds..."

"Wait, from the Ludds? You got it from a terrorist group that hates everything about CIPHER? They blew up Moloi's lab, for god's sake! Nothing good can come of them. You and Sam are crazy!"

"You're right... I didn't want it. But Sam thought the program might be useful, and we had a CIPHER tech look at the code. You see, there were so many ways that our plan could go wrong. We needed to have options. We saved it in our CIPHER storage, just in case. I didn't want to use it, but there was no choice. What I did was brutal and unforgivable. I know that."

"It was. Right now, though, I'll focus on helping Gareth. I'll deal with you later."

"About that. The program has a kill switch."

He handed her an envelope. Cathy hadn't noticed it before. He must have conjured it. A single word was written on it: *Auslösung.* Of course, it was a German word. So, she still remembered German. Cathy recalled that the word had several meanings, including release and solution. There were other meanings as well. She tried to remember what they were.

"Whenever you want, you can recall this envelope to you," Rick continued. "Open it. The kill switch code is in there. Run the code and I will be gone."

Rick paused as he set the envelope down, his face relaxing into a calm smile. "We need to begin our search. It's time for you to come down with a mild case of habitat vertigo. You can tell Tim you need some time to rest in your cabin. Your badge access to the maintenance areas should still be good. Hopefully, no one will notice that you're missing for a while. Once they do, they will know that you've gone down below. We won't have much time then."

Rick glanced at the envelope again, then stood up and said, "Ready or not, Moloi, here we come!"

Rick left the lounge, ending the visit. As the observation lounge faded away, she remembered another meaning of *Auslösung*: redemption.

The Breakup
September 2093

Sam and Gareth spent the rest of the trip on the *Lowell* barely speaking to each other. They shared her small suite, slept and ate together. The sense of intimacy was all but gone now. Sam became more distant and less active each day. Sammie continued to be restless, still trying to tell Gareth something.

There were no more dreams, no more memories rising from his subconscious. He wanted to confront Sam. Why pick me? he wanted to ask her. There were so many Experiencers. Was he so obviously gullible that he was an easy choice? Was it Alex? It must have been. Sammie squirmed. What does that mean? Was he right? Was he wrong? Does it not like Alex? Can't blame it. His old friend's betrayal still hurt. He bitterly felt the lack of someone in his life that he could trust.

I don't trust Sam. Her gradual withdraw is mysterious. She's getting what she wants; the reason she spent all this time and energy manipulating me. We're going to Mars, to Doctor Moloi. She should be happy. Does she feel guilty? Some regret? No, not her. She still thinks the end justifies the means. So, why the melancholy mood? It's out of character.

He couldn't find any way to coax her out of it. Each day was filled with routines and rituals that had no meaning. Each day was like the last. He got up and made coffee in the morning. Sam was useless in that regard. How can a grown person not know how to make coffee? Especially one who loves it so much. Then, he would collect his gym bag and head out to the fitness center. He also practiced zero-g navigation to prepare for the transfer to Phobos Station. He would hear her stirring and rolling over again as he left.

As far as he could tell, she never left the suite. When he returned, the bed wasn't made, and the kitchenette was still cluttered from whatever meal she'd had. Gareth would shower, make the bed, and clean up. He would order in dinner, and they would eat in silence.

This went on for sixteen days. The gym workouts became more intense. He became more reckless in the zero-g training, colliding with his partner. He mumbled an apology. His partner shrugged. "You'll get the hang of it," she said. "Well, fuck you!" was his response. Gareth apologized immediately, but he lost a training partner.

I'm losing control. My anger with Sam keeps looking for an outlet. Sammie also projected a growing sense of dread, expecting some impending confrontation. Then, three days out from Mars, Sam no longer got out of bed. It's no use, Gareth thought. This must stop. I need her for what happens next when we get to New Nottingham. He sat on the bed next to her. "Sam, look, you need to get up. We need to talk. Whatever it is, whatever you are trying to keep from me, you need to tell me. We need each other."

Sam rolled over, pushing the sheets aside. Gareth reached out, placing his hand on her shoulder, hope stirring in him. She glared at him and brushed it away. "Need?" Sam hissed. "Just need? That's the best you can come up with. Oh right, you think that I never loved you, never cared for you? Fine! Need, let's settle on that. We need each other. Need for what, exactly?"

Gareth felt the weight of the last few weeks break down the walls that surrounded his feelings. Everything he had kept carefully hidden ever since he was a child. He had reached out again and had been rejected—again. Never let them know how you feel; he should have learned that lesson by now. That's how they hurt you.

How many times have I watched that happen? he wondered. Just watched...and learned. Poor Alex had never learned that lesson, and the bullies had come after him. Like sharks smelling blood in the water. It had always been wrong to bully Alex simply because he'd had the courage, or naivety, to say what he felt. Unlike Gareth, Alex had no filter.

It had always been wrong that Gareth never said what he felt. Anger always frightened him. It meant losing control. It made him a good Experiencer. An Experiencer needs to stay in the moment, keep control of the situation and maximize its value. Losing control could jeopardize that. Over time, it became easier for Gareth to maintain control. It made him feel less like a human being, too.

He could feel Sammie stirring, the viral program running on his CIPHER. It added to his sense of rage. He felt his control weakening, anger entering. "Sam, what the hell!" He grabbed her by the shoulders and shook her. She looked at him in shock and surprise. She began to cry. Who the fuck cares? he wondered. He felt the freedom in the ultimate release of pent-up anger. Anger that had been building from the frustration of the recent weeks. Like potential energy, it builds until it cannot be denied.

"Gareth, please. You're hurting me! Please stop. This isn't like you."

"Maybe it is me, you bitch!" He raised his hand to strike her. She cowered, bringing up her hands, attempting to fend off the blow. He struck her, his hand crashing down through her protection.

He felt the sting in his hand. What am I doing? Gareth thought, shocked at himself. How could I even? He collapsed on the bed next to Sam. "Sorry," he said, the anger dissipating as quickly as it had formed. He looked at his red hand. Sam shrank back when he reached out to touch her with the other hand. "God, I don't know who I am anymore. There's no excuse for what I did. I've never hit anyone before. What have you done to me? You've messed with my head. MiXe'ing me with *EmpHance*, deleting our encounters from my memory. I know you did that. Did you ever think about what you were doing? What you have done to me? Ever since Alex messed with my CIPHER on the spacewalk, I don't even know how I feel." A small smile formed on his face. "I was never good at that to begin with. Now it's worse."

"You bastard!" cried Sam, sobbing on the bed. "You hit me and now you blame me! Take ownership of yourself for once!" She climbed out of bed, found her robe and wrapped it around her naked body, seeking some shelter.

She wiped the tears away with the sleeve of the robe. Somehow, the tension on her face dissipated. She had stopped crying; her face composed itself. "I know I've hurt you," she said. "But there was a reason. Empathy, we wanted to create something that would increase empathy between..." Sam began, trying to explain herself.

"Bullshit," Gareth said, the rage still there, but under control again. In a quiet voice, he continued, "Empathy, what the fuck do you know about empathy? OK, you know what it is, you can define it. You know the dictionary definition. But you, you really don't understand what empathy is, do you? If you did, you would never have done all this to me."

"Gareth, if you had experienced ...," she started again.

"Just stop it! I now remember every time you invaded my consciousness. That time I got my CIPHER 3 implants, you told me about empathy. But how could you do what you did to me and claim you have empathy? You wouldn't have used me the way you have! You and Rick, you wanted this for yourselves, to recreate something you long to have again. This isn't about other people; it's about what *you* want. If you truly had empathy, you wouldn't need this," Gareth said, pointing at his head, "my CIPHER 3 nanobots."

"Rick," Sam said with a puzzled expression, "how do you know about Rick?"

"How do I know? You told me about him during the procedure. You thought I wouldn't remember. And I can feel that part of you, that avatar you sent me—it lights up when it hears the name. You love him, don't you?"

"Sorry, Gareth, but yes. I do," Sam said as she sat on the sofa.

"Good, now we are getting somewhere," he said, sitting next to her. "There's more you need to tell me. How did you pick me?"

Sam slouched back on the sofa. "Cathy," she said.

"What?" Gareth asked. "What do you mean, Cathy? My Cathy? She told you about me? How? Why?"

"I should have told you sooner. You're going to find out anyway when we get to New Nottingham. I've been putting it off. Please try not to be angry with me."

Gareth felt Sammie relax. This is what it's been dreading—when I would find out, he thought. It's odd; why am I not more upset by this latest revelation? It's just one more thing, he realized. How is it I've been able to blunder my way through life like this and still be alive? Maybe Sam lacks empathy, but me? I'm too trusting. I'm not suspicious enough. Paranoia is a survival trait. I need to work on that.

"You were lovers, weren't you?" he ventured, feeling the truth of it. "Somehow you met, I'm guessing at an Isolators' meeting or at a protest? And she would have mentioned me, her ex-husband, who was an Experiencer. Did you love her? Or did you just use her, too?"

"Gareth, I, I don't know. I think so. It's possible to love more than one person, right? I mean, I loved both Rick and Ruth, didn't I?"

Again, Gareth felt Sammie's joyful reaction at the mention of the names. "Maybe you did." Gareth paused, memories of Cathy flooding back, their fights and lovemaking, invaded by images of Sam with Cathy and their lovemaking. Everything I have has been co-opted and corrupted, he thought. There's nothing that's genuinely mine. I exist only in relationship to others. So, who am I, then? Gareth shook his head, overwhelmed.

"Cathy loves you, Gareth. She still does. She, she was afraid. Cathy couldn't bear to lose you to Fugue, so she left. I was just a safe place for her to be."

Gareth nodded, remembering the day she left. How defeated she had looked. What could I have done differently? he wondered. If I had listened to her, not taken the job at *Multitudes,* none of this would have happened. That's always the problem. How do you know which decisions will tear your life apart? Did I have a choice, really? I was being sensible, a realist. I made the best choice. But Cathy didn't see it that way, and now here we are. No, I can't blame her. It was my choice. I created this problem.

"What happens when we get to New Nottingham?" he asked, now accepting his lack of choices. "Are we going to be just one big happy family? You, Rick, Cathy and me? How do you think Cathy will react when she sees me? When she sees me with you?"

"She knows you are coming. I'm sure Rick has told her. He will have told her about us. You can bet she will be as angry about this as you are. Gareth, I know this is a lot. I've been putting this off as long as I could, dreading telling you."

"What choice do I have? You've backed me into a corner. My only other option is to go back to Earth. We already decided that's a non-starter. I have to go to New Nottingham." Cathy had been right all along, he realized. CIPHER is wrong. It's ruined the lives of so many people trapped in Fugue, and the families of those victims. I didn't care about them until now. I just wanted to get rich and retire early. But now I see the reality of it, how what I do affects others. I share the guilt for what's happened to these people, not directly maybe, but still guilty.

For people like Rick and Sam, CIPHER's a toy.

Something to lose themselves in. They think it will make them better people, more than they are. But will it? Will it really make them any better, any different? It's like the myth of the Philosopher's Stone, the stone that would turn base metals into gold. They think that CIPHER 3 and creating this empathy connection will change them, transmute them. They are wrong. CIPHER is no Philosopher's Stone. Of course not. There is no such thing. Base metals remain unchanged, base people, as well. He decided.

"I will go along with you. I will give Doctor Moloi whatever she needs from me. Then, I want her to disable my CIPHER and you will leave me and Cathy alone. I want to live the rest of my life with her, if she will have me."

Off To See The Doctor
October 2093

Cathy had spent a week gathering supplies for the expedition. Her backpack was now loaded with provisions—hydration packs and algae protein bars. This should hold me for five days, she thought: two days out and two days back, with supplies to spare. It is just after midnight, with the fake darkness complete and no fake moon tonight. I've already sent Tim the message requesting time off. So, it's now or never.

"OK, Rick," she said to the unwelcome guest in her head, "I'm heading out."

"Great," replied Rick. "I've got the route ready. Once we get to the first access point and pass through, we shouldn't have any risk of detection."

As Cathy exited her cabin, she looked at the path

leading away from her cluster. She was not looking forward to what she had to do next. Once she diverted from the path, there would no longer be the benefit of lighting. It would be pitch dark. Cathy could handle the route to the access door during daylight, but she could quickly get lost now. She would need to let **CIPHER** guide her.

She took the first step off the path. *Cipher, Cathy sent, engage the visual overlay.* Her visual input was now replaced by a feed that she and Rick had created earlier. This is what an Experience must be like, she thought. Instead of a dark wooded area, she now saw a daylight-illuminated path through the trees. She could smell the floral scent of the banyan trees, breathing much-needed oxygen into the habitat. Cathy took a couple of tentative steps. As odd as it was, her mind and her body managed to synchronize with each other. The visual input updated in real time as she progressed down the path.

It's curious. My **CIPHER** should not be able to do this, Cathy thought. Only **CIPHER** 2 has the required integration with the senses. When Rick suggested this plan, it made little sense. But it's working—somehow. Was the virus that Rick sent to her able to reprogram her nanobots and create new connections, as well as create an avatar of himself? She never got a straightforward answer from Rick. It must have integrated her nanobots with her brain's visual processing, replacing the input from her eyes with the visual input Rick had created. She resolved to come back to this question after they found Moloi.

The path was straight for the next few steps, so she continued until it curved away. This is easy, she thought. I'm getting the hang of it. She confidently followed the path around, then felt her foot catch on something and she fell. The visual overlay tried to catch up, but she couldn't make sense of where she was and what she saw. A sense of vertigo built as her mind fought with her body in strenuous disagreement.

"Cathy, calm down. Take a few breaths," Rick said. "You just tripped. It must be a bit of trash someone left on the trail. Just give yourself some time to reorient yourself. Feel around for the path."

"OK, gimme a minute."

"No problem. When you are ready, feel behind you for the path, then to each side, and finally in front of you. You can use that to recalibrate your visual input."

Cathy felt the ground behind her, searching for the path. But the vertigo came rushing back. "Your mind and your senses are fighting each other," Rick's voice in her head said. "Until you get everything recalibrated, shut down the visual feed."

Cathy shut down the feed, and it was pitch black again. Now that her mind and senses were back in sync, the vertigo dissipated. She felt around as Rick suggested, orienting herself on the trail. Her hand hit upon something in the direction she figured was ahead of her, in the direction she had been heading. It felt rough, kind of like a tree branch. Which was probably exactly what it was. *That's what I stumbled over,* she thought. *I'll need to have a word with trail maintenance when I get back.* She tossed the branch to the side. Confident that she was now pointed in the right direction, Cathy stood up. *Cipher, engage visual overlay.*

Her vision jittered briefly, then settled down. "Good, Cathy," said Rick, "let's not do that again."

"Right, you wanna try this? It's not as easy as it looks, no pun intended." She took a few careful steps, and the visual feed kept up again. She kept her steps small, being careful to keep her weight rooted. *Sam's Tai Chi lessons are finally paying off,* she thought. *Full and empty, being sure the weight is fully on the foot not moving, and no weight on the foot moving to take a step.* Just the way Sam taught her, so long ago. It had only been months, but Sam and Earth seemed a distant memory.

The memories were too complicated to deal with now. She pushed aside the memories of Sam and focused on the path. Without further incident, she reached the door leading to the cradle at this level. "Good job, Cathy!"

"Yep, no thanks to you." She swiped her access card and heard the door open, even though it still appeared to be closed. Of course, thought Cathy, the CIPHER feed is still active. *Cipher, stop Visual Overlay.* The door disappeared as she was once again peering into the darkness. She took a few more steps and heard the door close behind her. Sensing her presence, the automated systems turned on the lights. She saw the hallway ahead of her. Ah, step one done, she thought.

"There's something I still don't understand," Cathy said as she continued down the corridor. "What does Isolde Phillips want with Gareth? Why bring him all the way here?"

"She wants what many people think they want. She wants to live forever."

"But how?"

"Well, who are you talking to? Right now."

"You, of course."

"And who am I?"

"You're the bastard who uploaded himself to my

316

CIPHER!"

"No, I'm just an echo of that person. *That* person is lying in a kind of fugue, back in the cell. I'm a simulation running on your CIPHER. Quite sophisticated, even for an AI avatar. I have some of his memories, just enough to help you. I don't remember where I went to school, my first sweetheart, or what I like to eat. In fact, that guy you were talking to at the café, Tim, there's a hint of a hint of a memory. It seems as though I should know him, but I don't. I remember Ruth and Sam. He gave me that, although I'm not sure that was a kindness."

Cathy stopped to open the next access door, which took her to the next level. She would eventually get to the last door of the enclosing structure. Then she would need to make it to the bottom, where, presumably, Moloi has her lab.

"OK, so Phillips needs more storage to hold all her memories. That just means a big cloud server."

"Yes, that's part of it. She can certainly afford it. I'm sure she wants to build that here, out of CRI's reach. Back on Earth, CRI would just shut it down. Here in New Nottingham, she would have free rein. There is still one missing piece. That is what Gareth is bringing."

"I still don't get it. What piece? What's missing?"

"Feelings, passion, love, hate. I remember Ruth and

317

Sam, but there's no sense of passion, just memories. There should be feelings of regret, fondness, all those things—and hatred. But a simulation doesn't feel. The CIPHER 3 Beta can get her closer to that. Remember what I told you about the Murmuration, how Sam, Ruth and I could share what we were each feeling?"

Cathy came up to another access door. "Why so many doors? This is getting tiresome," Cathy said, frustration creeping into her voice.

"It allows for the habitat to be sealed in case of damage. You know that. Have a little rest when we get through and then have a snack."

After the door closed behind her, Cathy sank to the floor and took out an energy bar. "Yes, I remember your kinky Murmuration. What about it?"

"The CIPHER 3 Beta would make that feasible for everyone, as it interfaces with the body's neuroendocrine system. That's a fancy way of saying that it can stimulate the endorphin and oxytocin responses in the host. That's why we want Gareth here, so we can work with Moloi to help us with that. We can copy his nanobot programming and duplicate it for ourselves."

"I see how that works for you and Sam, but how does that help Phillips live forever? When she dies and uploads to the cloud, there's no longer a body to produce those responses."

"Oh, but there are. There are many bodies at facilities like *Happy Meadows*. Every Fugue victim is a potential host, if she can access it. She needs to access only a portion of them. Then the simulation will have a human host feedback loop. It would be very much like being alive."

Cathy thought back to what had happened to Sam at *Happy Meadows*. She had figured Sam had hallucinated seeing her father during the brief time she was in Fugue. Maybe she really had seen him? Still active in some version of reality, a reality that Isolde Phillips had constructed to create her dream of immortality. Well, that raises the stakes. I not only have to save Gareth, but Dad, as well.

"Why didn't you tell me this before?"

"I don't know."

"What do you mean you don't know?"

"Like I said, I'm just a simulation. I didn't tell you before, because the me that uploaded this echo of me to you wouldn't let me until now. Why he never told you, I don't know. You'll have to ask him if you ever get a chance."

Cathy took a last drink and stuffed everything back into her pack. She stood up. "I'm not thrilled with either of you right now. I have little choice but to keep going. Do you have any idea what we'll do when we find Moloi? Or can't you tell right now?"

"I honestly ..." started Rick.

"Don't say it!"

A Late Message From Mars
October 2093

Gareth sat down on the sofa in the suite. Soon it would be time to leave for Phobos Station; it was time to pack up and prepare for the last part of the journey. Sam had finally returned to the land of the living. They had reached an accommodation, a cease-fire of sorts. The conditioning that Sam and Alex had spent so much time and effort on, to make him attracted to Sam, to trust her, was still there. At least now he was aware of it.

He heard the shower running. Now he had time to look over the message from Cathy. It had arrived days ago, but he had neglected to check his messages. He hadn't expected any. Gareth brought up the message on his tablet, regretting not having looked at it sooner.

Gar, the message began, I know you are traveling with

Sam Brown on the Lowell. How I know that is a long story. Maybe you already know some of it .

Yes, Gareth thought, I do. I'm still having a hard time not being mad at you. Sam used you, too. I understand that, but we had barely split up, and you went right to her. He skipped much of the text—the parts he already knew. Then he came to the bit about Rick.

Maybe Sam has told you about Rick. He and Sam were lovers. They had another partner, Ruth. She fell into Fugue when the three of them experimented with CIPHER NF-sharing. Trying to recreate that experience and somehow rescue Ruth from Fugue are both driving this plan he has. He's working with Sam to get you here, and that part of the plan must be working because you're reading this message on the Lowell.

I can't argue with that.

Things haven't gone so well for Rick here. I don't think Sam knows this. He fell into Fugue after being accused of blowing up a communications satellite. I suspect he could not message her after his arrest. Rick had asked me to visit him in his cell, and then he sent a virus to my CIPHER and loaded a copy of himself into it. He's in my head now and talks to me. I have a hard time not thinking that this could all be a figment of my imagination. But I know it's real.

God damn Rick! Gareth jumped up from the sofa, looking for something to pick up and throw. No, settle down. One broken mug is enough. He collapsed back into the sofa. If only this had come through sooner. Would it have made a difference? Probably not. Sam had already told him everything.

Well, I guess we both have a passenger. I have Sammie, and you have Rick. At least Sammie doesn't talk—not yet, anyway. He felt the anger creeping up on him again. For all their talk about empathy, Sam and Rick keep violating people. First me, now Cathy. She doesn't have the training I've had, the skills to keep reality and Experiences separate. I'm struggling to do that myself, with everything Sam has done to me. But this, what Rick did to you, Cathy! It's wrong! I've got to get to you. None of this would have happened if I had listened to you. I have to fix all of this somehow. He went back to reading the message.

I need to find Doctor Moloi. Rick knows where she is, hiding some place in the cradle that holds New Nottingham. I'm not sure what to think about Rick. I hate that he's always in my head; I hate that I had no choice in that. Over time, Rick seems to have changed. He is not as arrogant as he was at first. He seems genuinely remorseful about all this. I think he might be an ally.

I don't know what will happen when you get here.

They want to copy your nanobots; I know that much. Rick says it won't hurt you. Then what? What about Isolde Phillips? She's going to interfere somehow. When I think of what she's doing to all the people in Fugue, I know we must do something. Sam and Rick care only about themselves. We're just collateral damage. But Phillips— she's dangerous.

I feel overwhelmed by all of this and wish there were someone who could help, but I think it's just us. This is all my fault. I left you and started a chain of events that has brought us to this awful place. I need to go now, Gareth. There is no point in replying; I won't get the message. I love you, Cathy.

The sound from the shower ceased, and he heard Sam rummaging around in the bathroom. Gareth set the tablet down. As she emerged from the bathroom, wearing a light robe, the sexual desire was still there as well. There's no denying that, he thought. Do I tell her about the message? I want to yell at her about what Rick did. But what's the point? It's done.

"Gareth, have you packed yet? We have just four hours to Phobos Station."

"Yes, all packed. Remember, I pack light. If you're done in there, I'll grab a quick shower."

"Sure, help yourself."

He stripped, threw his clothes on the bed and walked into the bathroom, closing the door. He saw himself then in the mirror. It had been so different seeing himself through Sam's eyes, back at Lagrange One—before things went wrong. Things had been wrong for a long time, he reminded himself. He just hadn't known it. Alex's double betrayal stung. First working with Sam, then the kidnapping attempt.

How did I not know he was using me? he wondered. Seems like everyone but Cathy is using me. Especially Sam. That hurt the most. I had felt so connected to her back at the resort, with CIPHER 3 and *EmpHance*. It was powerful and intense. I can see why Sam would want that for herself. My connection, the feel of it, was stronger than it was for her. That's why she wants CIPHER 3. Now I carry a part of her with me, the avatar. It's quieter now, as Sam has revealed everything to me.

He stepped into the shower and turned it on. A brief pulse of water, just enough to lather up. It was a luxury most passengers didn't have. The NF-connection with Sam had been a kind of sharing. But was it sharing, though? I still filtered everything through my sensibilities. He took another burst of water to rinse off, and he stepped out of the shower.

Yep, that's me again, looking in the mirror. The man

in the image looked skinny. He had short brown hair and a small belly, nothing special. *I don't see the attraction, really,* he thought. *Sam did; I felt that. I experienced that with her.*

I keep circling back to that. Is what Rick and Sam want wrong? Others could experience what I did. Would that be bad? He lathered his face and warmed the razor, taking scrapes across his face. *Maybe it is bad, this feeling right now, so morose, almost self-loathing. It's a kind of withdrawal. Without that connection to her, I feel incomplete: not a whole person.* He wrapped the towel around his waist, hiding what he could before emerging from the bathroom.

"That was quick, Gareth. Why the towel? Shy all of a sudden?"

"I, uh, no, of course not. Just not dry yet."

With a concerned look, Sam asked, "Gareth, you are still running *EmpHance* MiXe, aren't you?"

"No, why should I? I stopped after our fight. It's not like we are ever going to get back together."

"Jesus, Gareth! I thought we had talked about this. You can't just stop running it; you'll crash. I've heard of some people killing themselves."

"No, that's crazy. I feel fine. You used that MiXe to control me. I'm not running it anymore."

"Please, we can taper you off, lower the level each day. You have to start it again. I know I have been little help lately, but trust..."

"Trust? That word again!"

"OK, I'm sorry. What I'm telling you is the truth. I know this is my fault. I should have been paying attention to you and not spent all my time sulking in bed. You've come down from a huge high on Lagrange One, and you've had a lot of things thrown at you. I can tell you're depressed. You are usually a more even-keeled, upbeat person, right?"

Maybe it was the message from Cathy, he thought. I don't know what I was thinking, taking on Sam and Isolde Phillips. I'm just a carrier of valuable cargo, nothing more. She's right; I am depressed. I can't afford that now. "OK," he said, "help me get back on track." He sat down on the sofa and ran the *EmpHance* MiXe. He felt his mood correcting itself to a more contented feeling. There was something I should tell Sam about, he thought. Was it in the message? No, maybe later. I don't want to ruin this mood now. It would just upset Sam. I don't want to do that.

###

Sam and Gareth finally arrived in New Nottingham. The trip from the Phobos station was uneventful. Gareth had been running *EmpHance* so much that he barely noticed anything. He still sensed there was something he needed to tell Sam but he could not focus enough to figure out what it was.

They emerged from the arrival elevator to a welcoming committee of enthusiastic Isolators. Gareth took in the view. It was so much like a park. He could see the curve of the horizon.

An enthusiastic young man greeted them. "Welcome to New Nottingham!" he said. "My name is Tim. You all have that 'My God, this looks so strange' look on your faces. Don't worry, you will adjust. We are here to help you find your quarters and get settled in. After being cooped up in a spaceship cabin for three months, I am sure you will appreciate your new living space."

It seemed to Gareth that Tim had made the speech several times before. Everyone was very nice on the way from Phobos to New Nottingham. Tim seemed to be very nice, too. Everyone seemed nice. Some woman in the crowd was waving at him.

He turned to Sam. "Who's that woman, Sam? Waving at us?"

"Where?" said Sam. "I don't see anyone waving."

Gareth looked back, and the woman was gone. "Sorry, she's gone now, anyway."

"Is there a Sam Brown or a Gareth Williams here?" Tim called out.

Sam raised her hand and waved to Tim.

"OK, if you two will come with me, I'll get you settled in."

After they had separated from the group, Sam asked, "Tim, where's Rick? He should be here." *So, they know each other,* Gareth realized. *Just how many people does Sam have working with her? Good thing he seems nice. OK, enough with the 'nice' stuff,* he told himself. *It's the EmpHance talking. Maybe the woman was an EmpHance illusion.*

"How is it you two know each other?" Gareth asked. "Oh, and there's something about Rick..."

"Rick who?" Tim asked.

"Rick Lewis," said Sam. "He was supposed to contact you upon arrival. He's working with us."

"I see. Well, that didn't happen. Rick Lewis? They say he blew up a communications satellite. He's in a prison cell. You really should have told me to expect him. I told you that too much secrecy would hurt us!" Tim said.

"OK, I'm sorry," said Sam, her voice sharp with annoyance. "You were right; I was wrong. Let's move on.

How do I get in to see him?"

"You can't, and it doesn't matter. He's in Fugue."

Gareth had been listening to the back and forth with increasing bemusement. Oh yeah, that's right—Fugue. Rick is in Fugue, he remembered. It was in the message. Why is Sam surprised? Didn't I tell her?

"Sam, didn't I tell you..." Gareth started.

"Tell me what?" Sam said, grabbing him. "Get a grip. It's the *EmpHance*. It's making you loopy. Try to focus."

"I am! It's about Cathy and Rick," Gareth struggled to get the words out. "I got a message from Cathy before, on the *Lowell*. She told me that Rick's in Fugue."

"Dammit, Gareth, why didn't you tell me?"

"Sorry, I haven't been able to think straight. Oh, and she mentioned something about needing to find Moloi."

"Oh, Jesus, Gareth—is there anything else?"

"Um, I don't think so. Why?"

"Tim, take me to Cathy now!"

###

Gareth could tell Sam was unhappy to find Cathy's cottage vacant. Tim did his best to plead his case. "How would I know I was supposed to keep track of her?" he pointed out. "No one told me."

Sam relented. "Tim, it's OK. I realize that now. I made a mistake. Tell me what she's been up to."

Tim regained his composure. "I remember, shortly after arriving, she was locked up in her cottage, with security monitoring her. I heard she was really sick, with a fever. This was just after she met Rick in his cell. He went into Fugue, and she came down with a fever."

"But she was OK, right?" asked Gareth. "She got better? She sent me the message."

"Oh, yes. She was fine after that. In fact, she spent some time working for me."

"Really," Sam said. "What work? Where?"

"My God!" Tim replied. "In the maintenance tunnels, in the cradle. Moloi's down there! I helped her get set up. Did Cathy go off looking for her? But how would she know?"

Sam sat down on the sofa, lost in thought for a moment. Gareth surveyed the cottage. Cathy lived here, he thought. For a bit. He noticed some clothes strewn about on the bed. Once a slob, always a slob. We had that in common, too. *EmpHance* is making it too hard to focus. I have to stop using it. I should just delete *EmpHance*. I need to focus. I can't afford this fog, and can't afford abrupt withdrawal. There is too much at stake. I need to taper it down. Not right now.

"Tim," Sam said finally, "you said that she was in a fever after leaving Rick?"

"Yes, Medical checked on her, and Security kept a watch. I think it lasted a few days."

"He wouldn't do that to Cathy, would he?" Sam asked.

Gareth noticed the concern in Sam's voice. "That was the other thing in the message. He sent a copy of himself to her. Like you did to me," he pointed out. "You two seem to enjoy doing that. Only his version is more sophisticated, right? It talks to her."

"Really Gareth? Was there anything else in that message?"

He shook his head. "No, I'm pretty sure that was it."

"The fever," said Sam, "that was her body spending energy to build up her nanobots to hold the copy. She must have some kind of mix now of CIPHER 1 and 2. I don't know what that means long term."

"Jesus, you two! Long term? You don't know!" said Gareth. "You just can't help yourselves, can you? Is it all worth it? I know you care about Cathy. What damage have you done to us?" Gareth rose from the table and started for Sam.

Tim, alarmed, moved to intercept him. "Hey," he said, putting his hand on Gareth's chest. He was much bigger than Gareth and easily stopped his approach. "Just slow down. I don't know you. But what we're trying to do here, it's important!"

"Fuck you!" said Gareth. He went back to sit down at the table. There's nothing I can do.

Yes, you are helpless, aren't you, young man?

What? Who said that? Gareth looked around the room. It's just me, Tim and Sam.

"What did you say, Sam?"

"What, no. Tim and I are talking. Give me a minute. Just try to relax, OK?"

That was me waving at you earlier. I'm trying to reach you.

Who are you? Do I know you? Cipher, who is talking to me?

Yes, you know me, and you know my son. You can trust me. I'll never lie to you like Sam. I can help you, but I need you to get closer. We'll be able to talk better then. Oh, and Cipher doesn't know about this conversation.

"Sam, there's someone else here. She's talking to me. At least, I think so."

"It's OK, Gareth! It's the *Emphance*; it's making you susceptible to NF. You're probably getting bleed-through from someone's CIPHER. Don't worry about it." Sam turned back to Tim. "Rick," said Sam, "knew where to look for Moloi. He was supposed to find her so that we could bring Gareth to her."

"Fine," said Tim. "It's just that Rick's kind of unavailable."

"Tim, this copy Rick sent to Cathy—it's something she can interact with. It can help her find Moloi. That's why he did it and why had to upgrade her CIPHER."

Gareth startled and returned to the conversation. "That's exactly what Cathy didn't want! She didn't want CIPHER 2, ever!"

"Yes, I know that Gareth! Christ, we lived together!"

"Right, thank you for that reminder! I feel much better now."

"Gareth, I'm sorry. But we don't have time for this. Tim, can you take us into the maintenance passageways? We need to get to the base of the cradle."

"I can do that." He gestured at Gareth. "Is he going to be alright? Do I need to bring someone else along?"

"No, he'll be fine. The fewer people, the better."

"When we get close," Sam said, "we'll connect to her cloud. Let her know we're coming."

Cloud? thought Gareth. Could there be another cloud? Did she come from there?

Cipher, Gareth pinged. Do you detect a Moloi Cloud?

Yes, Gareth. I detect two.

"Sam, my CIPHER says there's another cloud. Shouldn't there be only one?"

"Gareth, do not connect!" Sam jumped up from the sofa. "Yes, there are two. I recognize the ID of one. That's Moloi. It's faint, as she's trying to keep a low profile. The other one has no ID, and it's incredibly strong. Tim, New Nottingham, it doesn't have a cloud, does it?"

"There shouldn't be. That would kind of defeat the point."

"Could it be Phillips?" Gareth asked. "Could she have followed us here?"

Sam nodded but moved on. "Moloi's cloud strength is too low, too much interference. I can't warn her. Tim, we need to get going." Sam headed for the door.

It was all moving too quickly for Gareth. "Wait, what about Cathy? Will she be OK? And are you sure no one else was here? I saw something; I heard someone."

"Gareth, it's just us," said Sam gently. "The *EmpHance* is probably causing some illusions. We need to go now. You've been through a lot, and that's on me. Right now, we need to be on the same page. If Isolde is here, we don't have much time."

"But isn't she after me?" asked Gareth.

"Yes, and the best place for you to be right now is with us and Moloi. We need to get to her as soon as we can.

I've queued up a message to warn her about Phillips. It'll send automatically once we are in range."

Sam walked over to Gareth and touched his shoulder. "Gar, I know you are worried about Cathy. I'm sorry about what Rick did to her. I think, I think we have made a mess of things, Rick and I. I want to fix this. But we need to hurry. The sooner we are within range of Moloi's cloud, the better."

Doctor Moloi I Presume
October 2093

Cathy activated the door to the final sync point. At least Rick said it was the final sync point. It had been a long day. Each point had a slightly reduced spin. If this is the last point, they would be zero spin and Mars normal gravity. She stepped through the door and noticed again a slight change in weight. The door closed behind her.

"Rick, is this it?" she asked.

"Yes, it has to be."

This was not a corridor, like the last sync points. It was much wider, and the curve was less detectable. At the outer edge, there were numbered doors, starting with 1 on her left and ending, she assumed, with 120 on her right. The doors seemed to be evenly spaced.

"OK, any idea which door to try? Do I just keep

opening doors and asking if Doctor Moloi is home?”

“I have nothing better to offer.”

Cathy headed for the first door, number 1. It opened for her as easily as all the other doors so far. Light came on as she entered, revealing a large space with several tables and chairs clustered in the middle.

“Looks like a break room,” said Rick.

“Great, I can use a break.” Cathy headed for a comfortable-looking chair and sat down.

“This is no time to chill out, Cathy. We haven’t got much time, you know.”

“Fuck off, Rick. I need a moment, OK?” She sank into the chair, the material conforming to her body, relieving some of the pressure she had felt building up during her journey here. It had been such a frenetic few weeks, she thought. All starting with the satellite explosion and Rick’s confession. No, that’s not when it started. It started when I fell ill after visiting Rick.

Is this *real*, then? Rick’s voice in my head. Is this all just a fever dream? Is this place any more real than the virtual *Bradbury* lounge? A remnant of that illness? This could all be in my head. Rick’s voice, the search for Moloi. I could still be back in bed, back at the cottage. Maybe this is just one big dream.

“Cathy...”

"Not now, Rick!" She shifted in the chair, no longer comfortable. *How do I confront someone who doesn't exist?* "You aren't even real! Why am I doing all of this? Why the hell would I even think Moloi's here? I'm sick, that's all. I need to go back, get help." She stood up from the chair.

"Cathy, wait! I'm real; this is real! Gareth is in danger! We can't go back."

"We? There's no we! It's just me and my imagination gone wild."

Cathy went to the door, preparing to leave. She heard a faint whining sound. "Is that my imagination, too? Any idea what that is?"

"Sounds like a maintenance cart. I've heard this sound before. It is getting closer. Don't leave the room. We don't want to be discovered now!"

"I do. I want to be found! They can get me out of here and get me some help!"

Cathy stepped outside. The sound continued to get louder. The cart came around the curve, driven by a black woman, her hair streaked with gray.

"Hello!" said the woman as she stepped out of the cart.

She had a pleasant smile, offset by a piercing stare. Cathy recognized her immediately, even though she had aged some. "Doctor Moloi! My God, it's you! You're real, aren't you?"

"Of course, child. Why wouldn't I be?"

"I'm sorry. It's just that lately I've been doubting myself. We came to find you, but I began to doubt him..."

"Doubt who? I see no one. Is he still in the room?"

"No, he's in my head, running on my CIPHER implant. My name is Cathy Mendez. We've come down here to find you. Instead, you found us. How?"

Moloi nodded at the ceiling, indicating a small object on it. "That is a camera. I set it to alert me if anyone came here. Normally, I would hide. But you seemed harmless, so I investigated." She paused, eyes narrowing. "Tell me about your companion."

"Not so much a companion as an uninvited guest. His name is Richard Lewis."

"Richard Lewis! Rick? Uninvited? How? What has he done?" Moloi shook her head. "Tsk, tsk. Such a silly, foolish man! Did he infect you? Did he send you the builder virus? He should know how dangerous that is."

"Yes, Rick mentioned that. What do you know about it—this 'builder virus'?" asked Cathy.

"It was something that I had worked on long ago. It's meant to let CIPHER evolve in a limited way. One could bundle it with a blueprint to create new nanobots and a monitor program to run on them. Here, Rick is the monitor program. It is very dangerous. I stopped working on it, but the Ludds got a copy. He must have gotten it from them. Or maybe ... Izzy? No," she furrowed her brow, "not her. It couldn't have been her."

"What do you mean? Dangerous, how?"

"The resources it takes from the body, everything it needs to create the additional bots, can cause a fever. That could kill a person. Were you ill for a while?"

"Yes, several days, with a high temperature. I thought that this might all be a leftover hallucination." I'm still not sure it isn't. "It is real, isn't it?" she asked again.

"Yes, I don't blame you for doubting. Truly, I am real. You were fortunate. The human mind can't handle two consciousnesses for very long. The doubt you feel is partially a result of that. It grows. The monitor program, Rick, is more than just a program. When you talk to Rick, it seems as if you are talking to a person, correct?"

"Yes, a very annoying person."

"I am sorry, Cathy, but before long, you will begin to lose your sense of self. That is why I abandoned the project. We must delete the monitor program!"

"I am good with that, but he seems so real. It would be like killing a person. Is there a way...? He said that you could transfer him out. Can you do that?"

"Easier said than done, child. We must go to my lab. We can take care of that there. Then, you can delete the program." She shook her head. "I knew they would be trouble, Rick and Samantha, all this nonsense about empathy and bird shit, I mean murmuration. In some ways, they're more dangerous than the Ludds."

"She was always a bit prickly, gotten worse in her old age," said Rick.

"Shut up!"

"He's talking to you now, is he? Tell me, why are you here?"

"It's a long story," said Cathy.

"Tell her Isolde Phillips tried to kidnap your ex-husband and that he has the CIPHER 3 beta."

"Look, I've come a long way to find you. If all this is real, then I have to assume that what Rick has been telling me is true. That is, a good friend of mine is in danger."

Why do you keep calling Gareth your friend, Rick said. You are married. Still married.

"Damn it, okay! My husband, we are separated. His name is Gareth, and he's on his way here. I think Isolde Phillips is too. She'd tried to kidnap him not long ago. I think she will try again, try to get him, somehow. Whatever she wants, it can't be good. Can we go somewhere I can sit and we can talk?"

"Isolde? Izzy?" asked Doctor Moloi. "Coming here? Why would she come to Mars? What does your friend have to do with it? Why would that voice in your head, Richard, care?"

"He has the CIPHER 3 Beta."

"Oh, crap. Yes, let's talk."

###

Moloi's cart had space for a passenger. They rode along the corridor until they came to an unmarked door. The outline was barely visible, but it was there between doors 70 and 71.

"How is it you've managed to hide here? And why?" asked Cathy.

"The Ludds, the damned Ludds. They blamed me for CIPHER. They blew up my lab, you know. No one was hurt, but someday, if I stayed on Earth, they would get me. I had no genuine connections there—a few friends, but no family. So, I left Earth."

As they got off the cart, "I knew the gentleman who designed and built the cradle for this habitat. Izzy had provided the funding. I still don't understand why she did that. Maybe she was trying to atone for CIPHER. I doubt it, though; she never regretted anything. My friend built this lab for me; he owed me a favor. I had never intended to collect on it, but I had to leave Earth. It was not just the Ludds. There were so many things that had gone wrong. So many ways I could see Isolde working to pervert CIPHER, and all those Fugue victims. I still don't understand that. The Fugue makes no sense. I sometimes wonder if the Ludds are behind it."

She opened the barely visible door, and they stepped in. "I needed to be alone, away from CRI and all that. New Nottingham seemed to be the perfect place to hide, to be safe from the Ludds. Now, though, everyone seems to be coming here. Maybe Izzy found out I was here. That could be it. She needs something from me. Something I have."

The door closed behind them, and Cathy looked around the room. It seemed to be a kind of antechamber, as there was a door at the other end of the room. The space was pleasantly lit with a pair of comfortable chairs and a kind of kitchen with a table and chairs. There was an Experiencer chair in one corner of the room. A refrigerator and cooking area with a sink were at one end.

"Please sit down. I will make us some tea." Moloi put a kettle on and searched for tea, debating which kind. "Lapsang souchong, OK with you?" Cathy nodded, and Moloi filled a tea ball, setting it in the teapot. They sat silently, waiting for the tea.

"Thank you, Doctor Moloi," replied Cathy as she sank back into the chair. God, it feels good to sit down finally, she thought. She felt her muscles finally relax. Her head still hurt from using CIPHER to navigate the path in the dark.

"Child, you look exhausted. The builder virus can take a toll. Please call me Nomie. I do not care to be called Doctor anymore. Be careful, the cup is hot," she said as she handed Cathy a cup of the freshly brewed tea.

"Now tell me about your husband."

"His name is Gareth, Gareth Williams. He's about my age. He took a job as an Experiencer. The job paid for his CIPHER 2 implants so he could record Experiences. That's when I left him."

"I don't understand. Why? There are many young men and women who have taken up such employment. People need to take the jobs that are available and for which they are suited."

"Because my father is a Fugue victim. Gareth's work made me think of all those who had succumbed. I couldn't bear staying with him."

"Ahh, Cathy Mendez. The last name seemed familiar. Your father was Walter Mendez, yes? I remember the story. It was all over the newsfeeds. You can't blame your husband for that. The Fugue is, well, something I never anticipated. It really shouldn't happen and continues to puzzle me."

"Does it matter? Whatever the cause, I was afraid it would happen to him. So, I left. Now, maybe because I wasn't with him, something much worse may happen. Please, Rick has made some vague conjectures about what Phillips wants, but he isn't clear, and I don't know what it might mean for Gareth."

"Ah, yes. You told me he carries the CIPHER 3 beta nanobots. I counseled against it, but CRI wouldn't listen. It's too integrated with the host's endocrine and nervous systems. There is too much that could go wrong. Just like the builder virus, it is too much for the human mind to handle. But some fools like Rick and Phillips think it's the Holy Grail for whatever they feel is missing in their lives."

"Hey, I resent that," said Rick.

"She can't hear you, you know...," replied Cathy.

"Nomie, I need your help with something. Rick keeps talking to me, and it's becoming tiresome. Can you help me get rid of him?"

"I told you how to do that, just say the word," said Rick.

"Yes, I know. It's just that you have helped me. Everything is moving so fast! I'd be alone again."

"Don't worry, you have Moloi now. You are in good hands."

"Please," said Cathy. "Rick has been helpful; can we somehow move him out of my head? In case we need him later?"

"Move, no; copy, yes. I can copy the simulation to my private cloud. There is a lot of space. After that, we will need to delete him. Did he tell you how to do that?"

"Yes, please—the sooner, the better."

Trial Separation
October 2093

Cathy listened as Nomie explained the process for moving Rick to her cloud server. "I have a private Moloi Cloud server. I hate that it's called that, by the way. Let's just call it cloud from now on, OK? Anyway, I need to grant you access, then we can proceed." Nomie produced a small device. "This device identifies your CIPHER and passes that information to my cloud."

Hello Cathy, you have been granted access, Cathy's CIPHER relayed the message from the cloud.

"Good, you have connected. You may now instruct your CIPHER to begin the upload process."

Did you hear that, Rick? It's time for you to go. Cipher begin the upload process.

It's been great Cathy, hope you won't miss me too

much.

Upload complete, Cathy's cipher sent.

Nomie seemed distracted. "Cathy, don't delete Rick just yet. There is something odd about your nanobot structure. I think the builder virus did more than just create new CIPHER 1 nanobots. It created CIPHER 2 nanobots. Are you aware of anything different?"

"Yes," replied Cathy. "I could replay a visual of the path from the cottage to the first access point. I thought that was odd at the time. When Rick copied himself to me, I was feverish and slept a lot. He said that a lot of new nanobots had been created to hold his avatar."

Nomie did not reply for a moment, lost in thought, then she said, "I have interrogated the copy of Rick in my cloud. It claims not to know how your nanobots were modified. I suspect the builder virus reconfigured the nanobot connections to your senses. What you described—the replay of a visual—should only have been possible with CIPHER 2. This is very disturbing. But then, as I think about it, he had CIPHER 2. Yes, that's it. The blueprint for your new nanobots was CIPHER 2, so you now have a mix. They are not additive, so you don't have one plus two, giving you CIPHER 3. More like an average, like CIPHER 1.7 or something."

"That's wonderful news," Cathy noted, with a tinge of

anger in her voice. "How did I get mixed up in all of this? I'm just getting dragged along by forces I have no control over. I came here to get away from all this CIPHER bullshit, joined the Isolators, and moved to Mars. And now I find out that my brain has been messed with. Damn Gareth, damn Rick, and damn you! You and your mice started all this!"

"Get in line, dear. The Ludds are ahead of you on that account," said Nomie. "I am sorry. You have been running away from many things, from many people. You let all the other forces push you onto a path; a path you never chose for yourself. I am guilty of that as well. I let the Ludds push me away from Earth and hide here. Even so, my legacy follows me. There is no escape, no running away. However, you have more control than you realize. We both of us need to exercise that control."

"How?"

"Rick told you that Isolde tried to kidnap your husband, Gareth. She had wanted to take him to Earth, but that failed. So, she will likely come here. Maybe she thinks that is for the better. She could use me and my cloud to get what she wants. I don't know how she intends to accomplish this; there are many cloud attack programs. She is a confident, strong-willed person. I know her. She will have a plan. We have an advantage, though. We know she is coming and can develop counter measures while there is time."

"I still don't understand. What does she want?"

"That is a bit of a story. There is a reason I am here on Mars and Izzy is spending her life on the *Mangala*," Nomie said. "I think it also explains why she is after your young man. Izzy is dying, or so she told me some years ago. She has tried and failed in the past to upload her consciousness into the cloud." Nomie shuddered. "I was with her when she tried. It nearly went horribly wrong; you see, the upload program was infected with a Ludd virus. After that happened, Izzy's paranoia grew. She no longer felt safe on Earth. In fact, neither did I. All of it made us quite worried. Izzy essentially moved onto the space yacht she had just bought. She would keep working on the code. She wanted me to go along. I declined. As a parting gift, she helped me set up all this, as she was the main funder of New Nottingham."

"She knows you are here then," said Cathy. "Is that why she's coming? Not just because Gareth is here?"

"Yes, I think so. I believe she wants to finish what she attempted before—to upload herself to the cloud. After the Ludd attacks, that's the only place she can truly control and feel safe. Gareth's CIPHER 3 is part of that. As I had told Izzy, the upload cannot fully replicate a person. There is no endocrine system; more simply put, there are no emotions. CIPHER 3 helps with that, but you would still need a human host. I have a notion of what she's planning, and it is not a happy notion. If she is dying, she will stop at nothing."

"Should we contact New Nottingham? Get their help?"

"Help with what? The only crime I know of is the one I am committing by being here and consuming habitat resources without permission. Wait a minute..."

Nomie paused with the telltale look of someone communicating with their Cipher. "It seems we need to move more quickly now. I have just received a message. It's a good thing you didn't delete Rick. You will need him. Izzy is here."

The Battle for New Nottingham
October 2093

"Here?" asked Cathy. "What do you mean, she's here? Where?"

"Not physically here, child. Don't be so literal. She has landed her yacht somewhere near here, near New Nottingham. I have just now received a warning from Sam. She detected a powerful Moloi cloud nearby. I think Izzy intends to crash her way into mine. We must protect it. You, Rick's avatar, and I must work together to hold her off until Sam gets here with Gareth."

"Gareth, he's on his way?"

"Yes, and he will either save us or destroy us. Not literally, but if Phillips gets her way, she will take over my cloud and add it to her own. She intends to upload herself to the combined cloud. Gareth is the pathway."

"Why Gareth?"

"He has the CIPHER 3 Beta implant. Their interface with the endocrine system would make a digital upload of a human consciousness more complete, more human," said Nomie. She frowned and added, "There is still a missing piece. I'm afraid that I know what it is. I didn't think that even Izzy would do such a thing. All those people..."

"Well, shut down your cloud, then!" Cathy countered.

Nomie sighed and said, "Don't you think I have tried, child! It won't let me. Izzy set this lab up for me, and she must have put in a failsafe to prevent that. I was too trusting. She always has a reason for what she does. It should have been obvious she had plans for it. She was such a good friend, but the Ludd attack changed her. I still have control over all other aspects of the cloud. I just can't shut it down."

"She still needs Gareth, though," said Cathy. "We can still stop Phillips, right? All we need to do is keep him away from her."

"That may not be enough. You say that she tried to kidnap him?"

"Yes, I don't have the details. All that I know is she tried to get him on her ship near LaGrange One by manipulating his implants."

"She will have learned from that failure. There is another way…," said Nomie. She paused and remained silent for a few minutes. "I apologize. I was consulting with my **CIPHER**. She does not need to get to him physically. She can use the strength of her cloud signal to connect directly to his **CIPHER**. If she can do that, she can copy their current programming and duplicate them. I have detected her cloud, even now, reaching out—searching for Gareth. Trying to connect."

"We can warn him, can't we?"

"No, we can't," said Nomie, frowning. "I can't reach him or Sam. I'm being blocked. Izzy's cloud is interfering, blocking communication. I can tell that Izzy is trying to connect to him directly. There are data packets going to him, trying to punch holes in his **CIPHER** firewall. I can't stop the attacks unless he gets closer. I hope he can hold out."

"If he can't? What then?"

Nomie sighed and said, "Then she can get what she wants. Don't worry, Gareth won't be hurt. Still, I'm afraid of what may happen to others."

"Is there nothing we can do?"

Smiling, she replied, "Yes, there is. We can defend Gareth. I'll need your help, and Rick's too. You will need to connect to my cloud. You and Rick will work to keep

Izzy from taking it over. Have you heard of the Cipher game, '*You shape it, you own it*'?"

"I'm an Isolator, Nomie. Until now, I only had CIPHER 1. I've never run an Experience, let alone a game."

"Of course, I had forgotten," Nomie said, apologizing. "It's a silly game, but my old friend Jagan Bhatnagar..."

"Wait, Jagan? I met him on the way to Mars. He's a Cloud Researcher."

"Indeed, he is one of the best. On Mars, you say? Maybe I can ... Sorry, later. The point is, he postulated that this game could be used as a Trojan Horse attack to gain control of the cloud. I need you to play the game to keep control of my cloud and protect it from Izzy. You and Rick will create a virtual world, one that you must maintain." Nomie pointed to a chair in a corner of the lab. Cathy recognized it: an Experiencer chair. "Please take a seat. The chair will tend to your body's muscles, keeping you comfortable when you connect to the cloud. I am ciphering you the passkey to my private cloud. Please connect."

What choice do I have? Cathy thought. Me, an Isolator, connecting to a Moloi field. She sat in the chair and felt how it molded itself to her body, adapting so that no part of her body would be stressed. I should have bought one of these for myself, CIPHER or no CIPHER. Well, no time to waste. Cathy connected. She found herself in the observation lounge of the *Bradbury*. She saw Rick smiling at her. "Hello stranger, long time no see."

"You keep turning up like a bad penny," Cathy countered.

"You know what they say: in for a penny, in for a pound. Shall we stop with the archaic sayings?"

"Any time. Now what? Just how do we stop this attack on Moloi's cloud?"

"Just be yourself. You are a strong person, Cathy. Nomie's field feeds off that strength. You and I, this echo of me, anyway, need to maintain our version of reality. This is how we keep control of the cloud."

"Right, I don't get it. How does that help?"

"It is how Nomie defined her security program," Rick explained. "The program blocks various attacks that Phillips launches at Nomie's cloud. Attacks similar to the way Rick attacked your CIPHER and uploaded this version of me. It finds holes in the firewall and exploits them to infiltrate and take over. The *Bradbury* lounge represents Nomie's cloud. My program and your memories overlay that, and the attacks manifest themselves as changes to the reality we project here. We detect the changes and revert them back, blocking the attack. As long as we maintain our reality, we have control. This is what Jagan was describing to us on the *Lowell*. We need to hold her off until Gareth can connect in. If she subsumes this cloud, then she'll be too strong for Gareth to resist. She'll pull him into her reality, and she can copy his CIPHER 3. We cannot let that happen."

"All right," said Cathy, "I get the concept. At least, I think I do." She noticed the door to the observation lounge; there was something different about it. A doorknob. This is a spaceship; there are no doorknobs in space. In fact, she hadn't seen one of those in a long time.

"You see it, don't you, Cathy?" asked Rick. "The door looks different. Try to remember what it looked like before."

"I'm trying. Why couldn't we pick something I'm more familiar with, like my apartment? I could hold that image better."

"Sadly, I've never been there. It needs to be a reality that we've both shared. This is the best I've been able to come up with."

The doorknob disappeared, and the door looked as it did before, as she remembered it. "Good," said Rick. "Let's try to keep that closed for now." The Experiencer chairs, the bar, everything was as she remembered.

Cathy turned back to the observation window. The last

image she and Rick had shared was the satellite launch. She saw it now: the small object that the *Bradbury* had ejected. It still looks like a satellite, so that's good. Hurry, Gareth, she thought, this reality is too big, and there's just me.

###

Gareth watched as Tim unlocked the access door. "There should be only one more after this," Tim said. It seemed to take forever to get to Moloi's lab, Gareth thought. How far can it be? How many levels are there? Sammie was getting more agitated with each level they passed through, as if it were under attack. Maybe it was.

"Sam, how much longer? I feel, I feel like we're moving so slowly, like we're not getting anywhere." His speech sounded slow to him, slurred. It would be better if I could connect to the Moloi field. I'm not used to this silence.

It's OK, Gareth. You are almost there.

You're Phillips, aren't you? thought Gareth. Isolde Phillips.

Yes, I am. I'm trying to connect, but you are somehow blocking me. A security program? I wasn't aware ... maybe Sam Brown sent you something... Yes. I see. No matter,

359

I'll break through soon.

Why, why are you doing this?

Simple, I want to live.

Sam grabbed him by the shoulders and looked into his eyes. Her frown deepened. "Gar, are you all right?"

"Um, yes. I, I think Phillips is trying to connect to my CIPHER. She keeps talking to me."

"Since when?"

"Since back at Cathy's cottage. Remember I said I heard someone else? You told me I was imagining it? Can you let go of me now?"

Sam released him. "Sorry, Gareth. I should have listened to you. Are you sure it's Phillips?"

"Yes. I don't know how, but I'm sure of it."

"Damn, she's trying to hack her way in." Sam frowned. "You can't let her. But she's Isolde Phillips; this should be child's play for her."

"I know, she says that I have some kind of security program that's stopping her. It's Sammie, isn't it?"

"Sammie?"

"Yes, it's what I call the program you sent me back at Lagrange One. I think it's the security program. Nothing else makes sense."

"What the hell are you two talking about?" asked Tim.

"It's an avatar version of me, Tim," said Sam. "Give

me a minute; let me think." She leaned back against the wall. "Yes, I think we can use this. Can you trust me one more time? Remember, earlier when we connected our ciphers, we let each other in?"

"What are you doing, Sam?" asked Tim. "You sent an AI avatar to him, like Rick did to Cathy? Do you have any idea how dangerous that is? Did you tell him?"

"Yes, Tim, and no. Now shut up. We don't have time for that. Gareth, you need to let me in again. I can strengthen it, better able to deflect Phillip's attacks."

"Do I have a choice? Sure, come on in."

Cipher, allow a direct connection from Sam Brown.

He felt her rushing back in. He sensed her rediscovering the part of her she had left behind—back at Lagrange One.

Wow, I'm surprised you held on to this program for so long, Sam sent. Somehow, you created space for it in your nanostructure. That's incredible. It's like what Rick and I have been wanting to create. Does it, does she, talk to you?

No, it's more like a feeling. It's almost another kind of intuition. But she seems to get stronger. I think that's OK. Should I worry?

Gareth, I really think this could help. I think we can defend against Phillips if we let Sammie help you control your CIPHER 3 endocrine level and calibrate EmpHance levels. I'm sending another packet. It will increase Sammie's sentience level. Make her smarter. Don't be surprised if she starts talking to you.

Sure, why not? What's one more voice in my head, more or less. Maybe Sammie and Isolde can have a pleasant conversation.

That's kind of what I'm hoping.

Gareth felt his mood stabilize, Sammie using his CIPHER 3 nanobots to control his hormone levels. Getting back to his usual self.

"Alright," said Gareth. "Sam, I'm feeling better. Tim, let's get going."

Better Late Than Never
October 2093

"Is this it?" Gareth said. "I see a bunch of numbered doors. Tim, do you know which one?" Sam seems comfortable letting me take the lead, he thought.

"It's the door between," Tim replied.

"Between what?"

"70 and 71, of course. This way, it's shorter."

Tim turned to the right. Sam and Gareth followed.

A few minutes later, Sam stopped and said, "I think I'm close enough to connect to Moloi's field. I'm sending the passkey now. I want to let her know we are on the way."

Sam didn't move for a few minutes, evidently communicating with Moloi, with a blank expression on her face. This transformed into a sense of concern and then panic. "Phillips has attacked Moloi's cloud," said Sam finally. "Cathy and Rick are defending it, but they can't hold it much longer. We can't wait until we get to Moloi's lab. Tim, can we get into one of these rooms?"

"Cathy," asked Gareth. "She's with Moloi. She made it?"

Sam ignored him, waiting for guidance from Tim.

"Sure," he pointed at room 95. "None of these are in use now." He opened the door, and they followed him in. The light came on and illuminated a large storage space with some chairs. They were Experiencer chairs.

"Great, this will work. Let's get these two chairs and set them next to each other. Gareth, sit next to me. Tim, continue on to Moloi, see if there's anything you can do to help."

"OK, what are you two going to do?" asked Tim.

"We will try to buy some time for Moloi. I hope there's something she can do. Now hurry! Gareth, make yourself comfortable. This could take a while. I'm sending you the passkey. Go ahead and connect to Moloi's cloud."

Gareth sat in the chair and ordered his CIPHER to connect.

"OK, I'm in. Now what?"

"We need to NF connect to each other like we did that day on Lagrange One. The connection will strengthen us, our **CIPHER**'s combining. After we connect to the cloud, find a place both you and Cathy know, then invite her."

"Why?" asked Gareth. "What good would that do?"

"Phillip's attack is a kind of hijack. Imposing her cloud, her reality, over Moloi's cloud—or reality—remember when we played *You shape, you own it?* It's like that game. It's a surrogate for the actual battle taking place."

"That game didn't go so well, as I recall," said Gareth.

"Well, hopefully this time you'll focus better. Besides, you have not only me, but Sammie and Cathy. Especially Cathy. You and Cathy have a strong connection. Yes, I know she left you. You're angry, blah, blah, blah. She should never have left, and you should have been a better listener. There's plenty of blame to share between you."

"I know that!" said Gareth.

"Despite everything that's happened since, that connection is still there. I could sense it back at Lagrange One. The two of you and your memories, all of that will strengthen Moloi's cloud. Please, Gareth, you need to hurry!"

She's right, Gareth realized. I didn't listen to Cathy. I knew she was trying to tell me something. Something that was painful for her. But like a child, I wanted my toy:

CIPHER. That's all I cared about. Now, I want to throw it away, into the garbage bin with the rest of the things that I had so desperately wanted but no longer have a use for. Cathy is what I should have held on to. I can sense her in the cloud now. This is not the way I wanted to see her again.

Sam says I need to pick a place, somewhere where we were happiest. Where could that be? No place is perfectly happy. Everywhere has a mix of good and bad memories. The apartment in Kalamazoo that we shared in graduate school, maybe? We were so young then, and our futures had just collapsed before we had even got started. Too many bad memories, not enough good ones. It must be DC. A lot of bad memories there, too. We were older back then; we understood each other better. If only I had listened...Stop that! He told himself. Like Sam said, there's plenty of blame to go around, plenty to share. DC it is, then.

"Gareth, pick a place! We don't have a lot of time here."

"OK! I've decided. It's the apartment in DC, then." He smiled. "I hope she's glad I saved all those knick-knacks."

The storage room faded away, replaced by Gareth's apartment. This is not an Experience, Gareth knew. It's a virtual reality I've created from my memories, helped by CIPHER. It feels real; the furniture is solid. That's what CIPHER can do; it can make the unreal real. Will it feel the same to Cathy? She has only CIPHER 1. But when I sensed her in the cloud, it seemed different, more somehow. That's right, the builder virus Rick infected her with—no longer just CIPHER 1. Maybe this will work.

He was standing in the living room. He saw the sofa, coffee table and easy chairs. Was it always so small? It had been perfect for him and Cathy. The open floor plan with the small kitchen. The door to the bedroom closed.

Not bad, sent Sam. Seems better than Cathy had described. It looks like you cleaned for company. You have a lot of knick-knacks. How many airport shops did you visit? That's a lot of things to keep track of. It is what it is, I guess. Remember, this is an analog for Moloi's cloud. As long as you can hold it together, the cloud is under your control, not Phillip's. Now invite Cathy.

Where are you, Sam?

I can't join you, not yet. There's too much tension among the three of us. I'm not ready to face Cathy. We need this image, this place, to be as real as you and Cathy can make it. I'm still connected to you via NF. Our CIPHER's are synchronized. I'll help anyway I can, but I need to stay in the background. Remember, Sammie is with you, too. Now, invite Cathy.

Gareth sent out to Cathy, Hi Cathy. It's me, Gareth. Of course, you know that. Look, I've created another space for us. We should be able to hold it better, the two of us. Come join me at our apartment.

Cathy appeared in the living room, across from him, in front of the sofa. "Hello, Cathy," he said.

Cathy replied, smiling. "It's so good to see you. I missed you so much more than I thought I would. I wish I had never left. This is all my fault."

She looks worn down, even this virtual image of her. She's been through a lot; I can feel that. He wanted to go to her, hug her, and kiss her. Tell her how sorry he was. Where do I start? How about the truth? "No, it isn't, not really. You tried to tell me. I think I understand now why you couldn't. If I had just given you more time. If I hadn't pushed so hard."

"Maybe, but I left you. Then Sam swept in. We were ripe for the picking, weren't we?" Cathy wandered over to the shelves hanging off the wall. She sighed and picked up the hippo figurine. "This was always my favorite, although a hyena figurine would have been nice." She set it back down.

"I know," said Gareth. "But there's always the feeling that they have no soul, right? They just look at you, and all they see is prey. Kind of like some people we know."

"Sam isn't that bad!" Cathy pointed out. "After all, we both fell for her. She had reasons for what she did. Someday, I'll forgive her."

That's what's holding me back, Gareth realized. "We need to exorcise the demons of that relationship. She used us both." He moved closer to Cathy. This image of her, it's not real. I know that. But it's genuine enough for now. He pulled her into himself. She did not resist. He held her, and she placed her head on his shoulder.

"It's OK," Gareth said. "We're together now. I feel so much, I don't know, stronger, more complete with you. I felt so lost after you left, buried in work. The things I've done..."

"Shhh," said Cathy. "Sometimes it's better not to talk."

OK, Gareth, Sam sent, that's enough. I'm sorry, but you need to focus on maintaining this reality.

That's what I'm doing. This is what's real for me.

"Sam's worried. I'm not, are you?" He felt much calmer now, calmer than he had been in a long time. It was easy being with Cathy again.

"Right, Rick's worried too. They make a good worrying couple." Cathy stepped away from the hug and went to the kitchen. "How about some tea? I'll put the kettle on. Jasmine, OK? The same cupboard?"

"That would be great. Everything is where you left it," said Gareth.

Cathy went to the cupboard. "Ah yes, there it is." She measured some into the tea ball and placed the ball in the teapot.

"What did you ever see in Sam anyway?" Gareth asked. "I was under the influence. What was your excuse?"

That's below the belt.

I'm just making our reality, Cathy and mine, stronger. That's what you want, isn't it?

You need to focus on the apartment, the god-damned knick-knacks. You need to maintain the reality.

Sam, the knick-knacks are unimportant; they were never important. That's not the reality I need to maintain. This is me and Cathy. We are doing this. Now, leave us alone.

"Sam is a lovely person," replied Cathy. "There were a lot of reasons to fall for her. She wasn't a rebound from you, if that's what you're thinking. We each found something in her we wanted or needed. Like she's two people in one. Maybe, those two aspects of her, they were what we needed to find a way back to each other."

The kettle whistled, and Cathy poured the boiling water over the loose tea in the pot. They sat down at the kitchen table, held hands, and waited for the attack.

###

Of course, it would be the knick-knacks, Gareth thought. Sam had a point. There were too many of them. First, the hippo statue tried to change into a mirror. Cathy noticed the change; they focused on it, remembering the trip when they had bought it. They reverted it back, a hippo once again.

"Sam was right," Gareth admitted. "This apartment is too cluttered. There are too many things to keep track of. We need to simplify somehow."

"Should we recreate the apartment as it was, just after we moved in? Before we made those trips?"

"I wish I could. The image needs to come from after I got CIPHER 2. That's how I can recreate it, make it real."

"Maybe," Cathy began, "we can change it ourselves, here and now. Let's move everything to the bedroom, just throw them on the bed and close the door. We can reduce the amount of reality we need to maintain."

"OK, let's get going."

They gathered everything by the armful and deposited them with little fanfare on the bed.

"Get the pictures, too," Gareth said.

Cathy went to get the picture of them shortly after they had met. "No, keep that," Gareth said. "That will help. It's just the two of us."

"OK," Cathy set it down. She moved on to the picture of her father. He looked so happy then, well before the scourge of CIPHER. It was the two of them together, dancing at the party after she and Gareth had married.

Gareth, something's happening, Sam sent. There's an opening in the firewall! She's found a way in. What did you do?

Gareth looked over at Cathy, still looking at the picture of herself dancing with her father. She was crying softly. "Oh, Dad, I'm sorry. I didn't understand," he heard her say. "It wasn't your fault. I know that now. Where are you now?"

"Cathy, what's happening? Look at me, please!". He couldn't get her attention. She remained focused intently on the picture. There was something not right about it. He laid his hand gently on her shoulder, trying to draw her attention back to him. His touch was insubstantial, like grasping at air.

The apartment was fading, the furniture vanishing. I need to focus and hold on to this reality. I can't lose her. She was fading now, too. "Cathy, stay with me. I just got you back. Don't go!"

Gareth, you need to keep her with you, sent Sam. Stop her.

I don't think I can. I'm not letting her go alone this time!

"Cathy, take me with you. Wherever you are going, take me with you. Let's go together."

Gareth, Rick and I will join you. Focus on her! Stay with her!

Gareth grabbed hold of Cathy and concentrated all his attention on her. He pulled every bit of their time together, the good and the bad, from his memory, mining his CIPHER for everything. Remembering the smell of her, the way they held each other, so many times. Remembering also shared moments when they were in on a secret no one else knew. When they were so afraid that the elephant would collapse the tent around them. Relief when it got quiet again and still held each other. The apartment faded, but he still had her. They were together. Wherever Cathy was going, this time, he would follow her.

A Family Reunion
October 2093

"Hello, sweetie," the voice said. So familiar, yet such a long time since she'd heard it last. "Hi, Gareth. Who are your friends? Oh, I recognize you."

Cathy saw her father sitting behind a workbench, looking at Sam. He seemed to recognize Sam, but they had never met. How could that be? That's right, she remembered. Sam described meeting him when she was in Fugue at *Happy Meadows*. This is the dingy workshop Sam had described so many months ago. She looked around the shop, seeing Gareth and Rick also there.

"Hello, Walter, it's good to see you again," she heard Sam say.

"You too, Sam. Who's your other friend?"

"This is Rick. He's an AI avatar of my friend Rick.

Did you ever finish what you were working on?"

"Oh, yes," he replied. "Isolde Phillips was quite pleased with it. I finished the other thing as well. That one she didn't know about."

"Sam? What are you doing here?" said Gareth. He pointed at Rick. "And who's this?"

"I followed you in. We're connected, remember?" Sam told Gareth. She looked at Rick, a smile on her face. "This is Rick. My God, I've missed you."

"Sam, you know I'm not Rick. Not really. This," he pointed to himself, "is just an echo, living on Cathy's CIPHER. I'm sorry."

"Yes, I realize that," said Sam. "Still, I'm happy to see even this echo."

"Dad, I'm so sorry!" interrupted Cathy, her voice shaking. "It's all true, then. What Sam saw. Isolde Phillips trapped you here somehow. All this time, I was angry with you for leaving us, but it wasn't your choice, was it?"

"Don't be upset with yourself. You couldn't have known. Phillips created a kind of virus; her grandson Alex coded it into some Experiences that *Multitudes* created. It targeted people like me, as well as others with a more artistic bent, placing us into a special kind of Fugue."

"Maybe, like Ruth?" asked Rick quietly, hopefully. "She's in Fugue and was a star programmer. Is she with you?"

"I don't know," Walter replied gently. "Maybe she is, but some people really are in Fugue. Phillips took ten of us with her on her ship."

"Wait," Cathy said. "You are here on Mars? With Phillips? Why?"

"Yes, I am," said Walter. "As to why, I'll get to that later, if we have time. I had to bring you all here to this cloud version of reality. We need to stop her."

"Wait," Gareth said, "you brought us here? I thought it was Phillips. How?"

It was the picture, Cathy realized. Somehow, her father could reach out. The picture of her and Walter dancing acted as an entry point. If not the picture, maybe something else—a memory, perhaps—could have worked. Had that picture always been there in the apartment?

"I don't remember that picture," said Cathy. "You weren't even at the wedding, let alone dancing at it. You were too busy, as usual. Somehow you planted the picture there, hoping I would see it."

"I wanted to be there, at your wedding," Walter said, looking down at his bench now, avoiding Cathy's eyes. "But I wanted to work more. I always thought I was so important. That the company couldn't do without me. That picture, it's what should have happened. What I

376

always wish had happened."

"How did you push that picture out to Cathy?" asked Sam. "Phillips was attacking Moloi's cloud. We were defending against her. How did you slip by and insert that photo?"

"Yes, well," Walter replied, looking at Sam now. "Phillips should have known better than to kidnap an entrepreneurial engineer and endanger his family. Sam, look around you. Do you see walls? The walls of the workshop that you visited?"

Cathy looked too and remembered what Sam had told her. Her father had said something about too many walls. They had to come down.

"No, I don't," replied Sam. "I see open doors and windows to other shops. So, you were able to do it."

"Yes, we've been able the find holes in the reality Phillips is creating. Holes I've been able to slip through."

"Phillips has been poking holes too," said Gareth. "She's talked to me."

"I'm not surprised," said Walter. "We're both taking advantage of similar exploits: weaknesses in the cloud and our CIPHERs." He paused and looked at Gareth. "Is she still talking to you?"

"No. Sam, she added some protection for my CIPHER. A way to block the attacks. Phillips is quiet now."

"Good. That leaves the cloud as the only way for her to succeed in her plan to copy your implant."

"I remember you were working on something," Sam said. "What was it she had you working on? You mentioned a new spaceship drive?"

"A Quantum Drive. We finished that, and it now powers the Phillips yacht, the *Mangala*. That ship made the trip from Earth in two days."

"She used you," said Cathy, shuddering. "She put you in Fugue and she made you work for her!"

He nodded. "Yes, we delayed the work as much as we could. We also got to know each other. When Phillips loaded us onto her ship, we created a small communications tunnel for ourselves. That was our chance to take the 'walls' down. We could talk and work together. We all hated her for what she'd done to us, and we worked on a plan to stop her. You know what she intends to do, don't you?"

"I think so," said Rick. "She's dying, isn't she? I figure she wants to upload herself to the cloud. But that's not enough for her, is it?"

"No, it isn't. That's why she wants me," said Gareth.

"Yes, your CIPHER 3 enhancements, which have been so well tuned with all the *EmpHance* dosing. Sam's

378

plans produced just the set of nanobots Phillips wants, and she needs them now. She is dying, and she can't accept that. Hence, the digital upload. What's the point of living forever in the cloud if you can't feel anything? She has us, this farm of people in Fugue, and more victims every day, a limitless supply. She intends to turn us into a repository of CIPHER 3 hosts, with the ability to mimic endocrine responses. When she uploads herself to Moloi's cloud, she can run that program on our nanobot infrastructure. Like how your friend Rick is running on Cathy's."

"That doesn't sound good, the way you put it," countered Rick.

"Shut up, Rick," said Cathy. "Go on, Dad."

"When she couldn't kidnap Gareth, she improvised this attack. She needed our help in creating the attack vector. We also embedded our own payload in it, to reach Cathy and bring you all here."

"So, instead of attacking us," Sam realized. "You brought us here. To counterattack in her cloud. How? What can we do from here?"

"There's the other thing I was working on. We finished that, too."

Sam's brow furrowed as she asked, "What was that, Walter? What else was there?"

Walter held out his hand. He was holding a small

horse statue. "Remember now? See how easy it is to change this reality? Add and subtract things from it. Like this statue. That's how the game is played. *You shape it, you own it,* it's called."

"Yes, Sam and I played it recently," said Gareth. He frowned. "We lost."

"Now, we are playing to win," said Walter. "At least, not lose too quickly. When I saw how Sam escaped Fugue, I had this idea. A way to create a hole, or tunnel, from this reality to Phillip's cloud server."

"Fine," said Cathy. "Then what?"

"Then," Walter said as the horse statue disappeared. "We send our horse through the tunnel."

Rick grinned, "A trojan horse attack!"

Walter ignored Rick and continued, "Moloi is here, correct? Is one of you physically with her?"

This is all going too fast for me, Cathy thought. I just got the chance to talk to my father for the first time in years, and he's acting like a general. Although this is war. "I am," she said.

"Good, I need you to take the program with you and give it to her. I'll load it onto your CIPHER. Is that OK?"

"How will that work? Will I need to disconnect from this? I've just gotten you and Gareth back!"

"We aren't really here," Gareth said. "If this works,

we'll really be together. I'm just down the hall, after all."
He smiled and hugged her.

"OK," Cathy said. "Load it."

Walter frowned. "Cathy, there ought to be plenty of space to load the program. But there isn't enough. I don't understand."

"Yeah, about that," said Rick. "That would be me. You see, Walter, I'm a program running on Cathy's **CIPHER**. I take up a lot of space. I think it's finally time for me to go." He turned to Sam. "Sam, come find me in the cell later. Maybe you can get the old version of me out of Fugue. Cathy, Moloi has this version of me in the cloud. You can visit me sometime later, perhaps. Right now, I'm just a waste of space. You know what to do."

"I've grown fond of this version of you, Rick," said Cathy. "But it will be nice to be just myself again. Especially since I've just found Gareth."

Cathy summoned the envelope Rick had given her earlier into the apartment. It was now in her hands, with the word *Auslösung* written on it. She opened it. It contained a sheet of paper with what looked like programming code. It required a codeword to run.

"Goodbye, Rick. I hope to see you again sometime."

Cipher, Cathy sent, run program codeword Auslösung.

Program complete, Rick deleted.

I hope you found redemption, Rick, thought Cathy. "OK, Dad, there should be plenty of space now. Load your program."

"Done. You need to go now, Cathy. Tell her the program came from a colleague of Jagan Bhatnagar. She'll understand. I hope to be back with you again soon. Goodbye, sweetie."

"Good luck, Dad." She hugged Gareth again. "I never wanted to leave you. It's just that I couldn't bear the thought of what might happen to you. After what happened to Dad. I'm sorry. Come find me afterwards."

"I will," said Gareth. "I know the way."

Then, the workshop and everyone she loved faded away.

Isolde Phillips
October 2093

Gareth watched Cathy fade away, not quite like a Cheshire Cat—but close enough. What will happen to me when I take on Phillips? he worried. Is she a Snark or a Boojum? Same author, just a different book. Will I just softly and suddenly vanish away? "Walter, am I the Bellman? Is Isolde a Snark? Does the hunt begin now?"

"What are you on about, Gareth?" asked Walter.

"It's okay, Gareth," said Sam, resting her head on his shoulder. "I know what he's talking about. He's worried. This plan of yours, Walter, it's risky, isn't it? Cathy is safe now, but Gareth and I are still connected to Isolde's cloud. Will we make it out, even if your plan works? Will we be trapped here in Fugue?"

"No, I, we will not let that happen. Yes, the plan is not

foolproof; there is a risk. We have to allow Phillips to get what she wants from Gareth: the altered CIPHER 3 beta. She'll need to inject that into the Fugue victims she has on her yacht."

"Jesus!" Gareth said. "What?"

"We are the human hosts she requires. After she uploads to the ship's cloud, she will use our combined nanobots to provide that upload with the equivalent of an endocrine system. She intends to add you to that, put you into Fugue, as well. Phillips created the Fugue virus, after all. That will make her upload as human as it can be."

"I don't understand how this helps," said Sam.

"It helps, because we have a way to extricate ourselves from the cloud. A way to get all of us out of Fugue, leaving Phillips behind. The timing is delicate. Cathy and Moloi, they need to activate the program. I'm sure Moloi will know what to do, and they can send us a signal. We need to delay Phillips until then. Soon, she will detect that you are in her cloud."

"What's taking her so long?" asked Gareth. He felt panic rising again. *If only I could take another hit of EmpHance*, he thought, *that would help. I can't, though. I don't really exist. My physical self is sitting comfortably in an Experiencer chair. This me is God knows where.* "Can't she just attack? Let's get this over with."

"Time is different here," Walter said. "There's little correlation between here and the real world. You know that. How long does it take to consume a 30-minute Experience, a walk in the woods, for example? Five minutes, ten? It's arbitrary. You are the observer, you decide."

"Gareth," Sam said, her voice soft, "remember what's different about CIPHER 3? There are many ways to put it scientifically, but it comes down to emotions and feelings—the added dimensions of fear, excitement, love, all of those things. CIPHER 3 controls them; you control CIPHER 3. You don't need *EmpHance* to calm down. You can do it yourself."

Gareth focused on his breathing, which is odd, he thought, since he had no physical body. Even so, it created a kind of feedback loop. His self in this virtual world, breathing in and out, and the physical self doing the same now. He felt calmer.

The room shimmered, the outlines of the workbench becoming indistinct. "It's starting now, isn't it?" Gareth asked. "Will you be coming with me?"

"Sorry, Gareth, no, not yet," replied Walter. "I can't. Phillips won't let me. Hang in there, son. I will join you soon."

"Sam?" he asked. I know the answer, he realized. I am

on my own now. But not truly alone. He felt the avatar Sammie, its presence stronger now.

"No, Gareth. But you still have Sammie. The enhancements to its programming that I sent earlier—they should be nearly complete."

The room continued to fade away, taking Walter and the workbench with it. Focus on Sam, he thought. I need to hold her for as long as possible. I forgive you, Sam, but I am still angry. Let it go, he told himself. The anger is not doing any good. It's just another wall that separates people.

Yes, Gareth. Let it go.

It was Sammie, stronger now. She's with me! I won't be alone. Sam faded, and he found himself in what looked like a dining area, a small room. He was sitting at a long, narrow table set with plates and silverware; chairs alongside it. Gareth sat opposite a picture window along one wall. He could see New Nottingham spinning in its cradle on the surface of Mars. So much red plain spread out before it. The red plain that he had seen in his dreams. Sam was gone now. At the head of the table, a young woman sat.

"Hello Gareth, welcome to the *Mangala*. It's good to meet you finally," Isolde Phillips said. "I've enjoyed our chats, but it's so much better to meet in person." He recognized her. She wore a traditional business suit. Much younger than the images currently on the net, but he knew it was her.

"You're looking good," said Gareth. "I thought you were dying."

"Soon, but I have some time yet."

"Where's Alex? Will he be joining us for dinner? I miss my old college friend and Cipher Tech buddy."

"Sorry, no. He's busy. Alex has some nanobots to harvest, I mean copy. He is copying their programming, so we can replicate them. We don't need your physical body, just your presence here in my cloud. He's encountered a minor problem. It seems your nanobots are corrupted, which is unfortunate."

She means me, sent Sammie. That's not a nice thing for her to say.

"Yes, my CIPHER picked up a hitchhiker."

"Sam, isn't it? Or an avatar of her, anyway? She's been very useful, preparing you. I was hoping this would go much more quickly. You and your friends have done well delaying me. Nomie is clever. I miss her. She's the only one who really understood me."

"I wouldn't know; I haven't had the pleasure yet. I'm sure she isn't happy with what you are trying to do. Tell me what makes you so special? I mean, why should you get to live forever on the backs of all these people?"

Don't poke the bear...

"I'm special because I am special. I think, therefore I am. If I continue to think, I will continue to be. Anyone can do what I am doing. I just had the courage to pursue and got there first. CIPHER wouldn't exist without me. Nomie is brilliant, yes. But she didn't have the vision to take her initial discovery to what it is today. It could be so much more. CRI, hah! A sorry bunch of accounting cowards. I will do what must be done. Thanks to you, I can do that now."

"If you defeat Moloi, then yes."

"I will, with your help, regardless of whether you give it to me freely. Really, this isn't so bad for you. You already have what you need—your nanobots so carefully curated—you could ascend with me. Join me."

Gareth, you don't need to be afraid, sent Sammie. You can be more confident. Just make the proper adjustments.

Gareth instructed CIPHER to decrease his adrenal levels and increase his serotonin. As his physical body calmed, so did he.

"Ah," said Isolde. "I see you've learned to control it, your CIPHER, interesting."

Gareth picked up the knife and fork at his place-setting. "Maybe. I'm feeling peckish. When do we eat? Oh, that's right, we don't exist, so we don't eat. I eat, therefore I am. We don't eat, so I guess we're not. What's keeping Alex, anyway? My nanobots are ripe for the copying."

Isolde picked up the steak knife at her setting, pondered it for a moment, and threw it, striking Gareth in the right shoulder. Pain shot through him, blood streaming down from the wound. He cried out in shock and pain.

"Yes," Isolde said, smiling. "You are ripe. You feel pain; therefore, you are. That is the missing element in this virtual existence. You're angry now, too, aren't you? You want to leap across the table and beat me to a pulp? That's what I need. That's what you will give me."

Gareth reached for the knife. Do I pull it out? If I do, I may bleed to death. That's what I've always heard. But I'm not real, so it doesn't matter.

You're right, Gareth, the pain is a simulated reaction. There's no knife, no you, no pain. Take it out.

Gareth pulled the knife out and grabbed the napkin by the plate. He wiped the blood off the knife and set it down next to his plate. He instructed CIPHER to adjust his hormonal responses. The panic and pain subsided. "Sorry about the mess. So, any other games while we wait for

Alex?"

Desperate Measures
October 2093

Where am I now? Cathy wondered. She felt the contours of the Experiencer chair, gently releasing her muscles. She felt uncomfortable; the chair nudging her to stand up. As she did, Cathy saw a short, older black woman, facing away from her, working on something. Yes, that's Moloi. I'm back in her lab.

Rick, we made it back.

Silence. Then she remembered: Rick was gone, deleted from her nanobot storage. To make room for something, a program. She stumbled. Losing her balance, she grabbed the chair. I'm not used to this kind of thing.

"Ah, you have returned," said Moloi, hearing the commotion.

"Did we win?" asked Tim.

Tim? Cathy wondered. "Tim," she asked. "What the hell are you doing here?"

"So, about that. Years ago, I was Doctor Moloi's graduate assistant. I helped with the original mouse trials."

"Yes, you screwed up the server connection, allowing the mice to learn from each other," Moloi added, smiling. "This is all your fault."

"If it is, I should have gotten the credit as well as the blame."

It was playful teasing, Cathy realized. There was mutual affection, as well as a sense of melancholy. A burden they shared.

Tim continued, "When Nomie needed a place to go, to escape, I recommended New Nottingham. I was able to carve out this space for her, off grid. I guess Phillips helped with that. Nomie could continue to work, and I needed to get away from the Ludds, too. Imagine the two people responsible for CIPHER joining the Isolators!"

"I didn't join them," Nomie pointed out, "just needed a place to hide. I need little company, so this lab is fine for me. Tim is a more social creature and needs the company of others. This works for both of us."

"Hey! Sanitation work is a bit of a come down from my last job! But yes, I've adapted. And I can keep Nomie supplied with essentials, including the odd bottle of

Martian Single Malt. It's amazing what you can get away with in the early stages of habitat development. Some cloud servers might go missing, and such like."

Enough small talk, Cathy realized. "To answer your question, Tim, no, we haven't won, not yet. I saw so much and can't describe it all. Phillips brought some people with her: Fugue victims. My father is one of them. All this time, I blamed him for falling victim. It was Phillips, some virus she had created."

"I'm not surprised about that," said Nomie. "I always wondered about the Fugue. It never made sense to me. Still, that Izzy would do such a thing ..." Nomie started. She paused momentarily, lost in thought, then frowned. "If she bought them with her, she must be sicker than I had thought, closer to death. She needs them now. As I feared, this could be her last chance. She means to copy Gareth's nanobots to them, creating a human infrastructure of CIPHER 3's she can run her avatar on. Oh, your father? He is one of them? I'm so sorry."

"Yes, he is," said Cathy. She smiled. "Phillips made a mistake there. My father is a brilliant engineer, and he sent something back with me: a program. Something that he says will help."

"OK, Tim set aside some secure storage on the cloud. We can transfer it there. Please sit back down, Cathy. This

393

won't take long. I am sorry you've had such a hard time. This is what I was afraid of with **CIPHER** and the way CRI has been recklessly pushing the technology. Humanity isn't ready yet; we are too selfish! Samantha and Richard are almost as bad as Izzy. Tim, I told you it was a bad idea to work with them."

Cathy sat back down in the chair at the small table and opened her **CIPHER** up to Moloi's cloud. The program began to transfer.

"I know, Nomie," Tim replied. "What they proposed sounded promising. A way to fix **CIPHER** so that it connected people, not isolate them. People constantly consuming Experiences, lost in other worlds, leaving their own world, family and friends behind. Even without the Fugue, **CIPHER** isolates people. It could redeem some of the damage we have done."

"None of this is your fault, Tim," Nomie said. "Science creates things that can do so much good. Sadly, someone will always find a way to use it for base, if not outright evil, purposes."

"I know! I just can't help how I feel. When I met Sam at a conference years ago, before Nomie retired, she tried to talk me into this project. I refused then. Nomie and I moved here. Sam sent me a message saying they had a plan. They would bring Gareth and **CIPHER** 3 to Mars, and we could convince Nomie.”

Tim paused for a moment, frowning, before continuing. “The guilt still ate at me, no matter what I told myself. So, I agreed. They asked for something else too. The builder virus, and I gave it to them.”

“You did what?” Nomie asked, jumping out of her chair. “That’s how Rick got it, and how he infected Cathy. How could you do that?”

“Yes, it was wrong! I know that now. I’m sorry. The plan was to meet Sam and Gareth and bring them to you. If it hadn’t been for Phillips, things would have been fine. Ah, the program has transferred. Give me a few minutes to check it over.”

Cathy stood up and began pacing. Waiting, always waiting, she thought.

“OK,” said Tim finally. “The code looks good. We’re good to go.”

Nomie still seems to be trying to digest what Tim told her. I can’t blame her. I know what betrayal feels like. But I need them to focus. “Nomie, he said the program’s loaded. Now what do we do?” Nomie sat back down at her lab desk.

“Nothing,” Nomie said, regaining her composure. “We wait. The rest is up to your friend.” Nomie went to a cupboard and took out three glasses and a bottle. “I like my Scotch neat, so I have no ice cubes. I hope that's OK with you." She poured a glass and offered it to Cathy. "Please sit down. This is one of the bottles Tim procured for me: a ten-year-old single malt from New Aberdeen. It's an acquired taste. We may have minutes, maybe hours, before we know whether the plan works."

Cathy took the offered glass and sat down. She sipped tentatively. "Not bad. You can almost taste the red dirt." She then heard a pounding at the door.

"Moloi, it's me! Sam. Let me in!"

Sam, Cathy thought, isn't she with Gareth? Tim went to open the door. Sam came rushing in, breathless.

"Sam, where's Gareth?" Cathy asked.

"I had to leave him. He's alone now, with Phillips, I guess. I didn't see that I could help him there, so I rushed here." She pointed at the glasses on the table and the bottle, "You're just sitting around drinking?"

"After everything you've done to us?" Cathy said, barely holding her anger at bay. "You've just left him there? You've only ever done harm, hurt people and when Gareth needs you, you've just left him? Where is he? In which one of these fucking rooms did you leave him?"

"Cathy, I'm sorry. I, I did what I could."

"We all need to stay together," Nomie said, touching

Cathy's arm. "The program your father created. When the time comes, we need to be here."

"No, you don't need me! Gareth does. I will not leave him alone. When he comes back from Phillip's cloud, I will be there with him. I've left him alone before. I will not do that again. Which room, Sam!"

"I didn't mean for this to happen..." Sam started; she shook her head. "Room 95; it's not far."

"Hey guys," Tim said. "I think the program is working." He looked at the display by the server. "Our cloud is opening connections to Phillips' cloud. It's tunneling its way in. You don't have much time, Cathy. If you're going to go, go!"

What Remains
October 2093

Alex is close to evicting me, sent Sammie. When he does, he'll be able to copy your nanobot structure and its programming. I'm sorry, Gareth. I hope we've bought enough time.

What will happen to you? After he evicts you, Gareth asked.

That will be it for this version of me. There is no copy.

I'm sorry, Gareth replied. He marveled at how different this version of Sam was from the original. Since she had come to him, back at Lagrange One, she had grown from vague impressions, sometimes even warning him about the original Sam, to what seemed to be a self-aware consciousness. Was his CIPHER 3 working together with Sam's upgrade? The additional interface to his endocrine system? Is this what Phillips expects? To have a living presence like this?

Are you afraid? Is this like dying? Gareth asked.

I don't know, never died before. Maybe I'll come back and let you know. There may still be a way. Maybe it will work.

"Alex has nearly deleted your friend," observed Phillips. "Then we can get started."

"You want what my friend has. A life lived on top of CIPHER 3. If that means living to you, then what you're doing, what Alex is doing, is murder. Did you hear that, Alex? You are murdering my friend."

I'm sorry, Gareth, sent Alex. Really, it's just a program, not an upload. It's nothing like a person. This is not murder! Please understand that I have to do this. My grandmother can't die! I need her; the world needs her.

Ah, Alex. You are there, sent Gareth. This is wrong, not just deleting Sam, but all the Fugue victims you infected with the virus. What about them?

Why do they matter? replied Alex. They're well taken care of. They have a good virtual existence. Better than I had while growing up. They've had their turn, taking advantage of people like me! We're the ones who write the code, make the tech work. The only one who recognized my value was my grandmother! Not you, not

Cathy. So yes, I'll do anything for her.

"You're harassing my grandson," broke in Phillips. "He's too easily distracted. I've closed that connection. Ah, he's done. Your friend is gone."

That's it, then, thought Gareth. There's nothing I can do now. I have to hope we stalled enough.

"Alex has made copies of your nanobot programming and created new implants based on it. It will be just like CIPHER 3 with all the enhancements Alex and your friends added. All that conditioning has made them special. Precisely what I need. It's more than the original CIPHER 3 Beta. CRI refused to enhance them in the way I needed them. Alex is injecting my passengers with them now."

She smiled at Gareth, the predatory smile that some people show when they want something you have and they're going to take it. Isolde Phillips was used to getting what she wanted. "You can stay here with me, you know. Alex can upload you, too. You'll need to die, of course. I would like the company. You are an attractive, intelligent young man."

Gareth frowned. "I'm flattered, but no. You're not my type."

"We can fix that. Alex can make a few edits to your upload. You'll be happy to be with me. It's been so long since I've had sex."

You'd better not!

Cathy, is that you? How?

Yes, I was able to connect after Sammie left. I had to wait until after the copying was done. You're not alone, Gareth.

"There, it's done!" announced Phillips. "Alex has started the upload process." People began appearing in the other dining chairs. He recognized Walter opposite him.

That's Dad! sent Cathy. He's just sitting there, not moving. What's happened to him?

"Walter," said Gareth. "Are you all right? What are you doing here?"

"He can't answer you. He's too busy running my download. I was unable to bring many with me; the Mangala is only so big. The ones I have, like Walter here, they are networked together using Near Field. Their upgraded CIPHERs allow me to feel, not just sense, but feel like a human being, not just a simulation of me. It's incredible!"

"No, it's horrible," said Gareth. "You can't use human beings like that!"

"Of course I can. That's why I brought them along. This gives their lives meaning. Look at them! They were weak, easily trapped by the virus Alex added to the Experiences. I will give them a purpose. There's so much more I can contribute now."

She paused. "I'm not inhuman. When we have more people, I can release some of them for a while. You and Cathy can even visit with Walter now and then. I am feeling different now. Not just thinking, but feeling! My physical self has finally died. Good riddance! I hated that old, feeble body. Alex, have you taken over Moloi's cloud yet?"

Alex appeared in the chair next to Isolde. "I am working on it. There are some issues, but I think I have them worked out."

"Alex, how can you do this?" asked Gareth. "We're friends. You were at our wedding. You need to stop!"

"I told you, Gareth! Some things, and some people, are just more important. I can't just let her die! This will be okay, Gar. You'll see."

"Alex, ignore him! Concentrate on the work. Let me know when it's done."

"I don't get it. Why take over Moloi's cloud?" Gareth asked Phillips. "You have what you came for. Why not leave?"

"I admit," Isolde replied, "that I was upset when we failed to grab you at Lagrange One. We were going to take you to Earth. This is better, though. There's no **CRI** here, no one to worry about a Moloi Cloud in New Nottingham. I can live here just fine. Also, there will be a supply to replace these," she waved at the Fugue victims gathered around the table, "when they die. Maybe I'll start with Rick. He's in Fugue in a cell, isn't he?"

"More importantly," she continued, "I need to take over habitat comms; I can do that from Moloi's cloud. It connects to the habitat's communications grid. That will be my way in. New Nottingham wants to isolate itself from the rest of **CIPHER** society. I'm more than happy to help with that. There will be so much I can do, so many people I can use. Are you sure you won't join me? One way or the other, you will."

"I ran into some difficulties, another program," said Alex, a puzzled expression on his face. He relaxed. "Ah, no worries. I've sorted it out. Starting takeover."

"Wait, what program?" Isolde asked, concern creeping into her voice.

"Nothing to worry about, Grandma; this isn't like what happened before. I know what I'm doing! Gareth, don't worry. It's not all doom and gloom. What Grandma said, she didn't mean it! You know I wouldn't do anything to hurt you and Cathy. We've been friends forever, right? Just cooperate with ... uh, wait a minute, something's not right."

"Alex," Isolde cried out, "talk to me! What's happening?"

"So, you feel panic now," taunted Gareth. "I bet you're not used to that as an avatar. CIPHER 3 is running now on Walter and the others. All the emotions they are causing you to feel. My CIPHER 3 was calibrated to me, not to you. Were theirs? It's hard to get the balance just right. You need to do that for each person. Didn't Alex tell you? How many did you say you brought along?"

"Shut up! Alex, show me the program!"

Gareth glimpsed some motion to his side.

Gareth, it's my dad. He's moving.

Walter seemed to take a breath, which, of course, he didn't need to. "Don't bother," said Walter. "My friends and I, we are that program, and we now have control of both clouds—yours and Moloi's."

"No, you can't have! That's impossible," said Isolde. "I've built in too many safeguards. You're just an engineer! You can't have created anything sophisticated enough to take my cloud!"

"On my own, no, I could not have. But you brought us together," he indicated the other passengers, the Fugue victims, at the table. Gareth noticed their expressions were now animated, their eyes alive.

"You had us work for you. We made the star drive that powers this ship. Did you think we could do all that and not be a threat to you?" Alex disappeared from the table. "You were arrogant. Working together, we created a program. The program Alex was worried about. My daughter Cathy loaded it onto Moloi's cloud. Once you merged the clouds, it was easy enough for us to trigger it. We control access to the combined cloud. We decide who stays and who goes. You aren't going anywhere. Oh, and say hello to my daughter."

Gareth startled and saw Cathy sitting in the chair next to him. No longer a voice in his head, but present in this cloud simulation. "Cathy, what's happening?"

"The program they created worked! We got it into the cloud, and they ran it." She looked over at Walter, concerned. "Now what, Dad? You said you control it now, the cloud. What happens when you leave?"

"I'm sorry, sweetie, you're right. I won't be leaving. There's no other way. I've cut off control for Alex. Each one of us sitting here at the table, we have joint control now. When the last of us dies, all the programs in this cloud will be deleted, including Isolde's."

"You can't do this!" Isolde said. "All of you, you're nothing! You don't matter! I do. The world needs me! You can't keep me prisoner here. This is all mine! I created it! No one can take it from me! Without me, there'd be no CIPHERs. We wouldn't be on Mars. I can take us to the stars!"

"We'll get there eventually," said Walter. "We don't need you to get there. No single person is that important. You and I, we will talk more later. We'll be here for some time. Not now. It's time for you to go." Isolde and the other Fugue victims, no longer victims, faded away. Only Walter, Gareth, and Cathy remained.

"Walter," said Gareth. "You don't need to stay. The others, they could stay; you could come with us. You have a family..."

"So do they," interrupted Walter. "We are all sacrificing something. We agreed to do this together."

"You could just delete her program!" said Cathy. "You don't need to keep it running. She doesn't deserve this kindness."

"No, she doesn't, not now. Maybe later, she will. Think of this as her own purgatory, a path to redemption for her. Purgatory means many things to many faiths. One of my fellows here is a theologian. He argued against deleting her program, as it may be a manifestation of her soul. I expect he will spend a lot of time with her."

Walter smiled at Cathy. "I've missed you so much. I'll be here for a long time. You can visit me. There are practical things to address, though. This ship is under our control, but we have physical bodies. They need to be tended. Your friend Alex and the other crew members must be released from the ship and possibly charged. Go to the authorities in New Nottingham and persuade them to help. It's good to see the two of you together again. I hope that, well, like I said, we'll talk more later. Oh, and one other thing, Gareth. We saved the kernel of that program you were talking to earlier."

"Sammie?" Gareth replied. "You were able to save her?"

"We hope so. The programming is interesting. I want to make sure we don't make a mistake. We'll let you know. Goodbye for now."

The dining room disappeared, and they found themselves once again in the supply room. Gareth turned in his chair, looking over at Cathy. He was relieved that it was over, that he could get back to his life. Her hands gripped the arms of the chair tightly.

He was used to the transition from an Experience to reality; from the virtual to the here and now. Gareth realized that this was new for Cathy. *My God, what if she's stuck? He thought. She could be in Fugue, spending the rest of her life in that cloud. I can't lose her now. No, she's fine, he realized.* Her eyes were opening, adjusting to the lighting in the supply room. The grip on the chair loosened.

"Cathy, it's over; we're back."

"Yes," she replied, "we are!" She got up from the chair, and Gareth rose to hug and kiss her. The welcoming feeling of her in his arms. I missed that so much, he thought. Cathy freed herself and turned away.

"What's wrong? We're back, we won!"

"Yes, but I thought I had gotten my father back, too. He didn't need to stay! This time, he really chose to stay. It wasn't his choice before, but he could have come back, too. I was wrong to have blamed him before. But now I don't understand. Why?"

She stood up from the chair and paced the small storage room. She picked up and set down the different objects, subjecting them to some private evaluation.

"I don't know," Gareth said. Do I go to her again, hold her? What good would that do? What does she want? What does she need from me? She wants answers, you idiot. But she already knows the answers. She just doesn't like them. "It's been hard, I know," he ventured. "It's hard to lose Walter again. But this is who your father is, isn't it? It's why I've always respected him."

"Respect?" asked Cathy softly. She inspected the object she had just picked up. It was a stained wine glass, red still around the rim. Probably some couple had stolen into this room while the habitat was being built, or after? Shared some wine and maybe something else. The remains of a tryst? She raised her hand, preparing to throw it, then set it back down.

"Maybe," she said. "He was always a little distant. I knew he loved and cared for me, but when I was growing up, he was always occupied with his business. Now this."

"Cathy, some people, they need something big; something that can't survive without them. He has a community now: the other Fugue victims. They made this decision together. Walt has a purpose now. He needs that, something that will drive him. He knows you are not like that. Maybe it doesn't make it easier to bear. He's given us a chance, too. I want us to be together again. I need you."

Cathy sighed, "I know that you're right about Dad; I just wish it weren't so. I guess I will visit with him later. I want to be there too. To help take care of them, the others keeping an eye on Phillips."

"I will too. We can do that together. I want to stay with you. I don't want to go back to Earth. Can we try that? Or do you want to go back to Sam?"

"Sam? God, no! I hate the way she used us. All the things she did to you." She smiled at him. "Do you want to go back to her? Just what did you get up to with her?"

He grinned. "Yes, there were moments. I can't say I didn't enjoy them." Gareth's grin faded. "I realize now that they weren't genuine. I could never go back to her. She didn't love me, and I can't be sure what I felt. That bothers me! With all that she had done, all the ways she used to create a connection—NF, *EmpHance*, CIPHER 3—none of that created what she was looking for. It damaged me in a way that I still don't understand. I want to go back to who I was before all this happened. Can you help me? I want us to try again."

"Yes, Gar. I would like that. We can help each other."

There's something else, too, Gareth realized. This moment, how I feel it. It's good. These last few months, since I got CIPHER 3, I've just been a passenger. Sam and Rick were the drivers, conductors; they decided where I went and what I did. Now I'm free of them. Almost. I can't let it happen again. There's one more thing to do.

"Can you help me get to Moloi?" Gareth asked. "Do you think she can fix me? Get rid of CIPHER 3, I mean, turn it off, whatever! You were right; I never should have gotten it! I want to get us back again. Please. This, always connected, always flooding our brains with the Experiences and feelings of other people." His voice shook. "It's too much," he continued. "I don't think we can handle it. We weren't meant for it. I honestly think I am losing my sense of who I am. I held it together with Phillips, but even then I had help: Sammie's virtual presence and you. As long as these," he gestured at his head, "nanobots are still active. I'll never know for sure if what I do comes from me; if it's what I want. I need to get rid of them!"

She went to Gareth and let him pull her into an embrace. "Yes, Gareth. I'll help you get to her. I'm sure she can do something."

This is real, feeling her so close; I need to hold on to this for now. I'm me. I know where I begin and where I end—mostly. I can feel Cathy holding me, and that she cares for me. There's no need to really see what she sees, feel what she feels. That belongs to her. We are two individuals. That is a good thing.

www.ingramcontent.com/pod-product-compliance
Lightning Source LLC
Chambersburg PA
CBHW010936140726
47988CB00010B/3481